FATHER TIME

A NOVEL BY:

TORTHELL ROBINSON

Published By AVP

A division of Arrogant View Productions

www.Arrogantview.com

November 2021
Paperback ISBN: 978-1-7377217-0-3
Hardcover ISBN: 978-1-7377217-1-0
eBook ISBN: 978-1-7377217-2-7

This book is dedicated to all the great fathers out there. More specifically, my grandfather, Russell Lee Ware Senior. I would not be who I am today had it not been for your leadership, protection, support, values, wit, wisdom, work ethic, and guidance. Thank you for being the best father and grandfather any kid could have. You are the inspiration.

CHAPTER 1

Nestled in the heart of downtown Atlanta, Georgia, in the wedge-shaped Flatiron Building, is where we find Kristine Teller. She is a literary agent who operates at a prestigious boutique agency in the city's second and longest-standing skyscraper. Kristine stares down her sharp nose and studies a sheet of paper. The phone rings on her cluttered mahogany desk.

"This is Kris . . . OK . . . OK . . . Great . . . Tell her I'll be with her in a few." Kristine finishes the call then darts a menacing glare at me as if she's ready to pounce. Kristine is a cute, freckle-faced brunette from Nashville. But do not be fooled by the princess with the pixie cut. At times she can be a vicious mountain lion.

"Where's the rest of it?" Kristine asks.

"The rest is coming," I say without confidence. I'm not sure what made me think I was slick enough to strut in Kris's office and try to finagle my way to a signing bonus with what is supposed to be my second novel, but is actually just a sheet of paper.

"There's no plot. There are no characters . . . there's no story! I need a story that I can sell, Trevor!"

"Is it all about money with you?" I ask.

"Uh, yes!" Kris says candidly. "That's why I'm your agent. I told you before we agreed to work together that I have no interest in representing a writer—I represent careers. I'm interested in projects that excite me. If it excites me, we make money. What you've written, if you can call it writing, does not excite me, therefore, we will make no money. Do you want to go back to being a beat writer for *The Atlanta Journal-Constitution?*"

I shake my head no.

"I genuinely believe in you and your work. I think you're a talented, good-looking man that should be writing a juicy book that I can sell."

"I didn't see my father growing up, and many people who look like me lost their fathers to the streets. I noticed a problem in my community and want to use my story to help fix it."

Kris balls up the sheet of paper and dares to chunk it at me. "Great! Bring that story in the size, shape, and form of a book that we can sell. You have one more week, or consider this a wasted opportunity."

I take a deep breath and stand up.

Kristine places a brown box on top of the desk. "Take this with you."

I lift the box off the table then shake it to hear what is inside.

"It's Armani's belongings."

"Nope." I place the box back on the desk. "I don't deliver bad omens. I told you before you guys started dating that whatever happened between you and him was between you and him."

"If it weren't for your brother, you and I wouldn't be working together."

"I understand all that, but can we focus on the money?"

"Oh, so now you want to focus on the money?"

I shrug my shoulders. "What else am I supposed to say?"

"Tell your brother to pick up his belongings by morning or I'm burning it!"

I swallow my pride then leave Kris's office.

My mind races a thousand miles per minute as I storm down the sidewalk of the bustling corporate area of downtown Atlanta. It is a frosty

Thursday morning, but I'm fuming hot under my Canada Goose Parka. How the hell does Kris expect me to write a book within a week? Don't get me wrong, I get it, I had over a year to write it, but life has been disrupting the process.

I approach the busy Peachtree and Luckie intersection. Anticipating the crosswalk warning light to flash the walk signal, I dig in my pocket, grab my phone, and dial a number. Several moments pass as the phone rings and rings before going to voicemail.

"This is Armani. I'm not in but leave a message for a faster response. If I don't respond, it's because I really…really…really don't like you. Ok… Bye now!"

I wait for the beep then shout, "Yo! Kris wants you to come and get your stuff by the morning." I end the call. The walk signal flashes, and I continue.

A few short years ago, I allowed my folks to convince me to allow my little brother Armani to stay with me. It wasn't the first time I allowed this to happen, but it damn sure was the last time. Armani had been in and out of jail and needed a change of scenery. I thought all would be well right up to the moment he moved in. Eating all my food, stealing my clothes, borrowing money he couldn't pay back, and throwing random house parties at my place had worn my patience thin. The straw that broke the camel's back was coming home early one day from work to find Armani and Kris compromising my bed.

Finding out the naked woman sitting on my brother's face was a literary agent allowed me to kill two birds with one stone. At the time, I was in search of a literary agent. Most of the agents I submitted to did not accept unsolicited material and preferred referrals from sources they trusted. Not only did I get a referral, but I was also able to kick Armani out of my place guilt-free. Kris then took on the responsibility of taking care of him, while I managed to get away scot-free.

After graduating from Howard University with a degree in journalism, I moved back to the south. I was a beat writer at *The Atlanta Journal-*

Constitution, dabbled in a little sports talk broadcasting, but writing was my thing. After the success of my first novel, I bought a high-rise condo at The W.

The condo has fantastic city views of the Mercedes Benz Stadium with the downtown skyline painting in the backdrop. The pad is a quiet corner unit complete with two outdoor spaces and two-bedroom suites separated by the kitchen and living area. It has an open floorplan, floor to ceiling windows with remote-controlled motorized blinds, new LED lighting, a custom water feature in the entry, a modern kitchen with custom cabinetry, a center island, slab granite counters, all new high-end stainless-steel appliances, butler pantry built-ins, a beverage fridge, and tile floors throughout with radiant heat in the master.

For around the same price I paid for this place, I could have bought a nice home in one of the surrounding suburbs with triple the square footage I am in now. But have you ever experienced Atlanta traffic ? At times, it's worse than Los Angeles traffic. Except for the airport, everything I need is within a decent proximity. Grocery stores, sporting events, clubs, and lounges are all downtown.

At first glance, it may appear that I live the perfect bachelor life, but the truth can be detected if you look on the floor of the condo. Scattered along the ground are LEGO pieces, Star Wars lightsabers, crayons, and action figurines. What was once a bachelor pad designed to lure women has turned into a cluttered playpen. That is because I let my girlfriend Eva Lopez, her eight-year son Dustin, and a spoiled Maltese named Princess move into my bachelor pad. Princess, at the moment, is growling at me.

I snatch her little ass up and stare her down. She avoids making eye contact. "This is my house! I'll box you up and send you to a wet market." I place her down and she walks over to her pink doggy bed next to the L-shaped leather couch.

When I met Eva, she was a cocktail waitress in her last year at Georgia Tech, majoring in Business Administration. She was dating one of the town's hottest after-hours DJ's, who was also Dustin's father . Eva and

I would catch eyes from time to time, but that was that. I admired her from a distance but didn't want to be another thirsty guy posing as a friend but secretly waiting for her to bust-up with her guy.

I knew if she wasn't the one, then she might be the prototype. I couldn't believe it was another damn crush. I respected her relationship until it happened. I had one too many Old-Fashioned drinks and got in her ear.

"If I were your man, I'd hit that shit like a parked car," I whispered in her ear. She giggled. Next thing I remember, we were having sex in a bathroom. Afterwards, she broke up with her son's father, who eventually died of a cocaine overdose. A couple of years later, we ended up in this condo turned playground.

It is daunting sitting here at my desk in front of my laptop with a blank Word document glaring back at me. Sprinkled across my desk lay index cards, pens, notepads, a pair of Bose headphones, and ear plugs. Above my workspace is a framed degree from Howard University. My phone starts to vibrate. I dig into my pocket, grab my phone, see it is Eva, and answer the call.

"What's up, babe?"

"We need to talk." From Eva's stern tone, I already know where this conversation is heading. Luckily, and to my surprise, I receive an incoming call from Kwesi Black.

"Hey, it's my father. I have to take this . . . Can we talk later?" Without saying good-bye, Eva ends the call. I switch over to the incoming call,

"Hey, Pop . . . Give me a second." I hit the mute button, place the phone on my desk, and wait several moments before jumping back on. Whenever Kwesi calls, I have to take a few moments to collect my thoughts.

"Sorry for the wait, Pop. What's up?"

"Placing me on hold like I'm a bitch. I know you do that on purpose!" an echoey Kwesi says.

"What are you talking about?" A thunderous fart roars through the receiver. "What the . . . Pop . . . Are you on the toilet?"

"Sorry, Son, I didn't know you could hear that."

Princess starts barking. "Get in your bed and shut up!"

"I can't stand a funky ass dog. You gotta do everything for them. Get yourself a cat. Those sum bitches take care of themselves."

"That's not too far removed from your method of raising children."

"Do you have to bring up old shit?"

A couple of awkward moments pass.

"Is there something I can help you with? I have stuff to do, Pop."

A couple more moments pass.

"Son . . . Are you gay?"

I pull the phone away from my head, then place it on my desk.

Through the receiver, you could hear Kwesi, "Hello? Son . . . Are you there . . . Did I lose you?"

I take a deep breath, pick the phone up, and place it up to my ear. "No, I'm not gay, Pop. Why are you asking me this?"

"Because you don't have any kids."

"So, having children signifies heterosexuality?"

"I mean . . . Yeah, kind of."

"A person's sexuality has nothing to do with having children. And I'll have children when the time is right. OK, Pop!"

"I'm just saying that you should have kids young so that you can spend time with them when you're younger. Don't wait until you're a 50-year-old man to be somebody's daddy."

"At what age were you planning on being somebody's daddy?

The only noise I can hear are the sweet sounds of courtesy flushes and Kwesi spraying air freshener. Several moments of awkward silence creep in.

"What are you insinuating, Son?"

"If I ever have children, I'm putting them in a position to win. Something you didn't do. I'll be in their life, and they'll lay the foundation for their children, so we don't make the same mistakes you made."

"Judge me when you have children." A sensitive Kwesi says as he ends the call.

Several seconds later, I receive an incoming call and notice its Kwesi calling back. I ignore the call and place the phone face down on my desk. A few minutes later, Kwesi calls back. I ignore the call again. At this juncture in my life, I'm wise enough to know that Kwesi will continue to call until I answer. The phone rings again and this time I answer.

"What do you want, Pop?"

"Meet me in exactly one hour."

"Meet you in an hour? No!" This time, I end the call. As soon as I place the phone on the desk, I receive another call from Kwesi. I ignore the call. Seconds later, Kwesi calls back. I ignore the call again. Kwesi is relentless and calls back again; this time I answer.

"I'm not asking you, Son!" Kwesi says with a firm tone. "You'll hear my side of this story. I'll text you the address." Kwesi ends the phone call.

CHAPTER 2

It's the middle of April but it feels like December already. I enter the warmth of a coffee shop in Atlantic Station and shake the frigid cold off of me. I scan the shop and spot a well-dressed, good-looking Kwesi, who's rocking a thick salt and pepper beard and sitting in a corner reading a newspaper. Mixed emotions are floating in me as I navigate the shop to get to my father. My stomach feels like there are knots in it.

As I approach Kwesi, we don't greet each other, nor do we hug or shake hands. Not one word is mumbled between the two of us as we stare each other down. Though we are not speaking to one another, you can tell from our body language that we are communicating.

Kwesi was a drill sergeant in the United States Army where he mastered the stare down. As a drill instructor, he's used to discipline and not breaking his bearing under pressure. Hundreds of troops under his command would say he was the pressure. But something is different in my father's eyes these days. His eye contact is not as intense as it once was. He's showing a little vulnerability.

"Want something to drink?" Kwesi asks.

"No, thanks. You want anything?" I ask.

"Nah. I hate coffee."

"What made you think I like coffee?"

"You wear those leggings, so I figured you'd be comfortable in a coffee shop."

"They're not leggings, Pop; it's athleisure wear. Anyway, why are we here?"

"I wanted to see you."

"For what?"

"To talk."

"To talk about what?"

"Us!"

"Us? Why are you in Atlanta?"

"Are you a federal agent? Asking all of these damn questions. I'm here for a trucking convention and heading back home to Memphis tonight."

A few moments pass as we stare at each other.

"Our relationship hasn't been the same since that one Thanksgiving dinner with your ex's folks."

"Relationship? We never had a relationship, Pop."

"That's because you don't stop by and visit me when you come home. You drive right by my place to get to your mom and grand folks' house. You never have time for me these days."

"I guess the tables have turned."

Kwesi nods his head as he acknowledges his mistake. He scratches his head as sweat beads form on the tip of his nose. "I deserve that, Son. Anything else you wanna add? How about a nice kick in the balls while your old man is down?"

"Wanna know why I don't stop by?"

"No, but I'm sure you're gonna tell me," Kwesi says.

"Because we always do this . . . We never communicate without it turning into an argument.

"Fine. We don't have to speak."

"I didn't come here to not talk, Pop. That's not productive. You said you wanted to meet . . . I'm here, so what's up?"

"I want to get to know you better," Kwesi says as his voice cracks.

"Why? Why do you care all of a sudden? Are you dying?"

"One day . . . Father Time is undefeated," Kwesi says with a sigh.

Not sure how to process that answer, I decide to get in front of this awkward conversation. "Look, Pop, I'm not mad at you. The benefit of not growing up with you was that I got a chance to spend time with Papa and Grandma."

Kwesi takes a few moments to collect his thoughts. "So that's why you changed your last name?"

"What? How did you find out?"

"Your Mama told me. She also told me you're writing another book. What's it gonna be about?"

"Did you read the last novel I wrote?"

"Well, no."

"So why would you care about the next one?" A tense cloud of awkward silence covers the two of us. "When did you and Ma start talking again?"

"When I found out you changed your last name from Black to Russell."

Brewing with anger, steam spewing from my head, I stand to my feet, then storm off.

"Wait, Tre!" Kwesi screeches. "Please . . ." Kwesi signals for me to retake my seat. I trundle back to the table.

"You reach out to my mother—the first time in 30-plus years—to see why I changed my last name? Come on! You know why I changed my name, bro!"

"I'm not your bro, I'm your father!" Kwesi roars as he slams his fist down on the table.

"Had you acted like a father you would've gotten that respect. You don't get the privilege of me calling you my father. You are Pop to me. And you should be lucky to be that."

"Look, son . . . I called your mother to apologize for my actions. I know I ain't shit. I'm sorry for not being there when you were a child."

"I thirsted for the type of dad that would take me fishing on the weekend or take me to a basketball game."

"That's your first problem," says Kwesi. "You thirsted for something that I ain't."

"You're right . . . You're just a sperm donor."

"Excuse me?"

"You heard me right. You're a goddamn sperm donor. Any dummy with a dick can be a father, but it takes a real man to be a dad, and you weren't either. You left your children out here to fend for themselves. And then you criticize me for not having children."

Kwesi grows quiet. For the first time, I could remember, he had no comeback.

"Son, I was conceived in the bed of my father's ole pickup truck. I wasn't supposed to be here—"

"I've heard this story a million times. I get it, Pop. You could've been a doctor, a lawyer, or a successful businessman. You could've been a better leader if you cared about your family as much as you desire women. Your children would've followed suit. But here we are."

"I want to do better . . . I didn't have anyone to teach me how to be a father."

"I'm not mad at you. I'm disappointed. But it is what it is."

Kwesi tries to slyly deflect the narrative. "Whatever happened to you and Sade? You sho'nuff were in love with her."

My scowl lightens as thoughts of an old friend flash through my mind. Kwesi notices a chink in my emotional armor, but I deflect to center the conversation.

"What's the purpose of this meeting, Pop? What's the reason you're all of a sudden interested in getting back in my life? Do you need money or something?"

"I don't need your money, Son!" A few seconds of silence creep in. Kwesi takes a few beats before he reveals his true agenda. "I have Alzheimer's disease, Son. I don't want the last memories of me tarnished by this illness. I didn't do for my kids, and I'm trying to care about this now . . . So, when I have no control of what I don't remember, you guys won't hold that it against me."

A few moments pass as I process what Kwesi said. "After all these years, don't you think it's selfish to try to reunite the family you abandoned?"

"It might be . . . But, Son, can you find it in your heart to forgive your ole man?" Kwesi pleads as a tear rolls down his pathetic face.

I rise to my feet. "You're closer to your demise so now you want forgiveness? When you were healthy, I barely heard from you. You didn't care for my forgiveness then. Now that you're sick, you want compassion?"

My eyes start to well up. I cannot let Kwesi see me get emotional because he does not deserve my sympathy, or my empathy. The only action that seems natural at this point is to storm out of the coffee shop. And that is exactly what I do.

CHAPTER 3

HUMBLE BEGINNINGS

Before I was born, my father Kwesi Black served in the United States Army as a paratrooper with the 82nd Airborne based at Fort Bragg, North Carolina. He promised to marry my mother Renita Russell if she waited for him after a dangerous mission to Central America during the cocaine wars of the early 1980s.

Kwesi returned to American soil, honored his word, and married my mother. Nine months later, I was born. Two years later, my brother Armani was born, which came as a surprise for both of my parents. Their young marriage was laced with heated arguments that stemmed from Kwesi's infidelities. He failed to mention he had gotten three other women pregnant at the same time, which led to my parents' final separation.

By this time, my mother had enough of Kwesi's philandering. She packed all our belongings and moved us to a small town in Arkansas called Blytheville, where my Papa and Grandma Russell lived. When a father is absent, young boys look to other male figures to set the standard for how to behave and how *to survive in the world. For me, it was Papa. Growing up, I thought Papa hung the moon. Papa Russell was the breadwinner for our family. He came from humble beginnings, growing up on a farm with a family of 11 children.*

Papa broke away from the pack to join the military in 1955. He married my grandmother, Lois Rice, a little after joining the service. The two of them had four kids: two girls and two boys. The two boys were stillborn. Papa served in the United States Air Force from the 1950s to the 1970s, a period of time that included segregation, the beginning of the Cold War, the Korean War, and the Vietnam War. Papa and the Russell bunch traveled many places around the world during his tenure in the military. They moved from place to place—from France, Taiwan, Spain, Alaska, and Maine—until the last stop before retiring at Eaker Air Force Base. This military installation was used for basic training camps during World War II and as both a tactical and a strategic bomber base during the Cold War.

I remember our first night in Blytheville. After a long journey on a Greyhound bus from North Carolina, we settled into our new home with Papa and Grandma. Later that night as we slept, a fire broke out at the next-door neighbor's house. Papa was the first to alert us of the dangers lurking next-door.

"Get Up! Get Up, gotdamn it, before I beat you in the head with a brick!" Papa said as he made sure everyone in the house was awake. He headed outside to warm up the car.

Mom donned a thick winter coat and wrapped Armani and me up in warm clothing. She grabbed me and Armani's nursing bag, and yelled, "Mama, come get Armani!"

Mom rushed out of the house and headed for the car, where Papa was waiting. Mom placed me in a car seat, and sat in the backseat. As we waited in the car, Grandma rushed out of the house with a suitcase, four of her favorite church outfits stacked on top of each other, two of her favorite purses slung over her shoulders, and the brand-new boots she had purchased with her JCPenney's account. Grandma entered the car with the rest of us.

"Where's the other baby?" Papa asked.

"Oh, lord, I forgot to grab the baby . . . And I forgot my teeth," Grandma shouted as she rushed out of the car to grab Armani.

The fire was contained by the next morning. By accident, the neighbors burnt down their house by trying to freebase cocaine on top of their stove. Though our home was safe and secure from the fire, there was the more significant danger of the crack epidemic right around the corner.

*****

There's a knock at the door that breaks my concentration. I step away from the desk and stride over to the door. Glancing through the peephole, I notice it is a UPS deliveryman then open the door.

"Trevor Russell?" the UPS deliveryman asks.

"Yes." The deliveryman hands me a device.

"Can you sign here for me?"

I take the device and sign my name. The deliveryman hands me the package.

"Thank you, sir. Have a good day."

I shut the door, stroll back to my desk, place the package on the ground, and get back to where I left off.

*****

THE ARMPIT OF AMERICA

If you look at a map of the United States and pinpoint where Blytheville is located, you'd think it's in the armpit of America. It's located on the I-55 between two major cities, St. Louis and Memphis. It's also placed next to the nasty-ass, mighty Mississippi River that is filled with catfish, dead bodies, and burnt up cars from fraudulent insurance claims.

There's not much to do in Blytheville, Arkansas. The place reeks of despair and hopelessness. Resources are limited, and so is inspiration. The winters were cold, and the summers cooked anyone foolish enough to venture outside. The spring and autumn were laced with terrifying thunderstorms. As for shopping, there's the Mall of Blytheville, also known as Walmart. At any given time of the day, you would see half the town's population in that store. There are a couple of grocery stores, a handful of restaurants, some family-owned retail stores, and a ton of churches.

Once upon a time, we had two operating public pools, but the Blytheville Police Department shut one of them down because someone got shot and killed there. We didn't go because we didn't know how to swim. Mom was more concerned about our chances of getting shot as opposed to us drowning in the pool.

Here's the kicker about ole Blytheville: in the summer, mosquitos will bite the shit out of you. Why do these filthy creatures exist? They do nothing for society. If I were on the board for animal extinctions, I would put them at the top of the list for termination. Last but not least, Blytheville is located along the New Madrid Seismic Zone. This means that if, God forbid, a big ass earthquake happens, the whole area could possibly be swallowed by the nasty ass, mighty Mississippi River.

*****

My phone vibrates. Another distraction.

I'm never gonna get this done. I grab the phone and notice it's Ma.

"Hey, Ma."

"Hey. I got a notification that says you got the package I sent."

"Yeah, I did. What is it?"

"Open it and find out, boy!"

When I open the package, I find a scrapbook with pictures from my childhood. Each page is dedicated to every grade level up to my senior year of high school. As I flip through the album, I begin to chuckle, looking at old school photos and reminiscing about ancient times.

"Thanks for sending the scrapbook."

"Oh, you're welcome. It's for your twentieth high school reunion."

"Uh . . . Yeah . . . Um . . . Ma . . . I'm not going to the reunion."

"Why not? You haven't seen any of your classmates since you graduated."

"I can go on Facebook. Most of them post their whole life there anyway."

"It's not the same thing, boy."

"I'll think about it, Ma."

"Papa would love to see ya if you're back in town. "

"OK. I'll come home . . . but only to see Papa!"

"Before I forget, guess who I saw today when I was at the salon?"

"Who's that?"

"Sade!"

"The singer? I love her music."

"Boy you know that Sade ain't coming to no damn Blytheville. I'm talking about your classmate, Sade Cole."

"You actually spoke to her?"

"Yep, and she said she's expecting to see you at the class reunion."

"Oh . . . OK . . . Look, Ma, I need to get back to work. I'll look at some flights and see what happens."

"OK. Talk to you later, boy."

"Love ya, Ma."

"Love you." The call ends, and I get back to where I left off.

CHAPTER 4

EIGHTIES BABIES

In the 1980s, Mike Tyson was "The Baddest Man on the Planet." He became the undisputed heavyweight champion and took the boxing world by storm. Eddie Murphy was the funniest man on the planet, and Bill Cosby was America's favorite father. The 1980s birthed Michael Jackson's "Thriller," Janet Jackson's "Control," and Prince's "Purple Rain." The 1980's gave us Whitney Houston, one of the best voices in our lifetime. There was Magic Johnson's Lakers versus Larry Bird's Celtics and the emergence of the Bad Boy Pistons up north in Detroit. The Jheri Curl, which should go down as the worst hairstyle ever created in Pop Culture history, was born in the 1980s. It was great to watch TV and see all these emerging talents living their best lives. But at some point, the TV shuts off, the nostalgia wears thin, and reality sets in.

The reality during those times was the crack cocaine epidemic that affected inner cities throughout The United States. Crack became an illegal multi-million-dollar industry that overwhelmed African American communities.

As a result of rampant drug use, crime skyrocketed, and many communities have yet to recover. Which leads to the question, "What role did the US Government play in allowing crack cocaine to enter the ghettos of African American communities?"

The "War on Drugs" was a phrase the media coined after a press conference given by former President Richard Nixon. Nixon declared a "war on drugs" that would lead to the imprisonment of all participants. Though drug usage during those times was equal amongst all ethnic groups in the U.S., the rate of African American incarceration for drug offenses was disproportionately higher.

The Reagan Administration took Nixon's racist drug war to a new level. During the first five years in office, Ronald Reagan signed the Anti-Drug Abuse Act, which reinforced drug enforcement by creating mandatory minimum sentencing and forfeiture of cash and real estate for drug offenses. These policies were far more detrimental to African Americans than any other demographic group affected by the new laws. Reagan increased the size and presence of federal drug control agencies across the country, which led to mass incarcerations over the course of the next few decades. Yet, white drug offenders, consumers, and dealers of the same crimes remained free.

The Reagan Administration authorized the CIA to aid the Contra rebels through funding, weaponry, and training. The Contras operated out of camps in neighboring countries, such as El Salvador, Honduras, Guatemala, Costa Rica, and Panama. The Soviet Union got involved in providing political, economic, military, and diplomatic support to the left-wing of the Nicaraguan government. If the Russians took over Nicaragua, they would be too close to The United States. After Congress banned U.S. support to the rebels, the Reagan Administration underhandedly continued to aid them financially and militarily.

While Reagan was a supporter of the Contra agenda, he and National Security Council member Oliver North were at fault for flooding crack cocaine into predominantly African American neighborhoods, which led to Reaganomics.

Reaganomics sacrificed a sector of people to aid the racist, capitalist domination of the United States. While stimulating economic growth in the U.S. during the 80s, the policies also broadened the gap between low and high income earners. Reaganomics tripled the national debt and aggravated the ever-worsening income and wealth inequality. Reagan administered massive cuts in social programs for the poor, claiming that the "welfare queen" and other lazy people were abusing the programs. The welfare system was set up so that if a welfare queen has no male in the house, they get paid more money. If a man lived in the house with the welfare queen, then she would receive fewer benefits. Along with mass incarceration, the welfare system was created to keep black fathers out of the house. It was designed to incentivize children to grow up without a father. The government funds single mothers more if the father isn't in the house.

In our community, if the mother fails, the child fails. If you were a struggling single mother and couldn't afford to keep your kids, the government would threaten to take them. That drove many young men to lives of crime. They would push dope on street corners to make ends meet to help their stressed mothers. Most of the crack dealers and crack fiends originated from families that were on welfare. When crack arrived, unemployed men in our community had two options: sell crack to put food on the table or smoke it to alleviate the pressure of being economically oppressed and not financially stable enough to provide for a starving family.

A father's responsibility in a child's life is to nurture the child's intellectual, emotional, physical, social, and spiritual development. As human beings, we grow up imitating the behaviors of those around us. When a father is absent, young boys look to other male figures to set an example for how to survive in the world. That is the reason why so many boys in our communities end up murdered in the streets, sent to prison, or in the sheets like Kwesi. The absence of so many fathers has decimated African American communities.

The crack epidemic was a reverse genocide engineered for African American and Hispanic communities to exterminate themselves. The reason most of my classmates and their parents have daddy issues originates from *the circumstances created by the systemic agenda orchestrated through Reaganomics. The Reagan Administration set up the private prison industrial systems in many states, which turned prisoners into lucrative assets by using them for cheap labor. The U.S. spent almost $1 trillion fighting the "War on Drugs" but did not invest one dime in rehabilitating the communities destroyed by the crack epidemic.*

*****

The front door flies open, then slams shut. Eva and little Dustin Lopez enter the condo.

"Hey, Tre!" Dustin runs over to give me a high five.

"What's up, little man? How was school?"

"It was good. We took a field trip to the zoo. We saw lions and tigers, but no bears, just pussycats."

"Pussycats, huh? Nice!" I say with a grin. Eva taps me on the arm to get my head out of the gutter.

"Go to your room, Mi Hijo. Trevor and I have grown up business to discuss."

The inquisitive Dustin asks, "Is it about the cat we're getting?"

"Mi Hijo, what cat?"

"The other night, you guys had grown up business to talk about, and I heard you."

Confusion strikes Eva as she grows curious about what Dustin might have heard.

"What did you hear, little man?" I ask.

"The other night, I heard mommy say she wanted you to beat up some cat . . . Then I heard mommy meowing."

Eva glares at me, but I look away and pretend I'm typing on my laptop.

Eva pats Dustin on the bottom. "Go to your room! And stop listening to grown people when you're supposed to be asleep, Mi Hijo." Dustin scurries off.

An anxious Eva paces back and forth on the floor, "Oh my god, Papi. Now we have to buy a cat along with the baby."

"Wait, what are you talking about, Eva?"

"You're gonna be somebody's daddy soon."

"You're pregnant!"

"Mommy's having a baby!" Dustin's faint voice shouts from his room.

"Mi Hijo, Cállate! Put your headphones on! Now!" Eva shouts.

Everything in my body shuts down as I grow numb. I can feel the air in my lungs dissipating. What did I get myself into?

CHAPTER 5

Drenched in sweat, I pace across the floor, not sure if I am angry or afraid. I am not ready to be a father. How could she have gotten pregnant? Of course, I know *how* she became pregnant. How could I have been so careless? She should have never moved in with me. I knew she would try to trap me. Thoughts race through my mind as I try to fathom Eva's pregnancy.

"Are you sure it's mine?" I ask in a whisper.

Eva storms toward me then smacks my face. I guess that answers the question.

I take a few steps away from Eva and ask, "How do you know that baby is mine?"

"I've only been with you," Eva says in a passionate whisper.

"How do I know that, though? Are you sure it's not Terry's? You do see him every day."

Eva takes a seat at my desk. "That was years ago, Papi. I only see him every other day because he's my trainer."

"Finding out yesterday that my live-in girlfriend muted the fact that she slept with her personal trainer, the one she still uses, is a hard pill to swallow. I wish I had the opportunity to have sex with a woman and later she would hire me to write her biography."

"I'm so sorry," Eva said. "It's the worst decision I've ever made to not be honest when you first asked me, and I made it worse."

The more I think about it, the angrier I grow. "How would you feel if I was all buddy-buddy with another woman that saw me naked, had sex with me, shared intimate moments with me . . . And I still saw her every day?"

Eva thinks on the question a few seconds. "I would be flipping out, Papi. I'm so stupid. It was an awful choice. I wish I could rewind the time. But now we're pregnant."

"What if I'm a bad father? What if I can't be there for my child?"

"Don't be like that. Those are irrational fears, Papi. I love your relationship with Mijo. You embraced him like he was your very own."

"We have to get an abortion."

"That isn't your decision to make . . . I'm not aborting my child."

I sit in my thoughts for a few moments, then take a deep breath. I stand up, rush over to my desk, and pack my laptop into my backpack. I scurry to the master bedroom, grab my suitcase out of the walk-in closet and pack up a few items, such as underwear, a few pair of socks, shirts, a couple of pairs of shoes, and some outfits. I zip up the suitcase and rush out of the bedroom.

As soon as I return to the living room, I find a bemused Eva standing in front of the door. I grab a coat, my wallet, keys, and phone then storm toward the front door. Eva tries to block the door to keep me from leaving.

"Papi, what are you doing? You can't leave like this."

I move her out of the way. "I don't want children!"

"Where are you going, Trevor?"

I wheel my suitcase out of the condo.

CHAPTER 6

My nostrils feel as if I snorted a tube of vapor rub. The moisture in my nose has frozen, and I am pretty sure I developed a crick in my neck sitting in the backseat of this Lyft ride. My head hangs halfway out of the window because the car smells like a bag full of assholes.

"Sir, if you're hot, I can turn down the heater." The Lyft driver says.

"The heater's not the problem, bro."

"Well, can you roll the window up? It's a little nippy out."

"If I roll this window up, I'll puke inside your car." And I would much rather let the frigid wind rake my face than inhale the fumes seeping from this guy's body.

"What airline are you flying, sir?"

"Southwest."

The Lyft driver pulls over to the curb and pops the trunk.

As soon as I get out of the car, I dig in my suitcase and grab my *Creed Aventus* Eau De Parfum bottle. I squirt myself a few times to get the car stench off me then tread through the sliding doors of the airport.

The line for checking a bag is longer than I had expected. You would think catching a redeye flight on a Wednesday night would be a breeze, but not tonight.

My phone vibrates. I pull it out and notice Eva is calling. I ignore the call and shove it back in my pocket. Growing up, I was always looking for love. Now that I'm grown, I find myself running away from it. Part of me wants to blame my daddy issues for this flaw. Maybe it's the commitment issues I have. My thoughts are all over the place.

"Next in line," the customer service representative shouts. I roll my suitcase up to the service desk.

"Hello . . . I will need to see a Government ID." I hand the representative my ID. "You're heading to Memphis?" she asks.

"Yes, ma'am, I am."

"Trevor Russell . . . Were you on one of those talk shows promoting your book *The South Hates Me?*"

"Yeah . . . Unfortunately, that's me," I say as we share a laugh.

"That was a great read. When's the next book coming out?"

"Sometime within our lifetime," I say. The representative prints out a label for my suitcase, tags the bag, then throws it on the conveyor belt.

"Enjoy your flight, sir! Next in line."

I walk through the TSA pre-check line, through security, head toward the terminal, and find an empty gate where no one is sitting. I pull out my laptop and begin writing where I left off . . .

*****

HURT PEOPLE, HURT PEOPLE

One of my favorite films growing up in the 90s was "New Jack City." It starred Wesley Snipes, Ice T, Chris Rock, Judd Nelson, and Mario Van Peebles, who was also the director. At the end of the film, right before the ending credits, a message flashed across the screen. The message read, "Although this is a fictional story, there are Nino Browns in every major city in America. If we don't confront the problems realistically without empty slogans and promises, then the drugs will continue to destroy our communities." The infamous Nino Brown was the arrogant drug kingpin character in the film portrayed by Wesley Snipes.

The "Nino Brown" in our community was Rack Daddy, born Raymond Cole. Rack Daddy's folks immigrated to Florida from Haiti. He was nicknamed Rack Daddy because he was the town's best pool shark. When it came to playing pool, he could out hustle any sucker holding a stick. Rack Daddy wore big gold chains, rocked a juicy Jheri Curl, and drove beautiful sports cars that attracted the ladies. Rack Daddy floated on a false sense of reality because he wasn't a good-looking man, but dough made him look like a young Denzel Washington.

Rack Daddy was from Miami Gardens, Florida. At the emergence of the crack epidemic, South Florida was dead smack in the middle of a cocaine war between Columbian and Cuban cartels, predominantly the Medellin Cartel. Due to the wars amongst drug lords, Miami became the "Drug Capital of the World."

On a humid summer day in the mid-1980s, Rack Daddy was doing community service near the Florida Everglades. He and the rest of the chain gang were tasked with removing a bunch of dead alligator corpses from the surrounding areas. The cause of death was unknown until Rack Daddy discovered a bunch of packages with white powder.

Turns out, the crocodiles were chewing on packages that contained pure Columbian dope and dying of cocaine overdoses. Back then, the Medellin Cartel was flooding dope in through all the nooks and crannies of the Florida Everglades. Rack Daddy, the shrewd hustler he was, talked his brother into purchasing a boat that they could use to sail in and around the Everglades to gather as much dope as they could get.

Rack Daddy knew he could not compete with all that was happening in Miami, and law enforcement pressure drove many significant players out of the picture. Numerous high-end stores and businesses closed due to the fighting between the warring cartels. Rack Daddy decided to take his talents to a quieter place, which happened to be Blytheville, and business began to boom.

Blytheville was a strategic hub for nuclear weapons during the Cold War and a distribution hub for Rack Daddy's drug empire during the 1980s and 1990s. Blytheville had access to an operational airport and a river port for more premeditated imports. You couldn't smuggle drugs into Memphis or St. Louis because federal agents had beefed up security at airports through the new drug policies.

Once Rack Daddy set up shop in Blytheville, he bumped into an Air Force crew chief stationed at Eaker Air Force Base. His brother stayed in Florida, fished for new dope in the Everglades, then transported what he found up to Arkansas when the stash was large enough to make a solid profit. Rack Daddy became the crack distributor for multiple military towns and the primary dope connection from St. Louis to Memphis. This made Rack Daddy and his family massive amounts of money. That money was then turned into legitimate small businesses around the town of Blytheville to cover illegal operations and other ostentatious schemes.

Rack Daddy's main crack house was located on Rose Street on the west side of town. Rose Street is a couple of streets away from where my grandparents stayed. Rose Street was known as "Crack Alley." As a child the old urban legend said that if you started walking on one end of Rose Street by the time you made it to the other side, you would have mutated into a crackhead.

At that age, I couldn't fathom the luxury cars and fancy homes Rack Daddy owned. What I did grasp was how attentive Rack Daddy was to his children. Rack Daddy had a lot of kids, like Kwesi. My father didn't flood the streets with poison, but he didn't take care of his children. Rack Daddy took care of his children but, in retrospect, destroyed the community by flooding the streets with cheap dope . . .

*****

My phone vibrates in my pocket, and it breaks my concentration. I receive an alert that my plane is boarding. I stuff my laptop in my backpack and head for the gate.

CHAPTER 7

"We've reached 30,000 feet. Large electronic devices can now be used. Flight attendants will be coming around shortly with refreshments," one of the flight attendants says over the intercom. As we ascend into the sky on the Boeing 737 aircraft, I pull out my laptop and get back to writing . . .

*****

PAPA WASN'T A ROLLING STONE

While Kwesi was out populating the world and Rack Daddy was selling cheap dope to crack fiends, Papa sold expired candy under-the-table to kids in the neighborhood. If you bought candy from my Papa back in those days, you might have come across Christmas candy around Easter or Easter candy during Halloween. And business for Papa was booming.

Everyone bought candy from Papa, including the badass neighborhood kids who would come through and get sassy with Papa from time to time. One kid was Jackson Reed's punk ass. One time he was in line, waiting his turn to buy candy and started talking smack to Papa.

"You don't have freeze cups?" Jackson Reed's punk ass asked.

"What you see is what you get," said Papa.

"The lady at the corner store has better stuff than you."

"That's fine. Go down there, then . . . Next in line!"

"Fuck you, Mr. Russell."

"Fuck you back! Get out of my yard, sapsucka!"

The little kid flipped off Papa then shouted, "Momma! Mister Russell cursed at me again."

Papa flipped the kid the bird right back, "That's for your mammy."

Papa wasn't afraid to curse a kid out. He didn't care if you were 8 years old or 80. If you disrespected him, he was coming right back at you. Whichever way you sliced it, Papa made his money legally selling candy, working as head chef at the local country club, and operating as the general manager of the NCO Club on Eaker Air Force Base. This was all while providing for children that weren't his responsibility. Papa didn't have to work anymore after retiring from the military. But because Kwesi wasn't there, Papa worked harder than he should have to help my mother keep a roof over our heads.

Papa was the ultimate hustler. He would gather other people's junk from off the street, keep what he liked, and sell what he didn't. Papa would collect old cans around the town and take them to the local recycling center to make a few extra bucks to provide for his family. At that time, Reaganomics was in full effect under President George H.W. Bush. During this administration, the needle would be off African American communities and onto the Middle East with The Gulf War in Iraq.

Papa would work his last day at the NCO Club. Around that time, the Base Realignment and Closure Commission recommended that the Eaker Air Force Base in Blytheville, Arkansas, be closed in a cost-cutting move. The base closed on December 15, 1992, the same day Dr. Dre dropped "The Chronic."

Armani and I split our time with our mother and Grandparents. Mom was either working or taking quick naps in between her second and third jobs. My father's absence allowed us to be around our old folks. Though living in Arkansas at times felt as if we were prisoners of circumstance, we had our best times with Papa and Grandma.

One day, Grandma had planted a beautiful array of flowers in her garden. Loraine gawked from a distance as she attempted to steal the next-door neighbor's 175-pound Rottweiler. You can imagine how that went. Loraine was an infamous Rose Street crackhead notorious for some of the most random crackhead acts of the era. If it weren't attached to the ground or your house, she would steal it then try to sell it back to you. It was a matter of time before she graced Papa and Grandma with her presence.

Later that night, Loraine knocked on the door. The mauled, bloody, and poorly-bandaged streetwalker dug up Grandma's freshly planted flowers and tried to sell them back to Papa. Grandma fussed and cussed about those damn flowers all summer long.

It was a hard knock life for Grandma, or so she complained. Grandma griped and complained and fussed and cussed about how stressful life was. She fussed when it was cold and cussed when it was hot. Grandma fussed during sunny days and cussed when it rained. If there were a competitive sport for fussing and cussing, Grandma would be crowned queen. The poor lady never worked an actual 9 to 5 job. Her main responsibility was to babysit the kids while my mother and Papa worked.

One hot, muggy day that summer, Grandma paced the cluttered living room floor. "I can't believe he cut my tree down . . . Nobody listens to me . . . I just wish I could run away," she mumbled to herself. Whenever Grandma wasn't fussing and cussing, she would gossip with her widowed good friend Mrs. Juanita Cole.

Mrs. Cole, who lived across the street, had a bittersweet story. When she was a child, her family was trapped in a burning house. Mrs. Cole managed to escape but courageously headed back in the fiery home to rescue her family. She ended up with severe 3rd-degree burns and an amputated arm.

Before there was Wendy Williams, there was Mrs. Cole. She and Grandma would gossip about everyone's business. Mrs. Cole was a nosey little lady. She wanted to know who you were, what you were doing, when you did it, how *you were doing it, when you did it, where you did it, and why the hell you were doing it.*

Mrs. Cole was Papa's foe because she was so nosey. She would always assert herself if she felt Papa was overstepping his boundaries at his own house. The operative words being "his house." Mrs. Cole, who lived across the street, walked across the way and over into Papa and Grandma's yard. She was usually accompanied by her cute, tomboyish 10-year-old granddaughter, Sade, who was always dribbling a basketball.

For Mrs. Cole to enter the house, she had to walk pass Papa.

"Juanita," said Papa.

"Russell," Mrs. Cole responded.

They greeted each other passive-aggressively for the majority of the time until this one day. A few days before, Grandma had planted a tree in the front yard and Papa had one of his workers cut the tree down because he was laying concrete down over the front yard to extend the driveway. Grandma fussed and cussed about that damn tree to anyone that would listen. Mrs. Cole decided to confront Papa about the tree.

"Why did you cut Lois's tree down?" Mrs. Cole asked.

Papa, who didn't like to be questioned by anybody, answered back, "This is my house! Take your ass in the house before I chop yo head off with an ax!" Mrs. Cole, appalled by the response, decided to let Papa have his moment.

Because Grandma and Mrs. Cole were good friends, she would let us play with Sade, even though her father was the drug lord Rack Daddy. Sade and I didn't like each other at first. I thought because her dad was some big-time drug dealer and had a lot of money that she felt she was better than me. We didn't hang out much because she lived in a big house with some wannabe big shot her mother had married. Whenever Sade and I were around each other, we were brutally competitive.

We didn't have basketball hoops in our neighborhood because we couldn't afford one. All we could afford at the time was the basketball. Maybe one house on the entire block had a hoop, but Papa didn't want us playing in other people's yards. Since Sade's Grandma lived across the street, there were alternatives to having a basketball hoop. We played a game called streetball. Streetball is a game where two people line up across the street from each other and toss a basketball at the opposing sides street curb. Whenever you hit the curb, you score 10 points and the first to 100 wins. Another way to win the game of streetball without scoring 100 points was to toss the basketball over an incoming car and still manage to hit the curb.

Sade and I tossed the basketball back and forth with the intention of hitting the curb. Sade tossed the ball, hit my curb, and shouted, "She's heating up!" a reference to the video game NBA JAM. Sade tossed the ball and hit my curb again. "Boomshakalaka! That's game."

Armani and Jackson Reed's punk ass laughed hysterically.

"You cheated! I wanna rematch."

"Fine. I'll beat you again."

We played streetball all afternoon and into the evening, and I had not won a game. Sade had beaten me four straight games. I'd never won a game against her, but then it happened...

A car crept up the road as we threw the ball back and forth. Sade threw the ball, missed the curb, and it bounced to me. I waited for the car to get closer then tossed the ball over the car as it drove past. The vehicle stopped in the middle of the street, the ball hit the curb and ricocheted off a brand new, bright red 1994 Chevy Corvette. On the hood, was a naked lady with her breast blurred out.

"I won!" I shouted with glee, but my win was short-lived. The driver of the new car was Rack Daddy, who was trying to turn into the driveway at Mrs. Cole's house. He hopped out of the vehicle and darted an annoyed glare at me.

"Daddy!" Sade shouted as she ran into her father's arms.

"Hey, baby girl! I got you something for you." Rack Daddy opened up the trunk and pulled out a Jordan shoe box with a pair of Jordan 9's.

"Aye, Kid . . . Come here," he said to me.

I hesitated but inched closer to Rack Daddy, the most feared drug lord in town. Rack Daddy pulled out a stack of $100 bills then handed me one. I'd never held that much money in my hand ever.

"Don't tell your folks where you got this from."

I nodded my head yes and stuffed the bill into my pocket.

"Take a ride with me, baby girl."

"I'll see you later, Tre!"

Sade tossed the ball to me, jumped in the car with her father, then they zoomed off. In most people's eyes, Rack Daddy was a monster because he sold drugs, and stories floated around that he murdered people. But at that moment, I didn't see a murderer or a drug lord. I saw a man living one of the most chaotic and dangerous lives make time to spend with his child while Kwesi was nowhere around.

*****

Suddenly, the aircraft rumbles so hard it knocks my laptop off the tray. "Ladies and Gentlemen, we'll be experiencing a little turbulence. A thunderstorm popped up and is surrounding us. The Air Traffic Controllers are doing everything they can do to get us around the storm," said the pilot. "We'll put the seatbelt sign on for now . . . Flight Attendants, take your seats." I place my laptop in my backpack and slide it under the seat in front of me. The plane rumbles again, and this time overhead bins come open, luggage falls all over the place, and the lights go dim. Lord, please don't let this be it.

CHAPTER 8

It felt as if we are being hit from the top of the fuselage with the hand of God. The turbulence lasts a solid 20 minutes as the plane bounces and sways. For 10 of those minutes, my balls hide in my stomach as the plane shakes, rattles, and jerks through the thick, stormy clouds. As my life flashes by, I grow angry.

Why am I on this flight in the first place? Is my destiny to run away from my pregnant girlfriend and abandon my child, like Kwesi did to me? Thinking about all that lead up to this moment puts everything in perspective. It's Kwesi's fault. Why did I allow him to come back into my life and drop his baggage on me? He's the reason I have trust issues. I might not have overreacted with Eva had I ignored Kwesi's call. Now I'm on a plane that is about to crash and . . .

"Ladies and gentlemen, we're clear of the rough areas. We have about an hour and a half until we reach our destination. The seatbelt sign will remain on, but you are free to move about in the cabin," the pilot says.

The turbulence has ended, and it is back to smooth sailing. I pull my laptop out and start typing . . .

*****

EVERY DOG HAS HIS DAY

Growing up, I didn't need to be entertained much because I had Papa and Grandma. Though there was a generational gap, sharing my upbringing with them was a blessing in a disguise. Grandma and Papa were two of the silliest people I've ever met in my life. They fought and bickered about anything and everything. Papa and Grandma argued every day from the time we moved to Blytheville until I graduated from high school. Within those 16 years of living with them, Papa must have uttered he wanted a divorce at least 11,680 times. That equates to about 2 arguments a day.

"I wanna divoce," he would say to punctuate their arguments. The "R" was dropped because of his southerner drawl. Papa could have divorced Grandma after their children had grown up, but I believe he stayed around to help support his children's children.

I remember Papa and some hired workers were out in the front yard setting up a 20-something year-old RV trailer for his candy business. He wanted to detach it away from the house in case of a burglary. The trailer wasn't that presentable. The paint had faded, and a couple of the tires were flat.

Grandma paced the living room floor.

"I don't know why he's putting that ugly thing in the front yard," Grandma said. Grandma dialed multiple numbers, but no one answered. She placed the phone down and paced the floor a few moments. All she wanted was to express her feelings about how the trailer was obstructing the house's view. She rushed back over to the phone and dialed another number, still no answer.

Grandma couldn't take it anymore. She stuck her head out and screamed, "Robbie! Why the hell you putting that piece of shit in front of the yard? We don't need no mo junk out there." A few of the workers chuckled, which humiliated Papa.

"That's it! Got damn it! I want a divoce," Papa shouted as he stormed toward the front door like a tank on the warpath.

Grandma panicked, then locked the front door. "Hide! He's gonna get us," Grandma said. Papa wasn't coming for me, I thought, so I sat on the living room couch while Grandma ran into the back and locked herself in the bathroom.

I could hear Papa shuffling through his keys to find the right one that fit the keyhole. Papa burst into the house drenched in sweat. He thundered through the house and rushed to the back door. Several moments later, Papa was in the backyard with a shovel, digging a hole in the ground.

"Papa, what are you doing?" I asked.

"I'm fixing your Grandmammy's bed," Papa shouted, but he didn't harm her. When he calmed down, he packed up his things from the master bedroom, moved three rooms down the hall into his own space, and my grandparents became roommates for the rest of their waking lives.

Papa was the king of selling wolf tickets, and he sold every one of them. Papa threatened to hit us in the head with hammers, books, broomsticks, shovels, telephone poles, bricks, baseball bats, golf clubs, shoes, and tree branches. Papa even threatened to beat us with Grandma. Papa hurled out extreme threats, so he didn't have to physically beat anyone. He wasn't at all physical when it came to discipline. His threats were scary and funny, like the Chucky doll.

The only time Papa got physical with us was the time Armani and I were up playing way past our bedtime. Papa had to be up early for work at the country club, and we were making all kinds of noise. We didn't see the smoke signals from Grandma's fussing and cussing.

"Armani! Tre!" Grandma yelled. "Go to bed right now . . . And I mean it, too."

Papa shouted, "I'm gonna crack your skulls open and serve that poisonous brain meat to the folks at the country club if y'all don't shut up!"

We were on a sugar rush from all the stolen candy we had eaten from Papa's store. We snickered and fought way past Grandma's bedtime. We were watching the "Arsenio Hall Show" when Grandma walked in and turned the tube off. "It's bedtime. You up watching this mess . . . Go to sleep," she said as she turned the light off and walked back to her room. We waited a few seconds then turned the TV back on. Grandma walked back in the room and turned the television off.

"Turn that TV off and don't turn it back on . . . And I mean it, too!" Grandma fussed and cussed as she made her way out of the room. We waited a few seconds and then turned the TV back on. Several moments later, Papa snuck in the room like a ninja and whipped us with a dry towel. He swung that thing around as if it were nunchucks. That was the last time he ever had to inflict pain on me because I knew Papa didn't play. We knew we could pull fast ones on Grandma because she was nothing but hot air.

Before cell phones, there were landlines. Grandma had her line and Papa had his. Whenever Papa was at work, Armani prank called Grandma's line and disguised his voice.

"Miss Russell, is your refrigerator running?" he asked.

"Give me a second," she replied, and we watched her walk to the kitchen and open the refrigerator to make sure it was working. Then we watched her walk back to her room.

"Yes. It's running."

"You better go catch it, bitch," Armani yelled into the receiver and slammed the phone down.

Grandma caught on to our shenanigans and made us get a switch from the outside. If you are unfamiliar with a switch, it consists of sticks from a tree. You wanted to stay away from the not so ripe ones. They hurt! Armani would grab a twig so that once it hit you, the branch broke. I would bring in a big tree branch that Grandma wasn't able to grip. Over time she folded, and we had our way with her whenever Papa was at work.

Papa retired from his last job as the chef at the Blytheville Country Club. For the first time in his life, he didn't have to wake up early and go into work. That also meant he would be able to spend more time with us. All he wanted from his retirement was a stiff drink and a break from Grandma's nagging. But Papa wasn't drinking to get drunk . . . He was getting lit like a 4th of July fireworks show. Grandma took her fussing and cussing to the next level that summer because of Papa's drinking. It had gotten so bad that Papa made a promise to himself to never drink ever again. The power of Grandma's nagging saved Papa from drinking himself into an early grave. Papa settled into his retirement and continued to sell candy to neighborhood kids. Grandma continued to fuss and cuss at Armani and me while Mom worked day and night to provide for us.

My mother wanted independence; she wanted to get away from Grandma's fussing and cussing. She found us a place on the east side of town off McGruder Lane and McHaney Street in Section 8 housing. It was a tiny, brown, two-bedroom apartment next to a trailer park.

Our oldest brother, Rod, lived in the same housing area and he would play with us. Rod was a few years older than Armani and me, so we didn't see him until after school was over. Mom took him in like he was one of her own. We played with Teenage Mutant Ninja Turtles figurines, ate pizza, and played NBA JAM and Street Fighters 2 on the Super Nintendo. Whenever it was Rod's birthday, we went to his house to celebrate. Whenever it was one of our birthdays, he came to our place. When our cracked-out next-door neighbors stole our Christmas presents right from under our Christmas tree, we were over Rod's house opening gifts with him at his home. We were inseparable, then one day he and his family moved away. Who could blame them? The neighborhood around us was in shambles.

There were times we didn't have enough food for the three of us to eat. I remember times Mom didn't eat so there would be enough food for Armani and me. She often fell asleep hungry. At times, my poor mother didn't have lunch to eat when she went to work. The little money she made from working at Walmart was spread thin. When the electricity bill was past due, and the lights were shut off, we improvised. She had enough money to buy candles, so we made do.

My father Kwesi was nowhere to be found during most of this time. Kwesi was paying child support, but it was $81 a week. That equals $324 a month, *a yearly total of $4,212. Divide all of that by 365, and it comes to roughly $11.54 a day for two growing children. Even though the cost of living was relatively low because we were in Arkansas, that's still a disgrace. $4,212 a year would have been great in the 1930s, but we're talking about the 1990s. I would understand that amount if Kwesi helped raise us.*

Mom caught wind that Kwesi had been living in town for over two years and had never contacted us. When he got out of the Army in the early '90s and relocated back to Blytheville, Kwesi was on the other side of town with his new family, living it up in his beautiful two-story, two-car-garage home. Kwesi bragged to his co-workers about the vacations he went on and the expensive fur coat he bought his current wife.

My mother didn't go to the government or beg Kwesi for money. She found a decent job at a local factory then got a second job delivering parcels for UPS. She took another part-time job as a clerk at Kroger, the local grocery store. I felt so guilty watching my mother struggle without help from our father. There was nothing I could do to save her. Mom worked crazy hours. She was sleep-deprived and cranky. Mom worked three jobs to keep the lights on, put clothes on our backs, put food on the table, and buy us the Christmas toys she'd beat us with whenever we got out of line. And trust me, most of those ass whippings Armani and I received were deserved, needed, appreciated, and kept us out of the streets. My mother had to discipline us because Armani and I were little shits. She named a belt after her favorite singer, Luther Vandross. Whenever she whacked us with it, we were hitting high notes like in that song "The Glow of Love." We hid that damn belt every chance we had.

Being a single parent took its toll on my mother. For years, she gave Kwesi enough time to do right by his children, but he wanted no part of being our father. Mom had enough with having to be the mother and father, and she took him to court. It is a shame that a mother should have to take her children's father to court for the father to spend time with the kids he laid down and conceived. Mom and Kwesi were in and out of court that summer for child support and visitation rights in the weeks leading up to this moment.

They finally reached an agreement. He agreed to pay a lower amount of child support with the stipulation that he would have visitation rights every other weekend. I am sure Kwesi took the deal not because he wanted to spend time with us but because it was a way for him to maintain his lifestyle and not have to pay more money. He needed to find a loophole somewhere that worked in his favor.

One rainy summer day, Armani and I were over at our Grandparents' house while Mom was at court. As the rain poured down, Grandma, Armani, and I all sat in the living room watching old reruns of the TV show "227."

"Hey, Granny . . . Wanna see a magic trick?" Armani asked.

"Sure, boy," Grandma said.

"It's gonna cost you one whole dollar."

Grandma pulled out a dollar then handed it to Armani.

"OK . . . Now for the trick . . . I need a $10 bill."

Grandma pulled out a $10 bill and handed it to Armani. He flipped it over to show Grandma both sides of the bill.

"Abracadabra!" he said as he stuffed the $10 bill in his pocket and darted for the bathroom.

"Damn fool," Papa said with a chuckle. It took Grandma a solid five minutes to realize Armani had hoodwinked her out of eleven dollars.

Mom entered the house drenched by the rain. Unlike other days when she came back from court drained and defeated, this time she was upbeat and cheerful.

"Where's Armani?" Mom asked.

Grandma stood by the bathroom door, holding a switch she'd picked out herself. "He's in the bathroom with my money, and he gonna give it back . . . I mean it, too!"

"How was court?" Papa asked.

"It went well . . . Starting next week, the boys will be visiting their father every other week."

I was nervous yet excited. I never spent significant time with my father, but after years of watching other kids spend time with their fathers, I was eager to spend time with mine. No longer did I feel like a worthless, fatherless child. I wanted my father to redeem himself.

The day finally came. We met in the parking lot of the Walmart near I-55. It was a quick exchange and felt like a drug deal as Mom stared Kwesi down.

"Sup, boys," Kwesi greeted us. "Ready to ride?" Armani and I both shook our heads, yes. Mom flipped Kwesi the bird, but he laughed it off.

We hopped in the truck, Kwesi dug in his pocket for his keys, then entered one in the ignition. He attempted to crank the engine, but it would not turn over.

There was a half a tank of gas in the truck, the dashboard lights and radio popped on. Kwesi took the key out, blew on it, placed it back in the ignition and the engine turned over. It rumbled like a monster truck, and we were in the wind on our way.

I could feel the power the truck exerted through the deep rumbling Flowmaster exhausts. Armani and I rode quietly in Kwesi's red 1989 Chevy Silverado truck as he sped along, reaching speeds of a 100 miles per hour down the Access Road of Interstate 55. My 10-year-old eyes studied Kwesi, and the arrogant aura that he exuded. I thought this was the coolest thing I had ever experienced. I was spending time with my father.

The song "Reminiscing" by Little River Band blared through the aftermarket Cerwin Vega stereo system as Kwesi sang along with the chorus, "Hurry, don't be late . . . I can hardly wait. I said to myself when we're old. We'll go dancing in the dark, walking through the park. And reminiscing."

We made a right into a nice, middle-class neighborhood and pulled up to Kwesi's home.

"Wow . . . You have a basketball hoop," I said, observing his house. This was a two-story home with a big yard and a trampoline up front. On our side of town, there were no two-story homes. We didn't have basketball hoops, trampolines, or a front yard because we lived in an apartment complex.

Kwesi grabbed our bag and guided us through the garage and into the house. In the kitchen we found Brandy, Kwesi's wife, cooking up a meal for 6-year-old Brice and 4-year-old Angelo.

"This is Trevor and that is Armani," Kwesi said to Brandy. "Boys, this is your stepmother Brandy, and your brothers, Brice and Angelo." The time it took Kwesi to unload us and introduce us to everyone was the amount of time it took him to get back in his truck and depart. I was ecstatic to spend time with my two new little brothers. As we settled in the house, there was a faint sound of a basketball bouncing in the house and then Sade emerged out of nowhere.

"What did I say about bouncing balls in the house?" Brandy asked.

"Sade? You live out here too?" I asked.

"Yes. Your dad stole Brandy from my dad."

"Sade!" an appalled Brandy screeched.

"It's the truth . . . Come on . . . I'll show you guys around."

Sade started dribbling the ball again and guided us through the house. Who could have imagined that Sade would be Kwesi's stepchild? It was unreal.

Rack Daddy and Kwesi had history. They were never friends but shared a connection. Kwesi was sleeping with a lot of women in town before Rack Daddy brought dope to it. Once the dope flooded the streets, Kwesi received unwanted competition. Kwesi and Rack Daddy slept with the same group of women. Once women grew tired of orgasmic, cheap thrills with Kwesi, they were bribed by quickies laced with expensive gifts from Rack Daddy. They would always go back to the charming Kwesi once they became tired of the physical abuse from Rack Daddy.

Rack Daddy and Kwesi never messed with each other's Queen piece. The queen was off-limits until Rack Daddy's business got sloppy. At the time, Rack Daddy's queen was Sade's caretaker Brandy. She was a beautiful Puerto Rican lady that kind of looked like Rosie Perez. Rack Daddy brought her to Arkansas to get away from the madness in Miami. All the guys around town wanted Brandy, but no one wanted any problems with Rack Daddy. But never tell a guy like Kwesi what he can't have. Like other women, she fell for Kwesi's charming bravado, and they eloped.

The disturbing part about this was not only did Sade have a rich dad, but she also had my sorry ass, deadbeat father. Sade was effecting the pecking order of the older sibling role. Sade was Superwoman to Angelo, Brice, and Armani. This made her an instant rival. We debated about everything.

She would say, "My favorite TV show is 'Seinfeld.'"

I replied, "It ain't better than 'Martin.'"

"'Martin' isn't better than 'Friends.'"

"What world do you live in? 'Friends' is the white version of 'Living Single,'" I said. "And that show ain't better than 'Martin.'"

"'The Fresh Prince of Bel-Air' is better than all those shows," she said, and I couldn't disagree with her because that was a great show.

"What about music? East Coast or West Coast?"

"East Coast. All day!"

"Tupac and Death Row . . . You already know," I said.

Sade gave my response a thumb's down. I remember us playing Street Fighter 2 on Super Nintendo. She was Guile and I was Ken. As she threw Sonic Booms and I was Hadouken-ing right back, a debate sparked.

"You're never gonna beat me," I said.

"Uh, you never beat me in anything, Tre."

"I beat you last time we played street ball."

"That didn't count."

"You win. Perfect!" the video game said. My mouth hit the floor. Sade beat me without me laying one strike on her.

"I thought you said I'd never beat you?" Sade asked.

"I want a rematch."

"I have something better than a rematch."

Later that night, Sade put together a basketball game amongst the siblings. The teams were Sade, Brice, and Angelo versus Armani, their mentally challenged neighbor Mike, and me. I never played basketball—hell, I barely dribbled a ball! I enjoyed watching the sport from a distance but never participated. Mike had more experience than I did because he lived next door. Sade had the advantage because she had excellent basketball skills. Rack Daddy invested in her training and supported her through AAU basketball tournaments. On top of that, did I fail to mention that there was a basketball hoop in their driveway?

The pickup game was over before it had even gotten started. Sade's team destroyed us. Mike scored most of our points because Armani and I sucked. Armani didn't care about sports at all. Every time the ball came to him, he would either dodge the ball or pass it. I couldn't dribble and I couldn't make a decent pass without Brice or Angelo stealing the ball. Every shot I attempted was an airball except for a few that hit the top of the backboard. But something happened.

One play, Mike was double-teamed by Brice and Angelo. He forced a pass to Armani who then passed the ball to me. As soon as I caught it, I threw the ball up in the air. The ball soared thru the sky a moment, hit the backboard, then went through the hoop. I made my first basketball shot ever.

"That was luck," Sade shouted. As I celebrated my moment, Sade stole the ball from Mike on the next possession then passed the ball to Angelo, who scored the game-winning bucket.

"Game!" Sade yelled. "Get off the court, losers."

Brice, Angelo, and Sade all celebrated as if they'd won a championship. Armani and Mike started to celebrate with them as if their team had won. I tucked my tail and walked off the court. I knew that this would not be my last time going head-to-head with Sade. It was official: anything we did from here on out, I would try to destroy her. I didn't care if it was sports, video games, or even school grades. It didn't matter what she decided to do, in my mind, I was hell-bent on being better than she was because she had a better life than I did.

Though we were having the time of our lives, the weekend flew by, and we didn't spend any time with Kwesi. On the last day of our visitation, Kwesi returned. We were all in the living room watching X-Men cartoons. Our stepmom Brandy didn't speak to Kwesi as he sat at the kitchen table with his sunglasses on.

"Armani! Come here, Son!" Kwesi shouted.

Armani and I both stood up and timidly crept close to Kwesi.

"I didn't call you, Trevor. I only need to see Armani." Kwesi pulled out a cotton swab and told Armani to open his mouth. He placed the cotton swab in a sealed container, and Armani returned to the room with us. At the time, we didn't know what that was all about.

Kwesi stood up from the table. "You boys all packed up? I gotta take you back to your momma."

It was an awkward ride back home. There was nothing to reflect on because we didn't spend any time with our father. We just sat there and listened to him sing his songs.

As we pulled up in front of our apartment, Mom was waiting outside. "How was it?" she asked.

"It was so much fun! We played games. We ate candy and played basketball with Sade. Did you know they have a basketball hoop?" I asked.

"He put a q-tip in my mouth, mamma." Mom threw a glare at Kwesi, and things grew tense and uncomfortable fast.

"Come on, boys!" Mom said. "Y'all go in the house. I need to talk to your father a minute."

Once we got in the house, Armani and I rushed over to the window. We caught the tail end of their dispute.

Mom shouted, "No! You'll never have one without the other."

"Listen . . . I don't think Armani is my child, and I refuse to claim him as my son if we don't get a DNA test."

"I hope you rot in hell, bastard!" Mom screamed then stormed back in the apartment. Kwesi hopped in his truck, cranked his engine, and turned up his music. "Picture me Rollin" by Tupac blasted through the speakers as Kwesi sped off.

I rushed away from the window and sat on the couch as if I hadn't heard anything. Armani sat on the floor and started to tear up.

"He doesn't want me," Armani said as tears rolled down his cheeks.

Mom rushed over to console Armani. "Don't worry about Kwesi," Mom said. "His day will come . . . Every dog has his day."

*****

"Ladies and gentlemen, as we start our descent into Memphis, Tennessee, please make sure your seat backs and tray tables are in their full and upright position. Put away your laptops and other large electronic devices. Make sure your seat belt is securely fastened, and your carry-on bags are stowed underneath the seat in front of you or the overhead bins. Thank you," a flight attendant says over the speaker.

I place my laptop in its case, slide it under the seat in front of me, and stare 30,000 feet down at a familiar land.

CHAPTER 9

The sky is gray but not yet threatening. A storm brews as darker clouds cluster in the west. I pull the Toyota Prius rental car into the driveway of a southern-style colonial home located in a cul-de-sac near a small lake in a Memphis suburb called Germantown. I shut the engine off and take a moment to cogitate. Why am I here? Why should I get out of the car? He doesn't deserve any of my time. This was a mistake.

Several moments later, I restart the engine and start backing out of the driveway. A car pulls in the driveway, stopping me from departing.

"Shit!"

The curly-gray-haired, middle-aged, physically fit lady gets out of the car then approaches the passenger side of my Prius. Seconds later, she taps at the window.

"Trevor! Is that you?"

"Yeah, it's me. Hey, Glenn!"

"Get out the car and give me a hug."

I step out of the car and greet Glenn with a hug. Glenn Black is Kwesi's fourth wife. She is a nice lady, but she's never done anything for any of Kwesi's children. Glenn is not friends with any of Kwesi's children on any social media platforms. She never reached out for holidays or birthdays, but why would she? Glenn is married to Kwesi. Glenn and Kwesi met in the most Kwesi-way. She was married to some guy and Kwesi was on his third marriage. They both cheated on their spouses to be with each other. They relocated to Memphis from Blytheville after she made partner at a law firm she had worked at for 25 years.

"Your father is worse off than he's leading on," Glenn says. "He was driving around in his ol' truck earlier today and couldn't find his way home. But go check on him; he'll be delighted to see you. Come!

Glenn escorts me inside the home through the garage then leads me through an entryway into a formal dining room. Sticky notes with scribbled reminders are plastered throughout the lakefront home. To my left is an updated kitchen with natural stone countertops, and a door that opens onto the backyard.

"Go on!" Glenn encourages me to proceed to the back without her.

A stoned, glossy-eyed Kwesi rocks back in forth in his rocking chair, staring off into space. He takes a big drag from the joint he's puffing on. The backyard has a great lake view. It has wired posts in the yard displaying where at one time an above ground pool was laid. Once Kwesi notices it is me standing there he does a double take to make sure his mind isn't playing tricks on him.

We both stare at each other for a few moments. We don't greet each other. Nor do we hug Or even shake hands. Not one word is mumbled between us as we stare each other down.

With confusion and distress, Kwesi poses the question, "Who the fuck are you?"

I can feel the tension around my eyes dissipate. My father's mind has grown bad. "Pop . . . It's Trevor! Don't you remember me?"

"Trevor?" Kwesi repeats as he takes a long drag from the joint.

"I'm fucking with ya . . . Have a seat, son."

"Why would you do something like that?"

"At least you care . . . I'm still whooping Father Time's ass. It's the early stages of Alzheimer's. You want something to drink?"

"Nah, I'm good," I say as I take a seat.

"Thanks for coming to see me, Son . . . Means a lot."

Both of us sit quietly for a few moments. The majority of the times Kwesi and I were in each other's verve, things were not always this tranquil. The uncomfortable silence gets to the both of us and at the same time, we both say, "So . . ."

Acknowledging that we were speaking on top of each other Kwesi offers, "Go ahead, son."

"No . . . Ladies first, Pop." We share a rare chuckle.

"Middle age is the awkward period when Father Time starts catching up with Mother Nature." Kwesi takes another drag from his joint. "If you ever find me somewhere in some hospital room and not able to talk . . . Pull the damn plug. Don't let me live like that. You got me, Son?"

The look in Kwesi's eyes gives me a different perspective. I nod my head yes. "I gotcha, Pop."

"When I die, cremate my body and sprinkle my ashes over the water. You got me, Son?" Kwesi asks as he points toward the lake in the backyard.

"Can we not talk about that stuff right now, Pop? We still have things to work out before that happens."

Kwesi nods his head, "That's fine, Son."

A couple more moments of stillness creep by as we stare out into the lake. "Sorry about storming out of the coffee shop the other day."

"It's all good. What brings you to town?"

"A class reunion and I wanted to see Papa . . ."

"So, you have no problem getting home to see your granddaddy."

"Pop, if you wanted that type of love, you should've been a better parent. I'm here now, so let's stay in the present."

Kwesi turns his nose up and takes another puff of his joint. He offers it to me, but I pass it up.

"How's the ol' truck?" I ask.

Kwesi perks up, "You remember the ol' truck?"

I nod my head yes.

"Oh, that baby's still running good. I keep that sum bitch in the garage and only bring it out for special occasions."

Seeing the excitement in my father's face brings a genuine grin to mine. "I hear ya, Pop."

"Wanna ride out?"

"Nah, Pop . . . I don't have time." We both grow silent as several moments slip by.

"Can we speak frank, Pop?"

"Always Son. What's up?"

I take a deep breath then ask, "Why are you like this now? You're suddenly all in your feelings and you care about establishing a relationship with me."

"I think it's all that damn soy I've been eating," says Kwesi.

"Soy?"

"Yeah . . . I read an article that said soy kills testosterone."

"You didn't want any part of my childhood and now you do, and it's all because of soy products?"

Kwesi takes a drag of the joint, blows out the smoke, puts the joint out, then says, "Son, like I was trying to tell you when we were in Georgia, over the years, I have made my share of mistakes. I have done some reflecting on the way I was. I grew up not feeling wanted. My biological parents didn't want me. Knowing those details at a young age damaged me. It made me selfish. My adopted parents were good to me and gave me everything I wanted. But they never taught me family values."

"Pop, I know the story. I get it."

"That's why I changed my last name to Black," Kwesi says as he lowers his head.

"No!" I exclaim. "You changed your last name to avoid paying child support and to get into your adopted folks' will."

Kwesi's face contorts as he darts a glare in my direction. "Okay . . . I'm not perfect by any measure, Son. A man is supposed to take care of his family. I understand that now. I understand my flaws and mistakes. I wanna make it right with all my kids before it's too late," Kwesi says.

The intensity in my eyes evaporates as empathy spreads throughout my body. "I guess everyone deserves a chance to redeem themselves."

The phone in my pocket vibrates. I pull out my phone and check the notifications. Eva has sent me several messages. One reads, "I'll do my best to give you space and wait for you to contact me whenever you're ready. I love you . . . I miss you already . . . I'm here when you're ready to talk to me again. Even if it's at 3 am, and you need to get stuff off your chest. Be careful."

My face contorts as a frown sprout across my face.

"Everything OK?"

"It's my lady . . . She's pregnant."

Kwesi poses the question, "Do you think the kid is yours?"

I nod my head yes.

Kwesi takes one last hit of the joint then puts it out. "You have to do the right thing if the baby is yours, regardless of if you plan to be with her. But Son, find one woman, love her, and have babies with only her. Don't have kids by multiple women. That is played . . . Learn from me. And make sure to get a DNA test if you aren't sure it's yours."

"I'm sure you're all too familiar with that, Pop!"

Several awkward moments pass as Kwesi, and I sit in our thoughts and look out into the lake. A brisk cool breeze passes through the screened-off patio. "Son . . . Help me get all the kids together."

"Together for?"

"For a family trip."

"A family trip?"

"Did I stutter? A family trip. I wanna take a trip up to the Rocky Mountains with all of my children."

"What exactly do you want me to do? It's not an easy task talking with your offspring."

"I know, but try to talk to them for me," says Kwesi. "Invite Sade out if you like. She seems to hate me the most. But please don't tell them about the health stuff. I have to be the one to tell them."

I study my father a few moments. "I gotta go, Pop. Got a lot of things on my plate." I stand up.

Kwesi rises to his feet, puts his hands on my shoulders, looks me right in the eye, and pleads, "Do this for me, Son?"

"I got you, Pop . . . I'll do my best . . . But I can't make any promises."

Kwesi pulls me in for a hug. "Thanks, Son. Thanks for stopping by, and tell your folks I said hello."

It feels good to reconnect with my father, but we have been down this road before. For my security, I curb my enthusiasm, and I leave Kwesi's house.

CHAPTER 10

What kind of fool would I look like trying to mend Kwesi's broken relationships? I know the Bible says to "Honor thy father," but I am a heathen. Kwesi was never a parent. To call him a parent is an insult to any parent that has actually done the work of raising children. Those rules do not apply to our situation. I have bigger fish to fry than dealing with Kwesi's paternal shortcomings. I am not that fool's keeper. I have a manuscript to finish writing.

As I drive north on the highway, I notice the dark, grayish clouds above me. Lightning flashes, then a sharp, thunderous crack rumbles the rental car. I spot Starbucks on one of the road signs then exit off. I pull over into the parking lot, grab my laptop, and enter the shop right before the shower pours down.

I approach the register.

"Hello. What can I get you started today?" the cute barista asks.

"I'd like a Venti Green Tea Lemonade."

"Will that be all?"

"Yes, thank you."

Her eyes squint and her head cocks to the side. "You look familiar . . . Are you from here?"

"I'm from up the road. My father lives here."

"Who's your father?"

"Kwesi Black."

"Kwesi's your father? That's funny, I just saw him last night."

I have been down this road before. Kwesi is not a big fan of coffee or tea. The way she bit her bottom lip gave me all the information I needed to know. I hand her cash for the drink and find a secluded place to sit. As soon as I pull out my laptop, my phone vibrates. I reach into my pocket and dig it out to silence it. I must minimize distractions, but I cannot help to wonder who is calling from a 404-area code.

"This is Trevor," I say with a stern tone.

"You have a collect call from a Fulton County inmate . . . Armani. Do you accept the charges?" the automated operator says.

"Hell, no!" I say then end the call. I place the phone on silent. My phone vibrates again. I forgot to put it on do not disturb. Another call from the same area code. I answer.

"You have a collect call from a Fulton County inmate . . . Armani. Do you accept the charges?" the automated operator says.

"I guess."

"Respond yes to accept or no to end this call."

"Yes . . . Got dammit!" A couple of seconds pass.

"Tre," Armani's crackling voice says. "Get me out of here."

"What do I need to do, Armani?"

"Can you call Kris. She should know more."

"Things are a little tense right now with Kris and me."

"Please, Tre! I don't wanna call Mama or Grandma."

"Alright!" I end the call. I dial Kristine.

"Did you finish the book?" she asks.

"I'm working on it . . . But, uh, Armani is in jail and needs you to bail him out, I guess."

"Call his other girl to help him out. Is there business stuff I can help you with?"

"Nope."

"Now that I'm thinking about it and Armani's out of the picture, you're fired." Kristine ends the call.

CHAPTER 11

It sounds as if marbles are thumping off the building as the rain pounds down. The phrase "When it rains, it pours" hits harder when life decides to punch you in the face. It is pouring down outside, and my life is in shambles. Eva is pregnant, my deadbeat father is dying, Armani is in jail for who knows what, and now my agent has fired me.

I buzz Kris back. She answers the phone in mid-thought, "He said his mother doesn't think I'm right for him. Well, he can go fuck her."

"You do know Armani and I share the same mother."

There is a slight pause.

"Oh . . . I'm sorry. This will be the absolute last time I date a client's sibling."

"You can't fire me right now, Kris."

"Yes, I can, actually. I just did."

"So, all of the things you said about believing in my talent was bullshit?"

"I believe in your talent . . . it just comes with a lot of bullshit."

"But I have ink on paper. My thoughts are flowing. I found my inspiration."

"Is it done?"

"No."

"OK . . . You're still fired."

"You can't fire me!" I shout with frustration.

"Why can't I?"

"Because you're fired," I end the call and throw the damn phone across the shop. This will not alter the trajectory of my career. I will finish this book with or without help.

Moments later, the barista walks up, places my phone on the table, and takes a seat right across from me.

"Thank you," I say as we both sit silently for a few moments.

"So, you're like Kwesi but the younger version, huh."

I took it upon myself to stare at her like Samuel Jackson's character, Lazarus looked at Christina Ricci's character Rae in the movie *Black Snake Moan.*

"Oh . . . I'm sorry . . . I thought because Kwesi and I . . . You know what . . . I'm so sorry . . . Tell Kwesi that Brittany from the coffee shop misses him." She gets to her feet and strolls back to the cash the register. I get back to writing . . .

*****

DADDY ISSUE

Do you know how embarrassing it is to hear that other kids at your school see your father more than you do? During my elementary and junior high years, I heard a few of the children I went to school with say, "I saw your daddy last night!" I could count on my fingers and toes how many times some random kid said they saw Kwesi. Why is that?

Many of the men in our community were out of the house for a significant amount of time. Some of the fathers in our communities were incarcerated for drugs, and some were murdered from the violence of the crack epidemic. A handful of my peers' fathers had to enforce the laws derived from the War on Drugs. Some fathers put their hard hats on and worked long hours at factories to provide for a family they barely saw. And some of those fathers were away because of the welfare system. Yet, none of those situations applied to Kwesi. Sure, he worked and made money legally. From what I heard, he was a hard worker. But his efforts were only to satisfy his lifestyle.

I was sitting in the cafeteria for lunch one time. I sat at a table with Sade, Pretty Boy Royal, Mike, Travis, Big Ted, and Jackson Reed's punk ass. He is a black-ass white boy. He was the only mixed kid in our neighborhood, and he was a little terrorist.

Jackson Reed flunked the sixth grade three times, so he was much older than us. Jackson Reed was a cheerleader for foolishness. He was twice as strong as the rest of us because he was three years older than us. Jackson's parents had divorced several years back. His mother, who ran the lucrative Rack'Em lounge, didn't want to be a part of the military lifestyle anymore. Jackson's father, who was a Colonel in the United States Air Force, received orders that sent him to Korea. Jackson's mom lucked up and remarried one of the supervisors that worked out at Nucor.

For some odd reason, Jackson had a problem with me. My first interaction with him was weird. We were sitting at the lunch table, and Jackson was looking upside my head. Jackson's eyes squinted, and his head cocked to the side. "I saw your daddy last night." At that very moment, I understood why he didn't like me.

My computer lab teacher, Ms. Harris, was on lunch duty. Lunch duty consists of monitoring the lunchroom to make sure the children were not fighting. I remember her scanning and pacing the lunchroom like a prison guard.

To look cool in front of the guys, I blurted out, "Hoe." Quiet enough she did not hear me, but loud enough for the guys sitting close to hear. I received a few chuckles, but it was not worth the consequences.

I guess I said it loud enough for the table next to me to hear and the one person I didn't want to hear me was this dusty, hood rat that rocked a juicy Jheri Curl. Her name was Xena Jones. She had a crush on me, but I wasn't into her. She sucked her thumb and occasionally pissed herself when she fell asleep in class. She was also known around school as the teacher's pet. Her tattletale ass got up from her table and ran straight to the teacher.

Realizing what was transpiring, I got up and tried to cut her off before she could tattle on me. But my efforts were cut short when Jackson Reed stuck his punk-ass foot out and tripped me up. A roar of laughter filled the cafeteria. Lying there on the floor, I knew I was done. I could see Xena pointing at me and mouthing the words, "He called you a hoe."

Lunch ended, and we all went back to our class for the second half. Sade, who sat next to me in class, wasn't in her seat, and all her things were gone.

"OK, class, open your science book to page 75," Mrs. Dean said.

There was a knock at the door. An unexpected guest, none other than Darth Vader herself, the principal Ms. Willena Aldridge, walked in. She whispered something to Mrs. Dean then pointed at me. "Come with me," the principal said as she motioned for me to follow.

Ms. Aldridge, a former teacher herself, had a rep as a stern educator. She was the meanest teacher I have ever had in my entire life. Ms. Aldridge was so hateful. She would beat your shoulders with a paddle. Ms. Aldridge was my English teacher several years before, and I thought because she was a friend to the family, I would receive special treatment, but she didn't show me any love. She knew Kwesi was my father because he had slept with some of the teachers at her school. I was a goner.

As I sat in the principal's office, all my mind could fixate on was, "Damn . . . O.J. Simpson and I were in the same boat. He killed a white lady, and I called one a hoe." Other thoughts flooded my mind, but the one constant thought was what my mother was going to do to me. I didn't want her to take off from work because she needed to work for us. But it was too late; the office secretary had already contacted my mother at her second job.

A couple of moments passed, and then the doors to the office flew open. "It's my mother," I whispered dreadfully to myself. But it was Jackson Reed. He was sent to the office after beating up a bunch of kids at recess.

Moments later, my mom burst through the doors. "What happened?" she asked sternly.

"I . . . I . . ." I stuttered. Mom overwhelmed me with her vicious temper. My mother is a Gemini, she could be the sweetest woman in the room, or she could be the meanest creature in the world—with a switch. There was nothing to be said. I was guilty as charged. I faced the music and confessed. "A girl told a teacher I called her a hoe." She grabbed me by the arm, and we rushed through the door of the principal's office.

Before this moment, I thought I feared the menacing Ms. Aldridge, but after Mom stormed into the office, Ms. Aldridge became afraid.

"Why is my son in trouble?"

"Another student said your son called one of our professionals an inappropriate name," Ms. Aldridge replied

Mom, who could have been a lawyer, challenged back, "We're going off 'he said, she said?' Some of your staff members say you're an asshole, but are you gonna fire them because I told you?"

Ms. Aldridge started stuttering then deflected, "As a faculty, we don't accept such behavior. Trevor will have to serve a three-day suspension."

Mom turned to me then shouted, "Come on, Tre, let's get out of the racist-ass office." Mom stared down Ms. Aldridge a few moments then uttered, "You're the damn grand wizard of the KKK."

"Excuse me . . . I am black," Ms. Aldridge said in her defense as we stormed out of the school.

Mom and I sat quietly with our thoughts as music played. At the time, my mom drove a 1994 Mitsubishi Mirage. Playing on the radio was Mary J. Blige's second album, "My Life." I sat in the backseat studying to see if Mom was mad at me or mad at the school. I could gauge her mood by the song she played on the radio. If she was reflecting on being a single mother, she would listen to "I'm Going Down." My mother played that song every damn day for at least three months straight. If Mom liked a song or an album, she would play the hell out of it. She also played the shit out of other artists such as Teena Marie, GUY, Keith Sweat, the BIG Luther Vandross, Anita Baker, En Vogue, Johnny Gill, Jodeci, and SWV, to name a few.

As the next song began to play, Mom turned the volume on the radio down.

"I'm sorry, Trevor . . . I shouldn't have acted like that at your school."

In a way, I wanted Mom to continue to take the blame for getting me suspended, but I should not have said what I said.

"Mom . . . I said it."

Mom darted a glare through the rearview mirror. I could feel her beams on me as I avoided making eye contact with her.

"Look at me, boy."

My eyes eased to the rearview mirror.

Mom pulled the car over right next to a cemetery. The look in her eyes gave me the impression she was about to activate an ol' fashion ass whooping.

"What did you say?"

I grew hesitant but worked up enough fortitude to repeat, "I called the teacher a hoe."

"You had me go up there and act a damn fool in public? I called that black woman a racist, Tre."

Mom spun around and glared me down a few moments. "I can't stand you looking like your damn daddy. I wish he did more for you."

As we approached Papa and Grandma's house, we noticed a bunch of unmarked cars in front of Mrs. Cole's house. The alphabet boys — DEA, FBI, ATF, and Blytheville Police Department — had the entire block surrounded.

Mom pulled up to one of the officers that directed traffic at the intersection. "Officer . . . Sir . . . We live a couple of houses down . . . Can we pass through?"

"Sure, ma'am. I'll direct you into the driveway."

As we pulled into the driveway, there were a bunch of "For Sale" signs posted all around my grandparents' home. Papa had gone to Walmart, bought a bunch of "For Sale" signs, and posted them everywhere. He posted them on the cars, the fence, the trees, and the RV trailer. Not to exclude different parts of their house, such as the big-ass satellite dish planted on the side of the house. Papa looked frustrated as he stood at the door, spectating from a distance.

"What's with the for-sale signs, dad?" Mom asked.

"Your mama is crazy as hell. I'm moving out! I'm getting a divoce!"

Mom lightened up as she giggled at Papa's extreme pettiness.

"What's happening across the street?" Mom asked.

"That damn fool Rack Daddy shot and killed a man on tape," Papa said. "The footage got to the police station this morning."

Word got around to Papa about the events that occurred over the weekend. Enough was enough, orders had dropped, and an arrest warrant was issued for Rack Daddy. He had been hiding out across the street a few days.

The lifestyle of a drug lord caught up with Rack Daddy. He didn't smoke crack but snorted coke that led to him having a God complex. The once shrewd drug lord broke the ultimate rule of the "Ten Crack Commandments," a song by The Notorious B.I.G that advised, "Never get high on your supply." Rack Daddy became messy with his moves, and his ego grew bigger than the city. The empire he built on crack was imploding right under him. He wanted out of the dope game and wanted the rest of the world to know who Rack Daddy was.

In one of several attempts to get out of the dope industry, Rack Daddy started a music label called Rack'Em Studios, which created a buzz throughout town. Rack Daddy was inspired by all the talent that was popping up in the 90s such as Nas, Jay-Z, The Notorious B.I.G., Outkast, Three 6 Mafia, UGK, Wu-Tang Clan, Mos Def, Prodigy, and Big L. At this point, nobody had seen Rack Daddy for several months. In some of the conversations around the city, Rack Daddy was thought to be the next Master P. In other conservations, some thought he could be the next Tupac. The rest of civilization thought Rack Daddy needed to sit his ass down and stay off cocaine.

Rack Daddy hosted an event that was his version of Soul Train. His rendition added a freestyle rap battle to showcase local talent and crown the town's best lyricist. Whoever won would receive a recording deal through Rack'Em Studios. The catch was you had to beat Rack Daddy in the rap battle.

Rack Daddy planned it all down the smallest detail. He hired a production crew to film the event, which was held at his club Rack'Em, which was located on Main Street in the old Walmart building he had bought some time ago. The event brought much of the town out. The building was packed to the max 30 minutes into the event, and there were still people outside in the parking lot trying to get in. The event was a success, and the rap battle was just beginning. The dance floor of the battle was set up like a boxing ring, where the performers would face each other. If the contestants had skills, the crowd would cheer and if they sucked, the crowd would boo.

As the aspiring artists lined up for their turn to get in the ring for the face off, Rack Daddy grew nervous. This was the first time anyone would see him as a rapper and not as Rack Daddy, the big-time drug dealer. Rack Daddy excused himself from the lineup, escaped to the bathroom, then snorted a significant amount of cocaine to numb his anxiety and enhance his lyrical flow. By the time Rack Daddy reached the stage to rock the microphone, the coke had taken its toll. His flows were offbeat, and his verse grew into an aggressive shouting cocaine rage that made most of the attendees laugh. For the first time in a long time, Rack Daddy was the butt of all jokes. The audience laughed and booed so hard that it was louder than the music pumping through the club's speakers. This only fueled his opponents, who weren't the greatest of emcees.

One of the artists got on the microphone and hurled insults at Rack Daddy. The contestant talked about Rack Daddy's dried up Jheri curl and how he looked like an uglier rich version of Shabba Ranks. The guy called him out for needing money to get women. Rack Daddy's ego couldn't handle the humiliation, and he pulled out a Smith and Wesson .45 pistol and shot the competitor in the head in front of everybody. And with one finger curl, it was all over for the Rack Daddy empire.

Rack Daddy grabbed the microphone then said, "This is how y'all treat me? I helped build this city. I gave you suckas an opportunity to make money, and this is how you pay your respects to a god?" The nightclub grew quiet as some patrons rushed out while some stared in disbelief.

"Five grand to whoever cleans this shit up . . . Drinks on the house for the rest of the night if what you saw tonight didn't happen."

He dropped the microphone and walked out of the ring. No expensive lawyer could save Rack Daddy this time because the opponent he shot was not only an aspiring rapper but an undercover cop.

After we got the skinny on what happened across the street, Papa looked down at me. "Why ain't you in school, boy?" Papa gave me that death stare. I'd rather get 20 licks from any principal than to get that cold death glare from Papa. I tried to open my mouth, but nothing came out. I burst into tears to make Papa feel sorry for me.

The room grew quiet as I balled my little heart out. It got to the point where I ran out of tears. I spat in my hand and placed it on my cheek to imitate tears, but that grew disgusting fast, and the left side of my throat began to hurt. Fatigue settled in, and I could not sell it anymore. Papa and Mom weren't buying it as they patiently watched me make a damn fool out of myself for several minutes.

That stoolpigeon mother of mine straight dimed me out, "Tre got suspended for three days for calling a teacher a whore."

Papa grabbed me by the arm. "It's one thing to be stupid, and it's another thing to be a damn fool. And ain't nobody hiring anybody stupid, you damn fool!"

All of a sudden, we heard a woman's scream. We all rushed to the front window to see what was happening. The emotional Mrs. Cole was blocking the entry to her front door. She pleaded with the law enforcement units, "Please spare my son. Please don't harm him. He has a family. He's done well for the community. Don't hurt my only child."

One of the officers' yelled, "He killed a federal agent and destroyed your neighborhood. Shut up and move out of the way."

The living room drapes were snatched down revealing an angry Rack Daddy. "Don't talk to my mama like that," Rack Daddy screeched.

The commanding officer yelled out, "Move in."

One of the approaching officers physically tried to remove Mrs. Cole from the front of the door. She started to fight back. Another unit pulled out a taser then placed it on her side. Not knowing she wore a pacemaker; the charge gave her a heart attack. Mrs. Cole's lifeless body flopped to the ground.

Several moments later, an ambulance pulled upfront, and paramedics rushed out of the vehicle. It was too late for Mrs. Cole. After watching his mother die in front of his eyes, Rack Daddy surrendered. I had never seen a man cry until I witnessed that man cry. I never saw a kid weep that hard.

I felt bad for Sade. Her grandmother had died, her father was heading to jail, and Kwesi was the icing on the cake. Word got around about Kwesi's affairs within the school, and a couple of the fathers found out. One day, all the guys got together and waited for Kwesi to come home. They beat the hell out of him and had him confess his wrongs to Brandy. She'd had enough with all the traumatic events that had occurred. Once Brandy caught wind of Kwesi's infidelities, she took matters into her own hands and began to have an affair with one of Kwesi's co-workers. She divorced Kwesi, put him on child support, and took half of his 401(k). She got the house they were living in, sold it, and remarried. Kwesi wasted no time and remarried for the fourth time.

*****

My phone vibrates. It is a phone call from my mother.

"Hey . . . What's up, Ma?"

"Armani is in jail again," my mother says, her voice laced with distress.

"I heard. What'd he do?"

"He got a DUI. Where are you?"

"I'm outside of Memphis. I'll be home in an hour."

"OK! He's calling me now. See you soon."

CHAPTER 12

The ride up Interstate 55 is the most lackluster, non-exciting, non-spectacular drive a person will ever make in their life. It is thousands upon thousands of acres of boring, flat farmland. This is where tornadoes come to practice their destruction. It is raining so hard I can barely see the hood of the rental car, but I see the "Welcome to Blytheville" sign as I enter my hometown. The population says 14,000, but that is trending downward. I take the second exit into the city and pass the Walmart.

Nothing has changed as I drive over the overpass and enter town. The road I am driving on turns into a highway that takes you right through to Jonesboro. I make a right on Walnut Street then make another right onto Franklin Street and cruise through the dilapidated city. I take this road a couple of miles north then make a right into a rural area called Ramblewood, a charming, family-friendly neighborhood where kids can play.

The rain stops as I drive along Ramblewood Drive. As I drive, I see a familiar face standing in front of one of the neighborhood's homes. I speed past so that the familiar face won't recognize me and try to talk to me. Unfortunately, the person standing in front of the house stands next door to my folks' home. In my peripheral vision, I can see this person has recognized me and is currently waiting for me to get out of the vehicle. I am not sure that this person understands that it would not be beneath me to sit in this car until they stop staring.

A few moments later, there is a knock on the car window. Not to my surprise, it is Jackson Reed's punk ass.

"I thought that was you. What's up, Tre?" Jackson says with some genuine enthusiasm.

"Oh . . . Hey . . . What are you doing around here?"

"My mom lives here . . . This is where I grew up."

My folks have been living here a few years, and I never knew Jackson Reed grew up in this neighborhood. The way this kid acted back in school, you'd have thought he grew up where I did.

"My mom and stepfather live here."

"Yeah . . . I know your stepfather. He's cool. Bro, look at this car." Jackson says as he circles the rental. "It looks like you stepped out of a vagina."

"Fuck you very much for your observation, but unfortunately for that immature joke, the car is a rental."

"Damn. Easy . . . I'm just teasing, bro."

I wonder if it would just be teasing if I sock him in the jaw and knock some of his teeth down his throat?

"You're here for the class reunion, right?" Jackson asks.

"Kind of . . . Not really."

"Why else would you come to town for?"

"I don't know, maybe to see my family."

"If you don't come out for the reunion, at least come over to my place for the after-party."

"We'll see . . . Well alright . . . Nice to see you. I'll catch you later," I say ending the conversation.

"OK . . . Good seeing you," Jackson says, but he doesn't walk back over to his yard. This gives me the impression that he wants to say more.

But *fuck that guy*, I think as I step out of the car and stroll to the front door of my folks' home.

It feels good to be home. I am ready for peace. I slide my key in the door, but for some reason, it does not work. There's a faint growl from a dog. I try another key, but it doesn't work either. I start knocking on the door, and the dog begins barking.

"One second," Cliff shouts from the other side of the door. The door opens, revealing my stepdad with a dog on a leash. Cliff extends his other hand to greet me, "How are ya, man?"

"Good . . . I see you got a dog."

Cliff pokes his chest out, "Yeah . . . I got a guard dog for your mama. Her name is Haley. She's a Labrador and Chihuahua mix."

Who in the hell thought mixing those two breeds was a good idea? I think while nodding in agreement with myself. "Wow . . . a Labrador . . . Chihuahua mix?"

"Yep," Cliff says proudly.

"Interesting mix . . . Let me know how that works out. How's Lil' Cliff?"

"Don't know. Haven't seen him in some years."

Cliff and Haley take a seat on the recliner.

I wheel my suitcase in then take a seat on the couch. Mom enters from the back, "Hey, boy!" I stand up and hug her.

Mom pulls away, then glares at me for a few moments. Her glares are more intimidating than Kwesi's. His glares lean in the direction of intimidation as opposed to my mother's glares, which trend toward the infliction of pain.

"I didn't do it," I say.

"Yeah, you did . . . How are you gonna write a book talking bout' how the south hates you? Boy, don't no south hate you. Why would you put that energy on you?"

"Ma, it's a fictional story."

"The character sounded an awful lot like you."

"The character was based on me, but the story was fabricated. The next one I'm writing is a memoir to highlight my upbringing."

"Boy, don't be putting people's business in that book."

"It's based on Kwesi not being around as a father."

"OK," Mom reconsiders. "Maybe you can put his business in a book."

Haley starts barking at me.

"Did you pet your step-dog?"

"I'm not kissing that dog's ass."

"Watch your mouth," Mom says with a chuckle. "Cliff spoiled the dog . . . Feeding her ice cream and all."

"I heard that!" Cliff says.

"So, what happened with Armani? Is he OK?"

Mom takes a seat on the couch.

"I'm not worried about that boy. He's a grown man. He'll figure it out."

I stare at my mother. "You're not worried?"

"Armani has been getting himself into messes all his life. It's not in me to care more than he does."

"Who are you, and what did you do with my overprotective mother?"

Mom chuckles then asks, "How was the drive in? Did you stop and see your damn daddy?"

Cliff and I both roll our eyes, "Yes, Ma."

Mom face contorts as she rolls her eyes and mumbles, "With his ugly self." She segues. "You going to church with me while you're here?"

"Nope. I'm full-blown heathen these days, Ma."

"City life sure done changed ya . . . Looking like your damn daddy," she says, shaking her head with disgust. "How's your lady friend? Y'all still together?"

"Yeah, and I think she's pregnant."

"If that baby is yours, you better do right by that woman. But if the baby isn't, I think you and Sade should get reacquainted."

I grow curious, "Why do you keep mentioning that woman's name?"

"I watch her on TV from time to time."

"When did you start watching ESPN?"

"When I heard Sade was a sports analyst. She's good . . . That girl knows her stuff and she's eloquent. Maybe you guys could catch up at the class reunion."

"Ma, I'm not going to that damn reunion." The dog starts to growl at me.

"Damn reunion?" Mom asks with a fierce look. "Who the hell do you think you're talking to, little boy?"

"Sorry, Ma, I meant . . . I am not going to the class reunion."

"Why not? It'll be fun."

"If I want to know what the rest of those bums are doing, I can easily log in to Facebook. Besides, I'm only in town for a couple of days, and I have to see Papa and Grandma."

"Boy! Go to your class reunion. It'll be nice to catch up with your old classmates."

I peek at my watch to end the conversation. "It's way past my bedtime, Ma."

"Ok, the room is ready for you . . . Have a goodnight."

"Goodnight, Ma."

I walk into the bedroom and over to mom's cluttered workstation. I roll my luggage into a corner then take a seat at the desk. Next to the desk are some old magazines. Under the magazines is an old scrapbook from my senior year. On the first page is a sheet of paper titled *Tre's Shit List*. This list includes Kwesi, Xena Jones , Pretty Boy Roy, Big Ted, and Jackson Reed's punk ass. I immediately scratch Kwesi's name off the list and stuff the sheet in my wallet for safe keeping. There's a slight knock at the door.

"Are you decent?" Cliff says.

"Yes. Come in."

Cliff opens the door, "Hey . . . Your mother is in bed. Meet me out back." From the look in his eyes, I know what has to happen.

CHAPTER 13

The backyard is completely fenced in, with a double gate on the east side. On the west end of the yard is a garden fenced off with a sizeable walk-in greenhouse. Cliff signals me over to a separate part of the yard where his tool shed is positioned. Bloodsucking sniping mosquitoes feast on me as I attempt to walk through the muddy, low-lit backyard. The shed is decorated with Arkansas Razorback memorabilia. It is wired, concreted, and even heated for winter projects, but it's not mosquito proof.

The portable speaker blasts Johnny Cash. Cliff opens a cabinet and gestures me to come over for a peek.

"Whatcha think?"

I lean in and notice several jars with cannabis stuffed in them. Cliff opens one of the jars then places it under my nose. Cliff pulls out a joint, lights it up, and takes a long drag. He hands the joint to me, and I take a big drag then exhale.

"This is pretty good."

"I grew this out in the garden," says Cliff. "It's a northern California strain called Blueberry Cookies. It was created by crossing Blueberry Tahoe and Thin Mint Girl Scout Cookie."

"So, you're the weed man now?"

"No, I'm not the weed man," Cliff says with a chuckle. "It's for medicinal use. I don't sell it. I mean . . . I do sell it . . . But only to the guy next door."

"Jackson Reed! You sell him weed?"

"I only make a little bit of profit if he sells what I give him."

"You grow weed in the backyard of your house and give it to someone to sell . . . You're the weed man."

Cliff scratches his head. "I ain't think about that."

"If he gets caught, he will bring you down with him."

"He won't do that."

I nod my head yes because Jackson Reed is a punk ass.

"Then I'll just tell the cops he robbed me," says Cliff.

"You're gonna tell the cops he stole weed from you? The same weed that he got arrested for."

"Why are we talking about something that hasn't happened?"

I hand him back the joint, and he takes a drag from it.

"What y'all doing back here?" Mom shouts from the backdoor of the yard. Cliff chokes on the smoke and starts coughing.

"Thought you were sleeping, Ma."

"I was, but I needed something to drink." Mom starts sniffing. "It smells like a skunk out here." Mom shuts the door then goes back into the house.

"You think she knows?"

"Nah . . . Renita doesn't have a clue," Cliff says. He must think my mother is a new fool.

"I'm gonna head back in. Don't let that fool next-door get you into trouble . . . He's bad news."

"OK. I won't."

I walk back into the house, enter the room, and situate myself at the desk in front of my laptop. There is something on the floor that catches my attention. It is an old baseball glove and a bag filled with a bunch of old baseball uniforms. I start typing . . .

*****

THIS MEANS WAR

Playing baseball was a ploy to get away from Armani. My folks thought it was a good idea that he and I spend every waking moment of our childhood together. Despite what the spankings I received during my childhood would have you believe, I didn't commit a lot of the mischief I was accused of. It got to the point where I received three extra beatings on top of the one I earned for the week.

The last straw was the time Armani stole a pack of cigarettes from a gas station. He went to the backyard in Grandma's garden and tried to light one up. But instead, that fool burned down Papa's privacy fence. Instead of Armani getting in trouble, we both were grounded for the summer. I refused to give up another summer for Armani's foolishness and I knew he hated sports. Therefore, I tried out for the Junior Babe Ruth League and that gave me space. I didn't know what I was getting into.

I had never gone to a baseball game, nor had I even watched a game on television. I remember watching the movie "Rookie of the Year," but didn't quite grasp the details of the game. My favorite athlete of all time was "Primetime" Deion Sanders. He played both football and baseball . . . Michael Jordan played baseball.

"So why don't I give it a shot?" I thought as if I had their level of talent.

Playing JBR baseball allowed me to witness what life would be with a father in it. Papa was the father figure in my life but there was a generational gap. Papa's love language was different than the fathers of the children on my baseball team. My grandfather grew up during World War II. People back then were a little hardened by the war, and public displays of affection were perceived as weak. I saw fathers playing catch with their sons, and it blew my mind that it existed.

There were 10 sponsored teams in our league: Farmers Bank Cardinals, 1st National Bank Yankees, Holiday Inn Rangers, Hope Furniture Indians, Hays Orioles, MotorSport Red Sox, NIBCO White Sox, Chamber of Commerce Astros, Ritter Communication Tigers, and the Nucor Yamato Shipping Dodgers. I ended up joining the Dodgers, which was sponsored by the same company and department Kwesi supervised. Most of my teammates' parents were either coaches or friends with the coaches who worked for Kwesi at the Nucor Steel factory.

Most of the guys I played with had been playing baseball since the Peewee League. Mr. Rocky Hoffman was the manager of the Dodgers. Coach Rocky was a father of four who worked at Nucor and sometimes substituted as a French teacher at the high school. Though a redneck to the core, he was quite cultured. He lived in France and several other countries before moving back to Arkansas. Coach Rocky didn't show favoritism towards anyone. He was an excellent father figure for me.

Coach Rocky treated all of us like we were his own. He cursed us all out equally. He demanded greatness, but he also treated us like men. We talked shit like we were grown men. I never heard the word "fuck" so much in my life. Everything that flew out of his mouth was, "This sum bitch! That sum bitch! Who the fuck! What the fuck! When the fuck! How the fuck! Where the fuck! Why the fuck? Fuck this! Fuck that! Fuck you! Fuck him! Fuck them!" Listening to Coach Rocky was better than watching "Def Comedy Jam."

The older guys didn't tease me much, but there was some hazing. Rocky Jr. teased me and told me one day at practice, "If you pee on your glove, it'll help loosen it up, and you'll catch the ball better."

That sucker almost got me until Coach Rocky caught me in the dugout with my pants half past my ass. "Tre! What in the fuck you are doing?"

"Rocky Junior said if I pee on my glove, it'll help loosen it up, and I'll catch the ball better."

Coach Rocky chuckled, "Fuck Rocky Junior . . . He's fucking with you. That's my boy, but he's a fucking asshole." Coach Rocky stared me down a few moments. "You Kwesi's boy, huh?"

I shook my head yes.

Coach Rocky chuckled then said, "You sure look like that sum bitch!"

Each one of the 10 Junior Babe Ruth baseball league teams had between nine and 12 players. Out of all the JBR teams, I got stuck on the team with Jackson Reed's punk ass. He was the starting leftfielder, but he never showed up for practice. Whenever he didn't show up, Coach Rocky would start me in his place. Jackson would pick on me because of that. Jackson Reed always got into trouble. He would flick boogers on me whenever we were in the dugout together. Jackson and I didn't converse much in school because Papa heard his name on the scanner too many times. The straw that broke the camel's back was the time Jackson broke into Papa's trailer. He stole all of Papa's candy and started selling it to the kids in junior high.

Mike Rodriguez was also on my team. He was a utility player. He played several different positions well but was exponentially better as a shortstop. This kid was great. At the age of 14, Mike was receiving recruitment letters from Ole Miss and Arkansas. He was a straight-up grinder, like a baby version of Derek Jeter. And Mike was solid in the batter's box. He smacked a homer right out of the park his first at-bat our first year of JBR. This kid played the game like he was here in a previous life. Mike's stepfather Alex "Gonzo" Gonzalez was an assistant coach. Everyone called him Gonzo or Coach Gonzo. Gonzo was a baseball fanatic and had mentored Mike since he was a baby. He never spoke to me. Coach Gonzo just darted glares at me from time to time.

I was petrified of swinging the bat at the ball, and I was OK with sitting on the bench. Occasionally, I would come in If we grew a convincing lead on a team, Coach Rocky would sit down the starters and sub me in.

One warm summer night that season, we were playing First National Bank Yankees, who were the reigning champs from the year before. I was in the dugout daydreaming and heard one of the coaches yell, "Tre, you're up!"

This was my first at-bat in a real game. Sweat dripped down my face. The pitcher looked familiar, but I couldn't make out his face. The batter in front of me he hit a single into right field and got on base.

The catcher shouted, "Man, it's hotter than a four-puckered Billy Goat!" The catcher for their team was Bobby Lee Phillips. He looked at me, and the first thing out of his was, "Damn, bubba, you're ugly!"

This caught me by surprise because Bobby Lee didn't talk much in school. We'd had a couple of classes together in junior high, but I never knew him enough to talk trash to. I knew the catcher's job was to crouch behind home plate to receive the ball from the pitcher, but I didn't realize part of the job consisted of shit-talking.

As the pitch zipped toward the plate Bobby Lee yelled, "Swing, bubba!" I swung the bat early and missed. The fastball flew by me and hit the catcher's mitt.

"Strike!" the umpire snarled.

Bobby Lee whispered, "Hey, father-fucker, that swing was ugly like you!"

The pitcher got the signal from Bobby Lee, and the second pitch was on its way. As the pitcher wound up the next pitch, Bobby Lee whispered, "I think the umpire shit his pants." I giggled as the second pitch flew right by me and into the catcher's mitt.

"Strike two!" the umpire roared.

The runner on base tried to steal second, and like clockwork, Bobby Lee threw a dart to the second baseman.

"He's out!" the umpire shouted.

Bobby Lee patted me on the bottom with his mitt then uttered, "You're next, bubba." The third pitch came through.

"Strike three! He's outta there!"

Bobby Lee chuckled, "Not only do girls swing better than you, but you also let one strike you out!"

I took another glance at the pitcher on the mound and to my surprise, the pitcher was not just a girl, but it was none other than Sade. I had not seen

Sade since her father was arrested. She moved to another part of town called Armorel.

Sade wreaked havoc on our whole team. Watching her eloquent progressions as a pitcher was mind-blowing. I witnessed her throw strike after strike. One batter after another batter struck out. She threw fastballs, screwballs, curveballs, and knuckleballs. I remember thinking, "Where the hell did she learn how to play like that?" Sade struck out the whole team except for Mike. He was 4—4 in the batter's box. Sade even knocked one out of the park. Our lead shrunk and Coach Rocky put all the starters back on the field.

We eventually closed out the Yankees in what was an impressive comeback. Mike smacked a line drive into leftfield that led to Jackson running to home base to end the inning. After the game, both teams lined up to shake hands. The first person from their side to greet me was Coach Willie Wiley, who was Sade's new stepdad. Coach Wiley had retired from the Air Force and dedicated the rest of his time to building a solid foundation for Sade, my little brothers, and their new twin siblings.

After we shook hands, I rushed over to Sade. "Hey."

She looked right through me and said, "You look like a chubby Teddy Bear. I'm gonna start calling you, Tre Tre Bear"

"Tre Tre Bear?"

I guess I had put on some extra pounds, but she didn't have to call me that.

Watching her walk away made me realize that I might have a crush on her. Then the unimaginable happened. Jackson Reed shoved me out of the way, walked behind Sade, patted her on the butt, and then kissed her. Watching them interact together, the way she laughed at his corny jokes and the way she played with her curly hair, made me feel some type of way. I don't know if I was confused, sad, or mad; probably a mixture of all three. How could Sade and Jackson Reed's punk ass be a thing? I knew then I had to declare war on my enemy, and that enemy was Jackson Reed's punk ass.

****

83

CHAPTER 14

PRISONER OF THE MOMENT

I grew more disgusted as the JBR season progressed. The reason for playing baseball was to get away from the bratty misery that was my brother Armani. Then I joined a team with a guy I despised who was also dating my Sade. Why did she like him? It had to be because he was older and had grown facial hair. I started seeing Sade at our practices and games, where she came to watch Jackson. Jackson began taking the game seriously and received notoriety in the local newspaper for his play. One thing the newspapers didn't highlight was Jackson Reed's off the diamond activity.

One day before school, I noticed the line out front of Papa's trailer where he sold candy was shorter than usual. Grandma paced back and forth in the living room.

"Somebody broke in Robbie's trailer. They stole his candy and our money. I just wanna run away . . . And I mean it too," she said as she stormed off to her room.

Later that day at school, there was a big crowd surrounding Jackson. I walked up to see what was happening. I found him selling Halloween candy in the middle of May. That was the only clue I needed. Papa was the only guy in town selling off-season candy. Jackson Reed's punk ass broke into Papa's trailer, but he didn't do it alone. I did my own investigation the next time I was over to Papa and Grandma's house. I circled the old rusty trailer, I noticed the hatch to the door was still attached, and there were no scratches on the door. Whoever got into the trailer used a key. Armani had something to do with it, but I needed solid evidence that connected him to Jackson Reed.

In the dugout the next day before the game, I stared Jackson down. Usually, I avoided him at all costs, but today I wanted all the smoke.

"What are you looking at?"

"My grandfather got you on camera stealing his money and candy." That put a significant chink in his tough-guy armor. The intensity in his eyes loosened up, and fear replaced it.

"You can't prove it."

"Try me!"

We stared at each other down a few minutes.

"I can't get in trouble again," a paranoid Jackson said as he began to tremble. "My mother says she'll send me to boot camp . . . Look, he told me to grab all the candy I wanted . . . Alls I had to do was bring him back a percentage of what I sold."

"Who?" Of course, I knew who. I just needed him to say it out loud.

"Armani gave me the key. I didn't take no money. I only took the candy."

The ball was in my court, and I finally had leverage to control the dynamics of both relationships wrecking my adolescent life.

"From here on out, you will stop picking on me," I demanded.

"Done," a humbled Jackson said.

"And you have to break up with Sade in order for me to keep my mouth shut."

Jackson lowered his head. A few moments passed. "I can't do that."

"Why can't you?"

Jackson took a deep breath. "She broke up with me this morning because I flunked again. Her parents said I was too old for her. She's dating Mike."

Jackson stared at Sade and Mike holding hands by the visitors' dugout. One tear rolled down the side of Jackson Reed's punk-ass cheek like Denzel Washington's character in the movie "Glory."

"I quit," said Jackson as he threw his glove on the ground and ran out of the ballpark. Part of me felt great to see Jackson Reed's punk ass get crushed, but on the flip side, I was hurt to see Sade with another boy.

As the season progressed, my passion for baseball started to fade. I'd often stare into the stands and see mothers and fathers sprinkled throughout the bleachers, rooting their hearts out for their kids. I understood the reason my mother did not come to my games was because she was a busy, single parent working multiple jobs. It was difficult for one parent to earn enough to support a family.

It was the last game of the season, and we were playing the Motorsport Bandits. It was the top of the second inning. I was not expecting any playing time because the game was close, which meant I could watch the game from the dugout. I noticed a man and a woman walking with a beautiful Golden Retriever. I had never seen a black person with that kind of dog. The black people I knew were dog parents to Pit bulls or Rottweilers.

As the couple walked closer, the man's face grew familiar. It was a black-eyed Kwesi with his new wife, Glenn. Once I recognized who he was, I ran in the other direction. Kwesi darted off after me. When he caught up with me, I cried.

Kwesi gripped me tightly, "I'm here, Son."

"I thought you didn't want me."

A long pause grew before Kwesi spoke. "What's your schedule next week, Son?"

"He's a child, Kwesi. He doesn't have a work schedule yet," said the graceful Glenn. "We're coming to get you guys next week for dinner. Have your mom contact me directly." She handed me her business card.

Kwesi uttered, "Get back to your game, Son. We'll see you next week." We both hugged again.

Coach Rocky and Kwesi made strong eye contact from a distance, then gave each other a head nod. Coach Gonzo glared from a distance. Kwesi was the supervisor of Gonzo and Rocky at the Roll Mill at Nucor. Rumors floated around the small town that Coach Rocky, Gonzo, and Kwesi had a big argument at work. Kwesi had an affair with Gonzo's wife.

I overheard heard my mother's phone call one night. I never listened to her conversations, but I did that night for obvious reason. I heard her say, "Her name is Glenn James . . . Homewrecker! Can you believe he divorced his last wife to marry the family law attorney that helped him in our child support case?" Mom said.

"And I don't feel sorry for her . . . She knew he was a liar and a cheater . . . Lawyers lie and cheat for a living. I guess that's why she was attracted to him. And now this fool walking around with a black eye because he slept with one of his employees' wives . . . Yeah, girl!" Mom said with a chuckle. "The guy found out and whooped Kwesi's ass at work in front of everyone!" she cackled. "Damn dummy."

Mom muted a few moments. "Kwesi does not do anything for his kids . . . They don't get gifts for their birthdays from him . . . No Christmas gifts or visits." Mom started to tear up as her voice cracked. "My kids deserve better than this. When the boys get older, Kwesi will need them more than they'll need him." I remember sneaking back to my bed and crying.

The season was over, and so was my desire for baseball. It was time to hang out with my father. I wasn't as giddy as I was the last time because I didn't know what to expect from Kwesi.

When we arrived at the front door of the house, Kwesi said, "Let's bow our heads."

We all bowed our heads and joined hands.

"Father God, I want to thank you for allowing us to make it home safe. In Jesus's name, we pray, Amen."

Glenn, Armani, and I all followed with "Amen." We entered the home.

Of all people, Kwesi had become a born-again Christian. He joined a small church, became an active member, and became Deacon Black. Deacon

Black was a self-proclaimed "Man of God." He had been Tupac not too long ago but now he was Kirk Franklin. I thought it was weird to see a man who swam in a pool of sex a year ago suddenly become a Jesus freak.

"You guys want something to drink?" Kwesi asked.

Armani shook his head no, then whispered, "I wanna go home."

"Yes, please," I said.

Kwesi walked over to the refrigerator, dug out a Sprite, then handed it to me.

"Thank you."

As I pulled the cap back and went for a swig, Pop stated, "You gonna pray over that, Son."

It caught me off guard, but I mustered up a prayer then took a big gulp of the soda. Armani was a different kid around Kwesi. He wasn't as sassy and problematic as he was with Mom and her folks.

We all took a seat on the couch in the living room. They didn't have cable because Kwesi thought it was the devil's poison. Kwesi sat next to Glenn. Armani and I sat next to each other.

"Before we have dinner, I wanted to ask if you guys want to take a trip with us to the East Coast?" Kwesi said.

"The East Coast?" Armani questioned.

"We're planning a trip to Washington, D.C., and we wanted to invite you guys. I can talk with your mother and see what she says. Or if you choose not to go, I'll give you each fifty dollars."

Kwesi's idea of talking with mom didn't pan out like I thought it would. Not only did he try to negotiate not paying child support for the week of the trip, but Kwesi also tried to leverage the vacation as a way to negotiate lower child support payments. Deacon Black had converted back to Kwesi, and Ma was not in for it. We elected not to go. By 'we,' I mean Armani. Once Ma caught wind Armani didn't want to go, there was no chance she would allow me to go without him. And we never saw that fifty dollars Kwesi had promised each of us.

****

My eyes grow heavy, and I shut the laptop. I reach for my phone and make a call.

"Hey, Son," says Kwesi. "Why are you up so late?"

"Been thinking about some stuff."

"What's on your mind, Son?"

"Let's make that family trip to the Rockies."

"Yes, Son! Let's do it! I was thinking maybe around Father's Day."

If music were playing in this sappy moment, the record would come to a screeching halt. "Father's Day is reaching, Pop. How about Thanksgiving?"

He mulls it over for a few moments, "Let's do it!"

"Ok. I'm gonna get some sleep, Pop."

"Stop by on your way out."

"Sure, I'll do that."

"Good night, Son."

"Good night, Pop." The phone call ends. Who am I to deny a man his redemption?

I lie across the bed and try to fall asleep. I hear a buzzing noise in my ear. I roll out of bed and turn on the light. I notice a few mosquitoes are stacked up on the wall. One of them lands on me, and I swat the bloodsucker to smithereens. I begin to smack the other mosquitoes up against the wall, then try to fall back asleep. The dog whines again. The whining turns into a growl. Then Haley begins to bark. I try to fall back asleep, but the whining, growling, and barking only grows louder. I think I'm in for a long night.

CHAPTER 15

Haley keeps me up much of the night with her whining. As I lay trying to fall back asleep on this twin-size bed, a familiar tune gushes through the wall and catches my attention. I rise to my feet and open the door. Cliff's radio is playing "Reminiscing" by Little River Band.

"How did you sleep?" Mom asks.

"Ask Cujo. That dog barked all damn night."

"Watch your mouth, boy! This ain't your daddy's house . . . You ain't speaking any kinda way in here, heathen."

"Sorry, Ma," I say with a chuckle. "I didn't get any sleep because of the barking."

"She's not used to people at the house," Cliff says, defending Haley.

"I wonder why? That dog runs the house." Mom conceals her laughter in an attempt not to instigate banter.

"I'll be back . . . Heading over to Papa and Grandma's house. I can't leave until I hear Papa calls someone a sapsucker."

"Are you going to your class reunion tonight?"

"I don't think so."

"You want me to go for you?"

"No, Ma."

"Then, you better go . . . Or you can go to church with me tomorrow."

"Hard pass on church. Still considering the union." I exit out of the front door.

As I head toward the rental car, I spot Jackson Reed's punk ass standing outside of his mother's house. As much as I want to avoid him, I don't have the energy to do so.

My feet direct me right toward Jackson. "Aye, my man . . . I need to holler at you a second."

"Sure . . . What's up, brother?" Jackson says.

"I know we went to school and all that, but do me a favor: don't come over to this house with that bullshit. We don't need my stepfather going to jail for some nonsense."

"Why are you coming at me with this?"

"You heard me, bro."

"Can I talk with you about something?"

"Not really. I'm heading to my grandparents' house. You remember that place, right?"

I storm off, enter the rental car, pull out of the driveway, and speed past Jackson Reed's punk ass.

Driving through the city of Blytheville in the daytime is similar to waking up naked in a bed with an unattractive person you thought looked good after taking 13 shots of Jose Cuervo. This city has been abandoned without a backward glance. Though there are pockets of decent neighborhoods, most areas appear rundown. Old parking lots are now where weeds socialize across the cracking asphalt, gathering and laughing at the emptiness. There are deserted homes with doors hanging by a few threads of their hinges, groaning with pain at every sway from the wind. Windows have long shattered in the weakness of their structures and rotting boards, some broken, others hanging try to cover the empty eyes of every abandoned home. I see old tumbledown businesses as I approach a railroad crossing that divides the east and west sides of the city.

The crossing bell sounds, the red lights flash, and warning handles come down. I check both ways and spot a train a quarter mile on the track. The conductor blasts the horn as the train glides slowly on the rails. I think I can make it over and cross the train track. I spot flashing blue and red lights in the rearview mirror.

The Blytheville Police officer approaches the driver's side of the rental car. The monotone officer firmly states, "Driver's License and registration."

I dig in my pocket and grab my wallet.

"I pulled you over for crossing that railroad while the crossing lights were on," the officer says.

No shit, Sherlock. "Yeah, I'm aware."

I hand the officer my license then make it clear, "I'm recording us, and to confirm . . . I'm reaching for the rental agreement in the glove box."

"I see you're still a wiseass and ugly," the officer says.

I'd recognize that voice anywhere. I hand over the rental agreement and look at the officer. "Bobby Lee Phillips . . . Is that you?"

"You damn skippy, it's me, father-fucker. Get out of the car and give me a hug, sum bitch."

I step out of the car and hug an old friend. Nosey drivers drift by slow as the two of us get reacquainted.

"You're not gonna shoot me, are you? I know your kind."

"What's my kind?" Bobby Lee asks.

"The shoot-the-shit-out-of-you kind?"

"Man, I haven't seen you since high school. What have you been up too?"

"Writing."

"Oh yeah. I read your book . . . It was shit," says a blunt Bobby Lee. "When you quit that journalist job to write a book, I thought you were bat shit crazy. But I bought four of them sum bitches to support ya! Looks like it's paying off."

"I don't know how to take that, but thanks, Bobby Lee. How have you been?"

"I'm happier than a dog with two dicks. I'm married with four children. There's nothing like fatherhood, bubba . . . It's hard work, but it's the most rewarding thing I've ever done."

"That's good to hear."

"Did you bring your old lady and the kids home for the class reunion?"

"No wife . . . No kids . . . I'm visiting family I have here in town, and I don't think I'm going to that class reunion."

"Did you bring your old lady with you for the class reunion?

"No, I didn't bring her, and I don't think I'm going to the reunion."

"And why the hell not? Think you're better than the rest of us?"

"Actually . . . Yes!" We share a chuckle. "In all seriousness, I came in town for a couple of days to check on my folks. I don't have time to get to it."

"What if Sade's there?"

"What if she's married and has 100 kids like you, Bobby Lee?"

"What if worms had machine guns?"

"What the hell are you talking about?"

"Don't answer a question with a question, sum bitch."

"Fine . . . What if birds had machine guns, Bobby Lee."

"Birds wouldn't fuck with em . . . If you don't show up to the class reunion, you can bet your bottom dollar, I'm writing yo ass a ticket, bubba."

"Don't do me like that, Bobby Lee. I thought we were boys."

"We still are."

The dispatcher from Bobby Lee's radio announces, "We have a potential 187 at McHaney and Clark St." Bobby Lee's demeanor changes. "Copy that. In route."

"Is that another homicide?" I ask.

"Yeah, bro . . . It's been happening every other day. These young kids live in a city where the ceiling is low. They don't know life outside of this Blytheville bubble. I gotta go, man . . . I'll see you tonight, right?"

"I guess I'll see you there."

Bobby Lee scurries back to the police interceptor, turns on the sirens, then speeds off. I get back into the rental car and continue on my journey.

CHAPTER 16

I pull into the driveway of my grandparents' home. I take a few moments to glance at the neighborhood I had such fond memories in. The neighborhood has changed a lot. Mrs. Cole's house across the street burned down, and a couple of the houses surrounding it are vacant. I reach the front door of my grandparents' home and place my ear to the screen. Not to my surprise, the two of them are fussing and cussing at each other.

"You always use the bathroom, and you don't spray," Grandma Russell shouts. "Nobody wanna smell that."

"That's yo upper lip, woman," Papa shouts in response.

"Sometimes I wanna run away."

"You don't have to run . . . You can just walk."

I knock on the door, and Grandma shouts, "Come in."

"You don't even know who it is . . . Talking 'bout come in," Papa shouts. "Come in and get her!"

"The door is locked!" I shout.

Grandma Russell tries to unlock the door. "One second," she shouts, "Your Granddad got all of these damn locks on the door. Nobody wants any of this junk."

"Keep on talking, sapsucka! I'm gonna chop yo head off!"

"You chop my head off . . . It'll be the last head you chop off, and I mean it too."

Grandma opens the door, and the tone of her voice changes when she sees my face. "Hey, boy!" I give Grandma a hug then walk over and shake Papa's hand.

"I ain't seen you in months and Sundays!"

"Good to see ya, Papa."

Papa exhales in relief then says, "I'm glad you got here when you got here, Tre. Your Grandma ain't got the sense God gave an ant. She's nuttier than a squirrel turd . . . I wanna divoce!"

"When you get into town, Tre?" Grandma Russell changes the subject.

"Last night. I didn't get much sleep . . . That dog barked all night."

"We heard you on the ole scanner," Papa says.

"Oh. That was nothing,"

"Did you get a ticket?"

"No, it was my buddy from high school. He's a cop now."

"You talk to your brother?" Grandma asks.

"Uh, yeah . . . Armani called me yesterday."

"What did he want?" Papa asks. "I know he wanted something. That sapsucka only calls when he needs something."

"It was brief ."

"I still can't understand how the two of you couldn't live under the same roof," Papa says with a frown.

"I still trying to understand how the two you stayed under the same roof."

"That's because your Grandma can't take a hint."

"I've been depressed these days."

"Why is that?"

"No one remembered my wedding anniversary," says Grandma. "Your Papa and I have been married 60-some-odd years."

"Ain't nobody studdin' that anniversary," Papa blurted with a frown. "I don't know why she cares to celebrate the worst decisions of my life," He grumbles to himself.

"How's your lady friend, Tre?"

"Good."

"When are y'all getting married?"

"Don't do it!" Papa says under his breath.

"Don't you guys want kids?"

"She already has a kid, Grandma."

"You know what a mean. Y'all getting married and having children. I wish you and Juanita's granddaughter got together. What's her name?"

"Sade. I saw her show," Papa says.

"You know today is my 20-year class reunion," I segue.

"What you say?" Papa says. "20 years, huh? We went to our 65th class anniversary."

"That's a lot of years."

"Sho'nuff. Harrisonite Dragon."

"I don't wanna go, but my buddy joked that he'll write me a ticket if I don't show."

"You better go! You don't wanna pay no expensive traffic ticket."

I receive a text message from my former agent Kristine. It reads, "I don't like to mix business with my personal life, but I decided to help Armani out. I didn't want him to stress you and your family out. Finish writing the book, and let's get it published."

"Thank God," I say to myself as I rise to my feet. "I got to get some work done. I'll catch you guys on the next visit."

"You watch out for that Weefee," Grandma warns. "I hear they steal people's information from being on the line."

"Weefee?" I question.

"You mean Wi-Fi, you damn fool," Papa says.

Grandma Russell and I hug each other, then I walk over to shake Papa's hand.

Papa whispers, "Please take your grandma with you."

"Not this time, Papa."

"There's some bacon on the stove if you're hungry."

"I don't eat pork, Papa. It's a filthy animal."

Disturbed by my comments, Papa glances over at Grandma then back over to me. "You Muslim now?"

"No, Papa," I say with a chuckle. "Catch you guys later." I head to the door and exit.

CHAPTER 17

I make a right onto Ramblewood. As I drive down the street, I see Jackson Reed's punk ass standing in front of his house hustling his two children into the backseat of the car. I pull into the driveway, and he glances in my direction for a few seconds. He gives me a head nod, but I do not reciprocate. We lock eyes for several moments. One of us has to stop staring at the other one, and it will not be me. The garage door opens.

"Tre . . . We need to talk," says Cliff.

I guess I have to be the adult and stop staring.

Moments later, we find ourselves in the muggy shed. Cliff passes a lit joint to me.

"Why are you messing up my money flow, Tre?"

"What are you talking about?"

"Jackson told me what you said to him. That's not good for my empire."

"What empire? We are in a shed in the backyard. You work at a factory. Besides all of that, you can work with anybody else who is not named Jackson Reed."

"What do you got against the guy?"

"He's bad news . . . Trust me. And don't get mom caught up in this."

"I won't . . . I promise," Cliff says. He passes the joint back to me.

"I think she knows."

"Why you say?"

"When Ma gets back, watch how she reacts. You know you can't hide anything from, Ma."

"With her nosey ass." We chuckle at the observation.

"I want to thank you for being there for Ma."

"Don't mention it, man."

I head inside the house and enter the bedroom, shut the door, and sit at the desk. I open my senior year scrapbook and flip through its pages. I reminisce on old photos of my high school days. I stumble across a picture of me with my varsity football teammates.

A door slams shut. "Who's smoking that skunkweed?" Mom shouts.

A few moments later, there is a knock at the door. Cliff pokes his head in the door and places his index finger over his lips to signal for me to keep quiet. Moments later, there is another knock at the door. "Come in," I say as my mother enters the room with a frown on her face.

"He thinks I'm a dummy . . . Out there smoking that stuff in the backyard."

"Who?"

"Cliff."

"What?"

"Yep. I saw him through the window, but he didn't see me. You know what they say about people that smoke that skunkweed?"

"No . . . Enlighten me, Ma."

"They call them crackheads."

"Ma, no they don't," I say with a snicker.

"Why are you defending it? You must smoke that skunkweed too."

"Ma!"

"OK . . . I'll let you be." Mom shuts the door. I open my laptop and get back to writing...

*****

HIGH SCHOOL BLUES PT. 1

High school taught me how to stay poor and do someone else's work for less. We learned geometry, science, and distorted history. And while we are on the subject, distorted American history lessons only inspire 76.3 percent of Americans. 13.4 percent of Americans are descendants of Africans that were in bondage. What was the identity of those African slaves before the 15th century's transatlantic slave trade in the New World? If that is part of history, why is it not taught in schools? To think that a group of people's heritage started with slavery is a bit delusional. But history is written by conquerors, not the conquered. Never have we seen films of Africans before the Trans-Atlantic Slave trade. Africans are always the captured or savages. Where are the stories of tribes and kings that influenced the world? There are many stories and films of Vikings murdering, raping, and pillaging, but we get the Harriet Tubman movie. Roots. "12 Years a Slave." "Amistad." "Gone with the Wind." Or Tyler Perry films.

Whoever you look up to changes who you look down on. The media paints images as if the descendants of the enslaved Africans originated from poverty-stricken, diseased-infected, uneducated, low-class criminal backgrounds. But in actual proven fact, black people have the most ancient, developed history on the planet. School systems in America taught us inaccurate facts about Christopher Columbus, who somehow discovered a land that already had people on it. The education system teaches European history yet insinuates that descendant of the enslaved African ancestors in American history originated as indentured servants. The school system shoves Harriet Tubman,

Rosa Parks, and Martin Luther King Junior down our throats, but never other historical influencers who contributed to this world.

Have you ever heard about the Moors? The Moors ruled Spain for 800 years from around 711 AD. They introduced fashion, hygiene, streetlights, hospitals, and public bathrooms to uncivilized regions in Europe. The Moors' immense influence penetrated throughout Europe. Most of us never heard of Mansa Musa. He was one of the wealthiest kings in history. Not just black history, History. He was the 10th king of the wealthy Mali dynasty between the years of 1312 to 1337 AD. He ruled the Mali Empire in the 14th century, which was located on top of enriched lands. Mansa Musa ruled most of modern-day Mauritania, Senegal, Gambia, Guinea, Burkina Faso, Mali, Niger, Nigeria, and Chad. This land was the world's most productive natural resource and contained an abundance of gold. At that time, many African kingdoms were thriving.

Much of Europe was in the middle of a war, similar to what is happening now in the Middle East. America's foundation was built by scoundrels denounced in their European lands that set sail west across the ocean. They docked their ships on American soil, committed a genocide that was masqueraded as a Thanksgiving dinner, and slavery wasn't too far around the corner. Other than the Indigenous people of America, no other ethnicity living in America would be here had it not been for the enslaved African ancestors and the Civil Rights Movement.

School systems in America teach meaningless subjects graduates will never use in their everyday lives. School systems don't teach anything about economics, nutrition, real estate, how to balance a checking account, how to save money, or how the credit system works. All of which a student will have to deal with every single day for the rest of their adult life.

High School was a joke to me back then. I spent most of my days in the principal's office or detention hall. I knew my body couldn't withstand the pain of playing professional sports, and I knew that the teachers had their pets, and their pets got extra attention. Classmates had their favorites as well.

The popular kids received all the admiration. So, I became a class clown. I couldn't help myself. It kept calling me and calling me. It was my pleasure.

I would find the elephant in the room and make fun of it. I was good at this because of my antagonistic brother Armani. He would say whatever the hell was on his mind and didn't care how you felt. Armani talked about your mama, your daddy, your siblings, your auntie, and her nieces. That fool would talk about your child, and he would fight your grandmother if she had a problem with it. The only way to defeat a person like that is to outwit them.

The smarter the teacher was, the more amusing my antics got. The dumber they were, the more ridiculous the antics would be. I remember one of my teachers, Mr. Stedman. He wasn't ignorant, but he was becoming senile. Mr. Stedman was in his last year of teaching, and he would retire after our class graduated. One day, I remember super gluing all his items to his desk. I put super glue on the remote control for the TV because I knew once he realized everything was stuck on top of his desk, he would turn the TV on to distract us from watching him try to figure out if he was crazy or someone was pranking him. It had gotten so bad that whenever another student did something disruptive, I was blamed for it.

My senior year marked the first time I could finally work a real job. My old folks would put Armani and me to work in the yard cutting grass, clipping hedges, planting flowers, and every other form of slave labor.

My great-grandmother's house was the place no grandchild wanted to go. She was known as the Crazy Cat Lady because she had a pack of wild cats that lived under her house. Whenever we were there, she would make us cut her yard and pay us $5 to cut over an acre of land. But she would pay the neighbors and drunks $100 for the same tasks. I ended up blanketing the town with job applications until I got a bite. That bite was from Burger King.

This Burger King opened right after the Y2K scare. Y2K was a supposed problem in the coding of computer systems that projected to create havoc in the computer networks around the world at the beginning of the year 2000. Technology was supposed to be advanced to the point that it would enslave humans . . . Or at least that's what we thought. We had no clue what any of that meant because we couldn't afford a computer back then.

I remember my first day on the job at Burger King. Mike Rodriguez, Big Ted Jones, and Jackson Reed's punk ass all worked there too. I remember working at the fry station. Dumb Lisa worked the drive-thru window. Dumb Lisa was given the name because, well, she wasn't smart. She was cute, but not the brightest lamp in the room. She didn't have a clue. She had book smarts but didn't understand life outside of school. I didn't understand why her name was Dumb Lisa until our first interaction.

"Did you put the fries on the salt?" Dumb Lisa asked.

"What was that?" I wanted to see if she would say it the same way.

"Did you put the fries on the salt?" Dumb Lisa said.

"Did I put the fries on the salt?"

"Are you deaf?" Dumb Lisa shouted. "Did you put the fries on the salt?"

"So, you want me to scoop the fries out of the bin, place salt on it, then place the damn fries on the salt?" I asked.

"You're so stupid!" she said, then stormed off. The whole crew burst into laughter.

Sade worked at Burger King too. All-day, we threw slick remarks at each other. She said things like, "You talk too much."

My response would be, "Give me a sample, and I'll shut up."

She teased me so hard that at one point, I lost control, grabbed her, and kissed her lips. She stared at me then yelled, "That's why I lick my boyfriend's balls and his asshole." Then she stormed off. I'm guessing either she didn't find my approach appealing or she is one nasty teenager.

One day at work, Kwesi walked through the entrance of Burger King. I took a second glance at him because I couldn't believe my eyes.

"Hey, Son. Can you take a break?"

"Yeah . . . Sure . . . Why? What's up?" I spoke with some reserve.

"How have you been?"

"Good . . . Working . . . Going to school . . . My first game is Friday. I'm a starter this year. You should come to my game," I said.

"What are you doing after high school?"

"I don't know . . . Why?"

"You should join the military. It'll make a man out of you."

Thinking on it now, I should've responded, "You were supposed to make a man out of me, not the government." But I passive-aggressively responded, "Thanks for the heads up . . . I gotta get back to work."

Senior year marked the first time I became a starter on my football team. I couldn't wait to go out on the field and do something spectacular for my mother to see. I envisioned her in the stands yelling, "That's my son" as she bragged to all her coworkers while pointing at my picture in the newspaper, highlighting how dope I performed on the field. I wanted to make my mama proud.

My senior year marked the first year of Armani's high school experience. Now that he was at my school, he was bound to get me into more trouble because that's how Armani is. This fool got into three fights within the first week of school. One of those disputes ended in a physical altercation with a girl who was pregnant. A lot of female students were getting pregnant by older men at my high school. Armani and one of the girls were having a verbal sparring match in class.

From what the teachers said, the pregnant lady got up and punched Armani in the face. He stood up and yelled, "I don't fight girls, but I'm about to beat a bitch's ass." In retaliation for getting punched in the face, Armani pushed the girl to the ground, took off his shoes, and politely kicked the pregnant girl in the head. He was always ready to fight somebody but he couldn't quite back it up physically. The pregnant girl managed to trip Armani to the ground, put him in a headlock, and then bounce his head off the ground like a basketball. Armani got suspended, and I was relieved of all conflicts at school for a week. He hung around the school bullies. He picked up their bad habits such as skipping school, smoking cigarettes, talking reckless to people, and picking fights. When he wasn't starting fights with me, he was fighting with everyone else. When Armani got to my high school, all I heard people say was, "Tre . . . You cool, but I'll fight your little brother." That got me into more conflicts because if I didn't help him, my folks disciplined me. I was chopped liver. I realized that, and I knew in some form or fashion, I needed a getaway.

*****

My phone is vibrating in my pocket. I receive an alert and notice I have a couple of missed calls from Eva. One of the messages reads, "I'm still here, Papi. We miss you! I refuse to believe this is over." Eva attempts to call again. I ignore the call and place the phone face down on my desk. A few minutes later, Eva calls again. I pick up the phone and ignore the request again. She sends another text message that reads, *"Call me ASAP! Something terrible happened to the condo!"*

CHAPTER 18

I have been calling Eva's phone for the last five minutes, and she has yet to answer. "Hello . . . You've reached Eva. I'm not in now. For a faster response, send a text message." The call goes to her voice message. I dial back and start to pace back and forth in the cluttered bedroom. I end the call then dial back . . . This time she answers.

"What, Tre?" Eva shouts through the receiver.

"What do you mean, what, Tre? You called me with the bullshit," I say in a whisper. "What happened to the condo?"

"Is that what it takes for you to talk to me?"

"Why are you playing games, Eva?"

"Because you're playing games with me, Papi! How are you gonna leave us like that?"

"I needed to get away for a couple of days . . . My father hitting me with news about his sickness and you dropping the news about a baby was too much for me."

"All you have to do is communicate that, Papi," Eva says with a slur.

"You're drinking . . . Are you drinking?

"Bitch . . . I might be."

"You're pregnant!"

"If you cared so much, why are you putting our child through the same fucked up childhood you had."

"Don't ever say that again!" I roar. "My childhood wasn't fucked up . . . You're fucked up."

"Fuck you, Tre! We are done. I'll see you in child support court, la puta!" Eva ends the call.

"Fuck you!" I toss my phone to the other side of the room.

Mom storms into the room with her trusted belt, Luther, in her hand. "Don't you be cursing in my damn house, boy."

"I'm sorry, Ma."

"You fix that mess you're in . . . Cussing in here like its "Def Comedy Jam" . . . I'll still whip your ass, little boy."

Mom glares me down then exits the room. It is frightening to see my mother get that serious. I have not seen her like that in years, and I don't miss seeing that side of my mother. I sit my humbled ass down at the desk and start typing . . .

*****

HIGH SCHOOL BLUES PT. 2

Game Day had approached, and it was my first football game as a starter. I told my whole family to come out, but I needed Mom to be there to see me. I wanted her to be proud to be my mother as opposed to the constant disappointment she got from Kwesi. Mom didn't have to work three jobs anymore. She'd become a full-time nurse and was paid enough to quit two of her jobs. Plus, the game was on a Thursday night, and she was off on Fridays.

The exhibition game was the Osceola Seminoles against the Blytheville Chickasaws. This wasn't just an ordinary exhibition game. There is a deep historic rivalry between the two former powerhouse football programs.

Blytheville sits 16 miles north of Osceola, who was considered the big brother city of the two cities. Though at one point, Blytheville was a 5-A Division school, Osceola was a 3-A Division school producing Division 1 talent for colleges and the pros. All the preparation, practices, film study, and fights were about to be put to the test.

It was a warm August night. As Bobby Lee, Big Ted, and I walked out as captions for the coin toss, Bobby Lee shouted, "It's hotter than Satan's asshole after eating Taco Bell." I looked up at the stadium, scanning to see if my mother was in the crowd. Osceola won the coin toss, and they chose to receive the opening kickoff. That meant we would be on defense first, and I would get my time to shine on the gridiron. On the first play, the coach called a Safety blitz. My number was called to blitz the quarterback. In my head, it went perfectly: I would wait for the quarterback to yell, "hut," the ball would be snapped, and I would dash right to whoever was holding it. But instead of making that play in my head, I woke up from taking a vicious pancake block. A pancake block is a move used by offensive lineman that leaves a defensive player flat on his ass, and the person holding the ball runs right by them into the open field . . . And that is what happened.

It was the hardest hit my body had ever suffered. I decided then that this will be the last year of playing any contact sports. This was in high school. I could only imagine what would happen in college or the NFL. But I couldn't think about retiring or any of that other stuff right now. We were in the middle of a game. The season had started, and I had to make my mama proud.

I knocked the dust off my jersey and got right back into the action. In between each play, I would look up at the crowd to see if I could spot my mother. Throughout the game, I made some good plays but nothing spectacular other than a catch on a 10-yard slant route. Even though we lost the hyped-up scrimmage game, at least my mother got a chance to see me do my thing.

After the game, I could not wait to hear what Ma thought about my game. At the time, we lived right around the corner from Papa and Grandma's house. Papa had bought some land on the west side of town a few years back and gave it to my Ma. Then we built a home that was be big enough for me to have my own space away from Armani.

When I made it home, Mom was getting ready for bed.

"What did you think, Ma?"

She grew confused, "What are you talking about?"

"My football game tonight . . . Weren't you there?"

"I didn't go . . . I thought it was tomorrow. I'll go to the next one," Ma said.

"What did you do instead?" I asked.

"I went on a date with a coworker . . . What else do you wanna know, Dad?"

I hesitated a few seconds, then smiled and said, "OK . . . Can you make sure you get to the next one? I worked really hard, Ma. I'll show you."

"OK . . . I'm heading to bed," she said as she went into her bedroom.

Our homecoming game was coming up, and this drove all the girls in school crazy. Most if not all of the girls in school wanted to be on the court. They yearned for the attention. Some were doing whatever it took to get on the court. I didn't know their game at the time because I didn't have a lot of experience with girls. I never had a girlfriend. Hell, my sheltered life kept me in the house. Some of the teenage girls I went to school with liked teenage boys that looked like grown men. Others were having sex with older men who roamed the streets. My nuts hadn't dropped yet, and I was still a virgin.

The seniors who played all 4 seasons of varsity football escorted the ladies during the Homecoming Court. Most of the guys in my class were in relationships, so it was obvious who they would pick. No one chose Sade because they were intimidated by her beauty, her crazy boyfriend, and her height. Sade was over 6-feet tall and towered over most of the boys on the football team.

I would have picked Sade, but her boyfriend, who was the leader of the Hearn Street Posse, threatened to shoot any one of us that chose her. Between the guys who were in relationships and the guys who were smashing everything else, the pickings were slim. Most of the girls I wanted to choose had either got pregnant, started a relationship, or gotten fat over the summer.

This marked the first time I learned a real-world lesson: you're either looking for a sucker or waiting to get licked. I fell prey to a cute hood rat named Xena Jones. Xena was a tattletale from elementary. She was a diamond in the rough and came from a poor upbringing. In middle school, she wore second-hand clothes. Both of her parents had been affected by the crack epidemic during the 80s. She had gone through five different foster homes because her mother was fighting addiction, and her father was killed during the raids after Rack Daddy's arrest.

Xena was mature for her age because she had to grow up fast due to her circumstances. This helped improve her appearance. Xena went from pissing on herself in elementary school to pissing on older men that paid her to dominate them. Who knew she was into sadomasochism so young? She would do what other girls wouldn't do to get what she wanted. Xena was not the prettiest but far from the most hideous. She worked three jobs to build up capital to pay for school in case she didn't get a scholarship. She did gymnastics, she was a cheerleader, and she was stuck up. That made her more appealing to me.

At one time, she dated Mike Rodriguez, who was a starter on our varsity basketball team. All the boys at my school were waiting for Xena to split up with Mike. Mike and I had been teammates before, so I never pressed her. Word got out that they had split, so I took a chance at asking her out.

Those thirsty boys were lingering around like lions waiting to pounce on a gazelle in the Serengeti. Mike was trying to get her back as well. Rumor had it that she was hanging around some older men. There was no way I wanted to compete with that, but I did hold leverage. She had never been on the Valentine or Homecoming Court. Xena had a close relative who was on my football squad. It would be a breeze.

His name was Theodore Jones. We called him Big Ted because not only was he bigger than a bus, but he was also the best player on our squad. He was a defensive lineman and as fast as the running backs. Several colleges in and around the state scouted Big Ted. He received attention from Grambling, University of Arkansas, Arkansas State University, University of Memphis, and the University of Missouri. Our sorry-ass football Coach Gwen Douglas, who was also the athletic director, had his own agenda. Coach Douglas rigged the Blytheville School system to work in his family's favor. Coach Douglas had his eyes on sending Big Ted to play with his brother, coached down at Hendrix, a small Division 3 school in Conway, Arkansas. Coach Douglas tried to funnel the best players produced under his regime to Hendrix.

When Big Ted wasn't abusing people on the football field, he wrote poetry, which was peculiar for a 320-pounder. I knew he was related to Xena, so I approached him after practice one day. Homecoming was coming up soon, and I wanted to get the scoop on her.

"I'll hook you guys up, and I wrote a poem you can give to her . . . Better yet, I'll give it to her." Excited to get a chance to play Cupid, Big Ted hustled along out of the Fieldhouse before I had a chance to read the damn poem. I didn't care because I trusted Big Ted . . . I mean, it couldn't be that bad, right?

Class life was a breeze during the first semester of my senior year. Because I was an athlete, some of the teachers let me get away with sleeping in class or not doing the classwork. Classmates let me cheat off their papers during quizzes. I half-assed my homework right before it was due, and I still received Cs or low Bs. The teachers tolerated me because intellectually, they knew I was smart. My classmates enjoyed my antics.

Sixth period was my favorite class in high school because of my English teacher Ms. Sullivan. She was the cool teacher. She would pick on me from time to time if I was daydreaming, sleeping, or not paying attention in class. It was also my favorite class because Xena was in it. I wondered if Big Ted had said anything yet. Big Ted and Xena should have spoken by now since they shared a class the previous period.

An assignment was due for our term paper. The teacher asked, "Trevor, have you found a topic for your term paper yet? If it's not complete today, it could affect your grade, and you'll have to see Mr. Clay." All the students' eyes crept on me.

Having memorized the infamous response former President Clinton had for his affair with Monica Lewinsky, I got to my feet and said, "I want to say one thing to the American people. I want you to listen to me. I'm going to say this again. I did not have time to do my homework, Miss Sullivan. I never told classmates to lie, not a single time—never. These allegations are not true. And I need to go back to work for the American people. Thank you." I strutted out of the class, and my classmates erupted into laughter. More importantly, I made Xena laugh.

Before our next home game, our school conducted a pep rally. It was held late Friday afternoon in the boys' basketball gym before kickoff. The pep rally was held to introduce all the players on the football team. Xena approached me right before the pep rally. "Big Ted told me you wanted to put me on the Homecoming court."

"Yeah . . . I did," I uttered. I didn't say that precisely, but I went with the flow because Xena was looking extra cute.

Xena flashed a come-hither smile. "I'm kinda seeing someone. He doesn't go to our school, but he has a girlfriend. I ain't trippin', though. I'm looking for my high school sweetheart," Xena said as she brushes her hand against my face. "Wanna hook up after the game?"

What did she mean by, "Wanna hook up after the game?" I felt all the blood leaving my head and flowing to my pants, "I . . . Uh . . . Um . . . Yeah . . . OK . . . Sure," I stuttered.

"Cool! I'll see you after the game?" Xena asked.

"Yeah, of course," I said.

"Good luck with the game tonight," she said, then leaned in for a hug. I stuck my butt back and gave Xena a one-armed, old-woman-in-church hug because I was in full-time boner mode. We went our separate ways. I had a football game to focus on.

Our opponents were the Memphis Treadwell Eagles. During the game, I looked toward the crowd between plays hoping Mom would get a chance to see me on the field. My focus was off that night. During a daydream session, a receiver from the opposing team broke loose and caught a 60-yard pass on the opening drive. During the duration of the game, I blew a few assignments on defense and dropped a wide-open touchdown pass. I had also suffered a back injury from a blind crackback block from an opposing wide receiver. Luckily for me, the game was over before halftime. We eventually crushed the team 35 – 0. Either we were good, or the other side sucked.

After the game, I hustled back home to get ready for my date with Xena. When I entered the house, I noticed my mother dolled up and not in her regular work clothes. "Where were you?" she asked.

"I had a game tonight."

Ma grew silent a few seconds, "I'm so sorry, Tre. I went to dinner."

"With . . ."

"Someone."

"Who?"

"Someone special," Mom said with a blush.

I had not been disappointed when my mother didn't come to any of my baseball games because she had work and why should she have? I sucked and was sitting on the bench. But I was a starter now. I stormed off to my room and slammed the door.

Mom burst through the door moments later. "I know you didn't . . . You don't close doors around here. Ain't no privacy. This my house."

"You never make time for me!" I shouted.

"Come here, little boy! Looking like your damn daddy."

I don't budge.

"Now!" she said through her teeth without moving her jaws.

I turned around and walked toward my mother. I didn't do it because she said so. I did it because the tone in her voice scared me.

"Who do you think you're talking too like that?" Mom glared at me as if she was ready to fight.

"You've never come to any of my games. You never even tell me you love me. You never do anything for me. You're worse than my father."

Mom smacked me so hard it knocked the sound out of my mouth. "How dare you compare me to that man? Yes, both of us weren't as present in your lives as much as I'd wish for. One of us chose to be away by choice and the other had to be out of necessity," she said. "Can you call your father right now and ask to stay with him?"

I shook my head no as tears rolled down my face.

"How the hell else were you gonna eat? Who is there when you're sick? Who's clothing and feeding you? Who's been there for your birthdays and Christmases? I'm always working for you guys. I lost my identity taking care of you guys, and I never made time for myself!" she shouted as a tear formed in her eyes.

"I'm sorry, Ma . . . I'm so sorry."

"One of these days, you guys will grow up, and you will leave me. I don't wanna be alone."

"You won't be alone, Ma! I love you . . . I'll always be here."

"Love you too, son." For the first time, we hugged each other.

I rushed off to my bedroom.

"Where are you going?" Ma asks.

"I have a date."

"Who you going on a date with?"

"Xena Jones."

"You talking about Sister Jenkins's fast-ass granddaughter, Xena?"

"Yeah. Why?"

"Uh . . . Be back home at 11 pm."

"But, Mama, it's already 9 o'clock."

"Good. That means if you hurry, you got two hours," she said sternly. "No son of mine will be out in them streets . . . You ain't bringing no damn babies in my house."

Moments later, I headed outside and waited for Xena to pull up out front. I was getting a little nervous because I didn't know what to expect from my date. Xena was a fast girl. She had quite a reputation, and on top of that, I knew she wasn't a virgin. Xena's personal experience intimidated me. Rumor had it that she lost her virginity at the tender age of 12-years-old. It was insane to me that 12 and 13-year-old children were having sex.

Unlike most of my peers, I was still the big V. Sex was never a conversation I had with any of my folks. There was no way in hell I was talking about sex with my grandparents. None of our adults talked about it, so we experienced it vicariously through our peers. My only sexual experiences were from the porn videos and nude magazines some of the guys on my baseball team got ahold of.

Xena pulled upfront in her Ford Thunderbird, and we were off. As we drove through the streets, I didn't know how to act. Should I be the class clown or should I be cool and suave. I tried to act confident, but my nervousness bled right through.

We ended up at the dark and creepy Walker Park. As we quietly sat in the car, I could feel her sexual energy. She was not like most of the girls in school who were overly sexual, but she did have her own not-so-good-girl stories. It didn't matter to me because I didn't want her stories. I wanted her. My mind drifted thinking about our potential, but Xena reeled me back in. She leaned over and asked, "Who are you picking to escort for homecoming court?"

"I don't know."

She got closer and whispered, "You should consider me." Xena stared me straight in the eyes.

As we sat there in silence, Xena asked, "Are you OK?"

"Yes," I said, but I wasn't.

"Why are you so quiet?"

"I don't know." All I could think was I didn't have a condom, and I wasn't bringing any kids home. I didn't know what was about to occur.

Xena placed her hand on my thigh then asked, "Why don't you care about school?"

This caught me by surprise. Here I am thinking about losing my virginity, and she's asking me about school. "What do you mean?" I asked.

"You're funny and all in class, but I feel you don't take school seriously. Don't you wanna get a good job when you graduate?"

"I'm not focused on that right now . . . I'm trying to get through football season." I wasn't comfortable going there. "Do you like me?"

"Yes."

I thought: could this be it? Could I be about to lose my virginity? My pants grew into a tepee from the massive woody I got. Xena started giggling because she knew what had happened.

"Wait . . . What time is it?" I asked.

She turned on the car to check the time. It was 10:59 PM.

"Sorry, Xena, I have to go home."

"OK." Xena cranked the car, put the car in reverse, and we drove off.

Moments later, we pulled in front of my house. "I hope you had a good time," Xena said.

"I did."

"Good. I did too."

"I think I want to walk with you on the homecoming court. Would you like that?"

"I would," Xena said with a twinkle in her eye. We hugged, she gave me a peck on the cheek, then I scurried off.

*****

I hear my phone vibrating. I look at it and notice Eva has sent me 31 text messages. Most if not all of the text messages read, *"Fuck You."* Every other message reads, *"Puta Perra!"* and a few have *"Puta Maricón"* sprinkled in as I scroll through our chat. I dial up Eva.

"Hello . . . You've reached Eva. I'm not in at the moment. For a faster response, send a text message." It goes right to her voicemail.

I end the call and text, *"Can we talk?"*

She texts back, *"Fuck you . . . I'm going out."*

I call her phone again and this time Eva answers.

"What!"

"Take your drunk ass to bed . . . Hello . . . Eva—" She ends the call. I start to pace the floor. What did I get myself into?

CHAPTER 19

I am five o'clock hot right now. This woman has my blood pressure boiling like a steaming kettle. Pacing the floor helps slow the thoughts running through my mind. I brought this on myself. There is nothing I can do to change my feelings toward Eva. Sure, I have tremendous love for her, but I am not in love with her. Had I been in love with Eva, it would not have been that easy for me to leave the way I did. The relationship has run its course, and I probably procrastinated the break-up later than anticipated. I will deal with her when I get back to Atlanta.

Another message comes through from Eva. Not to my surprise, it reads, "*Fuck you.*" I put the phone on silent, throw it on the bed, and take a seat at the desk; I take a deep breath and get back to writing.

*****

HIGH SCHOOL BLUES FINALE

My senior year marked the last time Mom and Kwesi would head to court. I was graduating high school and almost 18, and he no longer need to pay child support for me. Kwesi wanted a paternity test done to see if Armani was his son or not. He denied Armani was his son to avoid paying the child support. This fool did many things to get out of paying child support. He denied children, he changed his last name, and he even tried to change his social security number. Kwesi treated all his children like collection accounts on a credit report. He claimed Armani didn't look like him and continued to claim that he was out in the streets, chasing women so he didn't have time to get my mother pregnant. But in the case of Armani, a 99.9% paternity result made Kwesi look like an ass—yet again.

After meeting in the park, Xena and I talked twice a day outside of class until the homecoming court announcements hit the school. Our football team would go on to lose three straight games before the homecoming game. All we wanted to do was look good for homecoming. We stopped caring about winning. We stopped focusing on the game and focused on everything the game was attracting. I suffered a back injury that took most of the season to heal, and I eventually lost my position on the field to Clifford James III, aka Lil C.

Lil C was faster than a hot knife sliding through butter. A track runner with blazing speed paired with high awareness, Lil C was a force to be reckoned with. He wasn't afraid to make tackles and knock your teeth down your throat if he caught you slipping on a slant route.

Whenever Lil C made a play, his loud country ass would shout, "Clifford James da Third!" Every game for the rest of the season, this fool shouted his name. It got to the point that whenever this fool did anything pivotal, he'd shout, "Clifford James da Third!" People loved hearing him yell his name after he made a big play. There was a song created by this fool, and all he did was yell his name the whole damn song. Lil C made big plays, but it didn't change the fact that our football team sucked. We didn't just suck, we sucked balls. Though he was able to do anything athletically on the field, he was academically challenged. If his brains were leather, he wouldn't have enough to saddle an ant. Lil C was in Wall Classes. Wall Classes in high school were for slower learners. If you were in these classes, you were considered dumb.

Homecoming Week was underway, but I wasn't thrilled. I was sidelined due to an injury. The homecoming game wasn't as exciting for me as it was for Xena. Who would have known Xena, the once dusty-ass hood rat that rocked a juicy Jerri Curl and sucked her thumb, would become Homecoming Queen? Once she was elected, the phone calls and conversation between us dwindled. The dialogue became strictly business between Xena and me. Xena was more concerned with how my suit looked than how my injured back felt. After we walked through the basketball court for the Homecoming ceremony, it was the last time that Xena and I spoke. Our football team won an ugly game 3 – 0 against the Jacksonville Tigers, who were ranked second in the state.

After the game, I hustled back home. When I entered the house, I noticed Mom was dolled up again. "Where were you?" she asked.

"I had a game tonight."

"Cliff and I were there . . . We didn't see you."

"I didn't suit up, but I was on the sideline."

"Oh . . . I wondered why I didn't hear your name."

The toilet in the bathroom flushed then and a tall white man stepped out of the bathroom.

"You're dating Opie Taylor?" I whispered.

My mother smacked me upside my head, "Be respectful!" she said.

I don't know if I was shocked that he was a white man or impressed that he was brave enough to come into our neighborhood at that time of night.

Cliff walked up to me and extended his hand, "I'm Cliff. Heard a lot about you."

"His son plays on your football team."

"Yep!" Cliff confirmed. "My son's a musician too. He made a song. You guys wanna hear it?"

"Sure," I said awkwardly. Cliff pulled a dubbed cassette tape from his front pocket and walked to the stereo system we had in the living room near the TV. The beat dropped and it sounded like a Three 6 Mafia song. Then things took a turn.

"This is my favorite part." Offbeat as ever, Clifford shouted, "Clifford James da Third . . . Clifford James da Third! Clifford James da Third . . . Clifford James da Third!"

I couldn't believe it. "Lil C is your son?" I asked.

"That's what you young folks call him. He's Little Cliff to us. He's the third Clifford Benson James."

All I wanted was for my mother to watch me play. The time she finally came to one of my games, I was injured. To add insult to injury, the guy my mother is dating is the father of the guy who took my spot.

The Homecoming Dance was held in the girls' basketball gymnasium. I remembered sitting alone, watching everyone enjoy the night, Xena especially. Donning a tiara, that skank shook and danced all night long with everyone except me. I sat alone in a corner defeated, deflated, and stewing in my thoughts. Why am I here? I thought. I didn't contribute to the game. The girl I escorted acted as if she didn't know me. All I could think of is how did I let Xena play me like that.

"What's up, Tre Tre Bear?"

I looked up, and it was Sade. She grabbed a chair and sat right next to me.

I barely saw Sade because we never had the same classes. She had advanced honors classes. I saw her a hand full of times over the course of the school year, but that was it. She was the big hype in school that year. She had become a 5-Star recruit in the state and committed to the University of Memphis on a full-ride scholarship for basketball and academics.

"How have things been?" Sade asked.

We notice Xena and Jackson Reed's punk ass making out on the dance floor. "My football career is over. I found out that my mama is dating Lil C's dad. Now your ex-boyfriend is kissing my homecoming date. I'm so stupid," I said, slumped over in my chair.

"I don't like how Xena played you. I thought you were smarter than that."

"I should have picked you, but your man-friend threatened us not too."

"He's not that much older," Sade said with a giggle.

"Can he go to the liquor store and buy alcohol?"

Sade does not answer my question. "I'm glad you didn't pick me. I don't care about that kind of attention."

Sade looks at Xena and Jackson Reed, grinding on each other on the dance floor.

"I read the poem you wrote her," Sade said. "You wrote her lyrics to an LL Cool J song? You're so lame! That stuff only works for LL Cool J."

I threw a tantrum, "Big Ted can barely read, let alone write. I don't know what the hell I thought when I let this fool write a poem for me."

"You might've dodged a bullet. We'll see in 20 years." Sade got to her feet and said, "I'll catch you around."

"You're leaving?" I asked.

"Yeah, my boyfriend is picking me up. You need a ride?"

"Nah, I'm good."

Then we heard the words, "Cash Money taking over for the 99 and the 2000!" Sade's eyes grew wide, then the beat dropped. She grabbed my hand and dragged me onto the dance floor and started grinding on me. She backed that thang up me. Of course, like any horny teenage boy, I grew a massive boner. My wang was harder than Chinese arithmetic. That didn't scare Sade, though. She grinded on me harder as the song played. It was almost better than losing my virginity.

Of course, us dancing on the dance floor got everyone's attention, including Xena's. Unexpectedly, Xena walked over and started to drop it like it was hot. Bouncing her ass right in front of us. Once the song was over, Xena sauntered away.

"Walk me out? I don't want any of your friends looking at my butt," Sade said. We headed out of the gymnasium together, and the speculation began.

After the Homecoming dance, there were little rumbles about Xena and Jackson Reed messing around. There were even rumbles about Sade and me because our classmates saw us walking around together before and after class more often.

One day while serving one of my many lunch detentions, Sade was waiting outside of the cafeteria for me. We walked in the other direction away from the center, where everyone hung out during the lunch break.

"What did you do this time?" Sade asked.

"Nothing . . . I guess teachers don't like being called by their first name."

"Do you call your mother or grandparents by their first name?

"No."

"So why would you call the teacher by their first name?" Sade asked.

"Because I have a problem."

"We all know you have a problem, Tre," she said.

A few moments glided by as we walked in silence. This would have been an excellent time for me to profess my love to Sade. But instead, I got cold feet and asked, "Do you really lick your boyfriend's balls and his asshole?"

"No . . . That's disgusting." Sade said with a chuckle. "I only said that because you were out of line."

"My bad . . ."

"You're good . . . Honestly . . . I'm still a virgin."

I stopped walking because this came as a surprise to me. "You're still a virgin?" I asked.

"Yep."

"Didn't you and Jackson? "

"Nope."

"Wait . . . So, you and Mike—"

"Never even kissed," she said. "You kissed me before my boyfriend even tried." We circled the school until lunch was almost over. We walked back to the area where all the other students were standing. Her boyfriend, Pretty Boy Roy, also known as Royal Jenkins, was sitting on one of the benches with a bunch of his cronies.

"I'll see you later, OK." Sade hugged me and ran over to where Royal sat.

There was a time that whenever Xena saw me in the hallways, she would go the other way. When we were in class, instead of laughing, she grew annoyed with my witticisms. One day before class, she tried to walk past me, but I blocked her from entering.

"What are you doing? You're making me late."

"Why have you been avoiding me?"

"Can you please move?"

"Not until you answer me."

She hesitated a few seconds, "You don't care about graduating. You act like a dumb jock, but you are smarter than that."

"That's the pot calling the kettle black. You're playing kissy-face with Jackson Reed's punk ass who flunked four times."

"At least he's being himself and not some act." Xena strolled by me and entered the class.

Xena was right. The whole time I was in school, I acted as if I didn't care about making good grades. I thought it was cool to be a dumb athlete. I acted as if I was sillier than I was. I only applied myself when I deemed it worthy of my time or if I needed to do well to receive a passing grade. Xena saw right through that. I found out Xena slept with all the senior football players except me, and of course, her cousin, Big Ted. We ended up with a 3 – 7 record in football that season.

It was hard to focus on class once the football season was over. Up until this point of the school year, I didn't do any of my work. My term paper was due in a week and a half and didn't have a subject to write about. If the term paper wasn't completed, I would not be able to walk across the graduation stage with my classmates. The pressure was on because the term paper determined my final grade point average. If you didn't turn in a term paper and held a high GPA, you still were able to graduate. But if you were me, the term paper would make or break your hope of graduating. This motivated me to get that paper done, graduate, and get as far the hell away as I could. I stopped procrastinating and put the pedal to the medal. I chose to write about events that occurred during the 90s.

The Internet did not exist for us back then, so I had to use other resources for research. Grandma hoarded old magazines and old newspapers. She stored them all in the spare bedrooms Armani, and I spent many nights in while my mother worked her third job. I grabbed all the newspapers and old magazines that Grandma had dating back to the early 1990s up to the Y2K scare. The more I read, the more I learned. But the more I learned, the angrier I became. We didn't know anything about the world economically. The trash courses they taught us during grade school were nothing but distorted fluff to pacify children while their parents slaved and worked to fuel the economy.

Most lessons we were taught had nothing to do with real-world matters. The term paper I wrote was about how we lack knowledge, economic literacy, and many other resources. I finished the six-page paper a couple of days before it was due. I became passionate about my thoughts and research. I turned it in and went on with my life. Mrs. Sullivan told me the following week that I needed to score a 79 to get my high school diploma. I knew that the paper I turned in would be good enough to pass, and I would graduate.

The following week in English class, I assumed my usual position, which was my head on the desk. Mrs. Sullivan handed out our graded term papers. She slid my essay under my head. I was pleasantly surprised. I received a 95, which was the highest grade in the class. Some of my classmates grumbled and complained that the teacher gave me a high score because there was no way that someone who went to sleep every day in class could score higher than most of the students who turned in their paper weeks before the due date. Xena, who was one of those chirpers, was disappointed with her score. Her grade on the paper was so low it dropped her GPA.

After class, Xena approached me and said, "Admit it . . . The teacher gave you a high score because she felt sorry for you."

"No, bitch," I replied. "I understand English better than your non-English-speaking ass." I knew once it rolled off my tongue, that I was in for a hell of a ride. Xena played me then tried to insult my intelligence. The irony is she worked her ass off to get a 3.1, and I half-assed my way through high school and managed to get a 3.2 GPA. What would have happened if I applied myself? Xena became the third person on my shit list behind Kwesi and Jackson Reed.

At graduation, we all sat antsy as the ceremony commenced. Some students knew this was the beginning of the end, and others knew this was the end of the beginning. Some of the students would go off to college, and some would head into the workforce. Some joined the military, and others went to jail. Sade was the National Gatorade Player of the Year, the Gatorade Female Athlete of the Year, and a McDonald's All-American. Sade was also the Valedictorian but opted out of her speech. Bobby Lee opted in because he was the Salutatorian. A few of the audience members chuckled as he made his way on stage. Everyone who knew Bobby Lee, knew he was about to talk his talk.

"I'm gonna make this quick and painless." He bellowed through the microphone. "My fellow graduates, over the last four years here at Blytheville High School, we have learned a lot. Ms. Sullivan, my English teacher, understood the artist within . . . And never forced us to do anything we didn't want to do. Mr. Clay taught us how to not get in trouble after the football season. And lastly, I want to thank the school district for hiring Coach Rocky as a foreign language teacher. Not only did he coach us to our first state championship in baseball, but I also now know how to curse in French. Thanks, Coach Rocky. Now . . . Va te faire foutre! Let's party!" he yelled, then took his cap off and tossed it in the air. The rest of the class followed suit.

As the students' parents migrated to the field, Sade approached me.

"Congratulations on not flunking, Tre Tre Bear," she leaned in and hugged me.

"Hey, son!" A man shouted. We looked over and saw Kwesi. The graduation would be the first time he attended any school function of mine. "Congratulations on graduating. Let me get a picture of y'all." Kwesi snapped a photo of Sade and me.

Sade darted a vicious glare at Kwesi. "I'll see you around, Tre," Sade said as Pretty Boy Roy stared as we hugged.

"Let's get that picture, Son."

Glenn held the camera and snapped a photo of us. Ma and Grandma walked up and hugged me.

"Congratulations, boy!" Grandma uttered.

It was good to see Grandma smile rather than give her typical scowl. Mom and Grandma were genuinely excited to see me graduate. I saw Papa sitting in the stands, and I knew he was proud.

Mama whispered to Grandma, "Kwesi taking pictures like he helped Tre get here."

Kwesi might have been extra happy to get me off child support, but I was glad he was there.

After the graduation ceremony, there was a party hosted in the boys' basketball gymnasium. Though I had now graduated, I still had a curfew until I officially moved out of my mother's home. One of my graduation gifts from her was a later curfew. She let me stay out as long as I wanted.

I joined Bobby Lee and Big Ted at the graduation party. "You sum bitches best put some pep in your step! This is gonna be the last time we see any of these clowns for a while!" Bobby Lee yelled as he danced his way onto the dance floor as "The Cha Cha Slide" by DJ Casper played. At the part of the song where it goes, "How Low Can You Go . . . Can you go down low?" Bobby Lee's perverted ass lay down on his back, and some chick sat on his face. That would be the last time I saw Bobby Lee. Big Ted and I rocked out until it was time for his girlfriend Jasmine to leave. I walked with them to the parking lot where she had parked.

"Are you ready for college?" I asked as we all headed to the parking lot.

Big Ted took a moment to respond then answered, "I don't want to play for some sorry Division 3 squad. But, if I can help them win a championship, I'll get my chance to play for a Division 1 school and possibly get to the pros."

"Fool, you didn't even lead us to a winning season."

Big Ted grew defensive, "That's because we were coached by a dumbass who doesn't know the game of football."

"So, you're gonna play for his brother?"

We chuckle.

"Are you coming back in?" I asked.

"Yeah, give me a second," Big Ted said.

As I headed back toward the gym, someone yelled, "Yo, Tre!" I turned to my right, and it was Sade's boyfriend, Pretty Boy Royal. "I heard what you said to my girl," he said as he got in my face.

"What are you talking about?" I asked.

"You called my girl a bitch!"

"I never called Sade a bitch," I said, baffled.

"Nah, fam! I ain't talking about her. I'm talking about Xena . . . My other girl." A couple of his cronies circled around me.

At this point, I did what any rational person would do . . . I lied. "Man, I don't even know Xena."

Some random person shouted from the side. "I bet you won't hit 'em, Pretty Boy Roy!"

"You talkin' with your tongue out yo shoe," Pretty Boy Roy said. "You walked her on the homecoming court."

Royal's brother Kane blurted out, "Enough with all this talking." Kane threw a sharp hook and caught me right in the jaw. It knocked me to the ground. That was one of the hardest blows I had ever taken. He hit me so hard I could taste the punch. Royal jumped on top of me and started kicking me. I wasn't the biggest, but I was stronger than him. I managed to wrestle him to the ground, get on top of him, and land a couple of jabs to his jaw.

I took a blow to the back of my head from Kane. He began to stomp on me. In between him and Royal's punches, I recalled seeing a timid Big Ted look on from a distance. He saw that I needed help and didn't want any smoke. Big Ted walked back into the gym. What made it worse was Jackson Reed's punk ass laughed while these guys whooped my ass.

Suddenly, a couple of gunshots cracked into the sky. Everyone scrambled. A couple of drunk graduates had decided to pop off a couple of rounds to celebrate finishing high school. I managed to sneak off to the side of the gym and hide until it was clear. I waited almost an hour until the last cop had left. Once it was clear, I strategically walked back home, lost in thought.

I woke up the next morning with a busted lip, an almost broken jaw, and a swollen eye socket from the fight the night before. I couldn't hide my injuries from my mother, so I told her what went down.

Someone banged on the door. I answered, and it was an enraged Papa. "That sapsucker stole my car when we were at Tre's graduation. Heard it on the scanner last night. Armani was riding in a car, smoking weed with that other sapsucker Jackson Reed and shot bullets at some house. Damn fools were arrested after a high-speed police chase on I-55. The car is totaled, but Armani's OK."

My mother had grown tired of Armani acting out and the trouble he caused. She knew his antics outweighed his contribution to the family and she sent him off to reform school. Mom knew I had to leave sooner than later. I added Pretty Boy Roy and Big Ted's names to my shit list. I licked my wounds; I quit my job at Burger King and vowed to get as far away as I could. The following week my mother dropped me off at the Greyhound bus station, and I was on the first thing smoking out of Arkansas.

*****

My concentration is broken by multiple vibrating messages and alerts from my phone. This time it is not Eva. Bobby Lee sent me a screenshot of a ticket and a message that reads, *"If you don't get here now . . . I'm processing this first thing Monday morning, you sum bitch."* Bobby Lee sends another text that reads, *"Sade's here, and she's hotter than the devil's armpit. She's got me over here sweating like a blindfolded lesbo in a fish store."*

I text back, *"LOL! I'm on my way!"* I rummage through my suitcase to find something to wear for this damn class reunion.

CHAPTER 20

A handful of overweight guests enter the lobby of the Holiday Inn. I have been sitting out front in this rental car for at least 10 minutes, scoping out the place before joining the rest of my old classmates. I crank the engine and place the gearshift into drive. As I inch the car out of the parking space, a car pulls up and blocks me. The car parks right beside where I'm parked. The person driving the car steps out of the vehicle. I instantly recognize her.

I shut the engine off and hop out of the car. "Xena . . . Xena Jones. Is that you?" She turns her head, and it is the gorgeous and voluptuous Xena Jones. Xena and I stare into each other's souls. She has a motherly glow, but deep within, there is a thirst for something refreshing.

"Tre!" she shouts ecstatically. "Wow! You look . . . You look amazing."

"Thank you," I say. "Father Time has been on your side, Xena."

"It's been some years."

"I know." We stare into each other's eyes for a few seconds. Not a word is said, but no words are needed because we have unfinished business.

My pocket starts to vibrate. I receive a flurry of text messages all from Bobby Lee that read, *"Hey FATHERFUCKER . . . I'm looking right at ya."*

I look up and notice Bobby Lee staring at me through the double glass door of the entrance. He opens the door and shouts, "Bring yo ass in, Buddy Ro!"

I enter Bistro Eleven 21, which is attached to the side of the Holiday Inn. We shake hands then hug each other. Bobby Lee, who is a sweaty hot mess, pushes me away. "Get off me . . . It's hot." He starts fanning himself, "I'm sweating like a priest at a little league game. I need a beer."

Bobby Lee leads the way into the bar as we walk through a flock of our former classmates who are staring at their phones. "I don't remember half of these sum bitches," Bobby Lee says as we shuffle through our classmates.

There's a bunch of small talk going on as we walk by a table filled with familiar faces. Mike Rodriguez, Big Ted Jones, and Jackson Reed's punk ass all sit together at a table. A few voices shout, "Tre! Is that Tre?"

Big Ted and I give each other a fist pound. Sitting next to him is an extremely hefty, greasy-skinned, pimple-faced lady with disheveled hair. She is wearing a filthy housedress and has a butch-looking face with short purple hair.

"Hey, man . . . This is my wife, Apple." She looks more like a rotten tomato than an apple. Apple's smile looked like she had been chewing on charcoal from all the rotten teeth in her mouth. She sticks her hand out as if she wants me to kiss it. I give her a fist pound as well.

"Nice to meet you," I say. "You know what, Big Ted? For years you were on my shit list because you didn't help me when I got my ass beat by those guys at the graduation party. Now that I see you with your lovely wife, I'll let bygones be bygones."

Mike Rodriguez randomly blurts out, "I do so much coke my dick stopped working!" Mike looks as if like life has not treated him well. He has put on about 80 pounds since high school. His eyes are sunken in with dark bags under them. Mike appears to not have gotten any sleep in the past few days. The little hair that's left on his head looks like it's running away from his face.

"Congrats on the accomplishment," I say mockingly." I'm sure you've made your parents proud."

"I haven't seen you in a minute. How come you don't post much on Facebook?" Big Ted asks.

"I only log into Facebook to unfollow people."

Bobby Lee interrupts, "Ain't that something with the Internet? Kids now have to deal with cyber-bullies . . . In my day, I'd just turn the phone off."

Jackson Reed places his hand on my shoulder. "Nice to see that you showed up."

A fake smile grows across my face. I still want to knock Jackson Reed's punk-ass teeth down his throat, but now isn't the time for that.

Big Ted chimes in, "Word around town is that you've gotten this far in life, and you still don't have any kids."

"That's because he's gay," Jackson Reed shouts.

"Bring your ol' lady around and let her find out how gay I am." The guys at the table erupt into laughter.

Bobby Lee whispers, "Watch out for ol' Jackson . . . He'd try to bang your wife if you had one. Mike was married to Xena and had a child with her. But they busted up when Mike found out that she was sleeping with Jackson."

"How did you find that out?"

"I responded to a domestic disturbance one night. Mike called the cops on Xena because she had beaten the hell out of him. Ain't that a bitch? You found out your wife is cheating on you, then you get your ass beat for finding out. I still can't understand how Mike and Jackson are still cool about it. Oh . . . Remember Clifford James da Third?"

"Yeah . . ."

"He was the biggest drug bust since Rack Daddy."

"What?"

We find two empty spots at the bar. "Hell . . . I tried talkin' with your ol' girl, Sade, but her stuck up ass acted like she didn't even know me. She has a stick stuffed all the way up her ass, man."

"Why would she come here if she didn't wanna talk to anyone?" I ask.

"She thinks because she's on TV, she's better than everybody else."

I scan the room, "Where is she?"

"She probably went to the pisser," Bobby Lee says as he signals for the bartender. "Can I get a Bud Light on draft?" He turns to me and asks, "Whatcha drinkin'?"

Xena and I are in the middle of a staring match from opposite ends of the bar.

"You didn't learn your lesson from high school? That girl ain't nothin' but trouble," says Bobby Lee.

"What happened to you, Bobby Lee? Not trashing your current career, but I wouldn't have pegged you as a police officer."

"I didn't either . . . I had a full scholarship to play baseball at Arkansas State, but my dumb ass tried to play football too. I blew out my ACL and my PCL at football practice. That affected my baseball game, and I dropped out. If I wasn't playing sports, there was no reason for me to go to college. I joined the force. But hey, that's life. At least I don't have student loan debt and I ain't out somewhere sucking dick for car payments. I learned how to speak French but never left the state of Arkansas," says Bobby Lee.

"I'm sorry . . . I'm waiting for the violin to play," I say. We share a chuckle. "You can always leave," I say.

Bobby Lee shakes his head no. "I can't, man. I can't leave my kids. I'm not doing that to my kids like my dad did me." Bobby Lee takes a swig of beer, "All's I'm saying is . . . Hell, I see why you don't come home much. There's nothing here. It's a ghost town. Businesses crumblin' . . . Unemployment rates spikin' . . . Crime risin' . . . I've seen more people die in these streets than I ever wished." Bobby Lee takes a big gulp of his beer.

"Anybody, we know?"

Bobby thinks on it a second, "You remember Pretty Boy Roy?"

"Sade's ex? Yeah . . . What happened to him?"

"He was shot and killed in a shootout a few years ago."

I dig in my pocket and pull out the piece of paper titled *Tre's Shit List* then scratch Big Ted's and Pretty Boy Roy's names off the list. I nonchalantly re-fold the piece of paper and stuff it back in my pocket.

Bobby Lee grows curious, "What was that?"

"Nothing. Continue with what you were saying."

"I love this town, but if I could, I'd move as far away from this sum bitch as possible. This town lacks resources and leadership. The kids can't dream because all they see is violence."

Xena and I make eye contact again.

"Enough about that stuff . . . Come over and meet my wife," Bobby Lee says. Bobby Lee leads me over to a table where a slightly obese lady is sitting. "Remember, my wife, Krystal. She said you were in her English class." I study Krystal's face, but I don't register it.

"Tre, is that you?" Krystal asks ecstatically as she recognizes me.

"Yes . . . It's me." She stands and gives me an uncomfortable big bear hug, "How ya been?"

"I've been . . . Been good." I try to fake my way through our interaction, but Krystal catches on.

"You don't remember me, do you?"

"Not even a little bit . . . I'm sorry."

"At least you're honest about it." Krystal continues, "We were in second period together. I remember you going to sleep every day and then got the highest score on our final assignment. We thought you cheated on the paper, and then you turn out to be some big-time writer. Looks good on you." Krystal throws a wink at me.

"Oh, yeah . . . Now I remember you . . . You are the 'Cha Cha Slide' girl . . . The one that sat on Bobby Lee's face that night?"

"Yep . . . I've been sitting on his face ever since," Krystal says proudly.

"That's so disgusting . . . I'm happy for you guys," I say.

Bobby Lee interrupts, "Baby, why don't you get us a couple of beers."

"OK, Daddy." She walks off.

"What was that all about?"

"We're kind of like swingers." Bobby Lee says candidly.

"What do you mean . . . Kind of like swingers?"

"Well, we're swingers. I didn't wanna just come all the way out with it."

What in the hell did I get myself into? I knew I should have stayed home.

"Don't knock it till ya try it, Buddy Ro."

I try to mask the awkward exchange, "No judgment here, bro." I was judging him.

"It's written all over your face . . . You're judging me," Bobby Lee says.

"Yes, I'm judging you . . . But if you like it, I love it."

"Do you really love it?" Bobby Lee finishes the last gulp of beer and stares into my eyes. "Because now that I'm thinking about it, you should get with ol' Sade and join us. I got one of them blow-up hot tubs, and the four of us can drink beer and catch up. You know what I mean?"

I scratch my head, "Nope . . . I don't know what you mean and I'm good on not finding out."

Bobby Lee covers the awkwardness with an uneasy chuckle, "I'm fucking with ya, bro." We both share an awkward snicker. "Unless you're gon' do it?"

Bobby Lee stares me right in the eye.

"I'll pass."

Bobby Lee stands to his feet. "I'll be right back," he says. "Gotta drain the ol' weasel." Bobby Lee fades off to the bathroom.

Now is my time to escape. I stand to my feet then stroll off to the exit. I walk pass Krystal.

"Hey, Tre!"

I wave goodbye then sneak out of the bar. Before walking out of the door, someone taps me on the shoulder.

"Where are you going, Tre Tre Bear?"

I stop in my tracks and notice when I turn around it is Sade.

"Sade!" I say as we give each other a hug.

I am so enamored by Sade's aura. A lot has changed over the years for Sade. She was a former WNBA All-Star turned basketball analyst who calls games for ESPN, TNT, and NBA TV. She was previously a reporter for the Washington Wizards and the Washington Football Team.

"You're too good to be true . . . Looking like a modern-day Vanity."

Sade is wearing a sexy black jumpsuit that wraps around her Amazonian figure. Her curly hair and nails are done immaculately. Her nails are low enough to dribble a basketball but sharp enough to draw blood.

Sade blushes but deflects, "Wow . . . Is that dirt around your face, or is that a beard? I don't know who this guy is."

"I thought you had left already."

"I was waiting on you . . . But I had to sneak away from someone," says Sade.

"Let me guess, Bobby Lee?" I asked.

"Yes! How did you know?"

"Because I had to sneak away too."

Sade laughs. That cute laugh of hers was always music to my ears.

"Bobby Lee said you were acting all stuck up."

"That's because he invited me over for a threesome."

"He hasn't changed much."

"I wouldn't have expected anything less from him," says Sade.

"It's good to see you. I mean . . . I only came to this damn thing to see you."

"I kind of only came to see you," Sade admits.

Mike Rodriguez, Big Ted, and Jackson Reed all walk out of Bistro.

"Hey, we're going to my house and play some cards? You guys should join," Jackson slurs as he leans over and places his arm around Sade.

"I'll pass. I have to drive back to Memphis."

"Are you sure, babe?"

Sade removes his arm and corrects him, "I'm not your babe, Jackson. But nice to see you again."

Xena follows behind and approaches me and Sade. She gives Sade a hug. "Good seeing you again, girl," Xena says.

Xena positions herself in between Sade and me, hugs me a few moments longer than I expect, then she walks away.

Sade rolls her eyes, "I still hate that fake bitch. Give me your phone."

I hand Sade my phone. We stare at each other in the eye a few moments, but neither one of us makes a move. Sade leans in, we hug each other, and she walks off.

Bobby Lee and his wife walk by me. "Babe, wait for me in the car, will ya?"

"Yes, daddy," Krystal nods. "Hope to see you again, Tre!" Krystal winks at me then scurries off to the car.

"I saw you and Sade talking," says Bobby Lee. "Is she down to join us?"

"We aren't joining you, but it was nice seeing you again."

"And where the hell you think you're going? You're not going home tonight." Bobby Lee places his arm around me. "Because tonight, we're getting fucked up!"

CHAPTER 21

Who would have guessed I'd be hanging out with Jackson Reed's punk ass? We are in his so-called man cave that's in his oil-stained garage. How tacky is that? Calling this place a shithole would be offensive to toilets. In this man-cave is an old sofa, an old dining table, and a cheap-ass beanbag that I'm sitting on. Jackson Reed, Big Ted, Mike Rodriguez, and Bobby Lee all sit at the dining table talking trash, playing poker, and pounding shots of Jose Cuervo. It is already bottle number four for these drunks. I hear fragments of the banter, but my focus is on my phone.

"It's obvious that there is still an attraction between us," I text Sade.

Sade sends a message right back that reads, *"I'm staying at the Peabody in Memphis over the weekend. What time will you be here?"*

To sound busier than I am, I text back, *"I'll check my schedule and see what works."*

"LOL! OK, Mr. Schedule. Text me when you get to the lobby . . . I'll be good after 3 pm."

I reply, *"That's too early and too late to do anything. But I guess I'll see you then."*

"Do you remember our pact?" Messages Sade.

"What pact?" I reply.

"You don't remember our pact?"

"No . . . What was it?"

"I'm not texting it over the phone."

"See . . . You're playing."

"LOL! We'll talk about it tomorrow. Heading to bed. Goodnight, Tre. 😊 "

"Wait . . ."

Sade replies with a question mark.

I text her, *"Send me a nip pic!"*

"Bye, boy!"

"Goodnight."

Amid all the commotion, Jackson Reed focuses his attention on me.

"Yo," Jackson shouts as he takes a sip of his drink. "Remember when Tre got his ass beat at the graduation party? Man, that was funny."

Big Ted snickers then covers his mouth to conceal his laughter once our eyes met.

"Wait a second," Bobby Lee says as his demeanor sours. "Tre, you got into a fight after graduation?"

"You were too busy getting your face rode on the dance floor. Pretty Boy Roy and his goons jumped, Tre. Correction, they whooped his whole entire ass," Jackson utters with a snigger.

"I did get my ass whooped," I say with a fake chuckle.

"And you didn't help?" Bobby Lee asks.

"Nope! But I laughed my ass off," Jackson Reed says with a chuckle. He then spells out, "L.M.A.O," to add emphases to the ass-whooping.

"What kind of fucked up are you?" Bobby Lee asks. "You're more of a bitch now than I ever thought. Who sits and watches a friend get his ass beat?"

Big Ted says nothing as he looks away, avoiding eye contact with everyone.

"It's all good. We were never friends in the beginning," I say with a fake smile as I glare down Jackson Reed's punk ass. A part of me would love to knock his teeth down his throat and laugh as he suffocates on the blood from his mouth. I take a mental note and file it away.

"If I were Tre, I'd beat yo ass right now for bringing that up, and you didn't help me."

"Whatever," Jackson says as he studies me for a few beats. He takes another sip. "You know who bought me that beanbag you're sitting on?"

"Let me guess . . . Nobody, because you stole it," I say because it's in his wheelhouse.

"No. Actually your daddy bought it," an inebriated Jackson says, slurring his words. "I saw his father more than he did."

Big Ted and Mike burst into laughter. Hell, I laugh with them, but I am not letting that comment slide. "These are all facts!" I say with a grin. "He's right . . . He saw my father more than I did because he was probably banging Jackson's mother while his daddy was at work."

There room grows quiet, then the guys erupt in laughter. Jackson doesn't find my response humorous.

"Why you gotta say that?" Jackson said.

"You started it with your punk ass," Bobby Lee says.

"That's kind of a low blow, bro."

"Stop acting like a bitch, Jackson," says Bobby Lee. "You've said and done worser things."

"Worser ain't even a word, jackass."

"Ain't ain't no word either," Mike mumbles to himself.

"Statutory rape is a word," Bobby Lee says.

"Actually, it's more than a word," says Jackson Reed's punk ass.

"Sum bitch flunked six times and wants to correct me. You're legit the only asshole I know that can attend the next six class reunions."

I take great pleasure laughing my ass off along with everyone else in the room.

"Fuck y'all . . . I was only held back four times," Jackson says defensively.

"In high school, Jackson was R. Kelly."

"The girls I smashed were in the same grade as me," Jackson says. "At least I was fucking. You no-pussy-getting motherfuckers. Y'all just mad because I probably fucked y'all's wives back in the day."

"Now hold on a second," Mike interjects, "I used to bang your wife back in the day. Hell, she was my wife before she was yours."

"None of y'all have slept my wife back in the day," says a very confident Big Ted. Everyone grows quiet.

"Yes, this is true. But let's be honest, you're probably the only one that wants to fuck your wife," Jackson says, calling out the elephant in the room.

Big Ted did not find Jackson Reed's response funny, but I did.

"At least I know I'm the only one that hit it," says a deflated Big Ted.

"That's something you don't ever have to worry about," Jackson says bluntly.

As much as I don't want too, I laugh my ass off at Jackson Reed's comment and I enjoy it. I thought Big Ted was a friend and he left leave me hanging. Listening to this incestuous banter gives me clarity that after tonight, I will never see any of these fools again. At this juncture in my life, I am fine with it.

"Where's the bathroom?" I ask.

Jackson says, "Through the doors on your right,"

I walk through the garage door and enter the house.

Krystal, Xena, Apple, and Mike's wife Leslie are all sitting at the dining room table playing cards.

As I walk through the house, the ladies grow uncomfortably quiet. Xena and I make eye contact. Though she's not saying anything verbally, her eyes scream, *take me.*

"Tre, you want next," Xena says seductively.

"Only if you can handle it," I say flirtatiously.

"I can handle it, baby," Krystal says as our eyes connect. Her eyes scream, *I'll let Bobby Lee watch you take me.*

"Nah, I'm leaving soon."

I walk through the living room and enter the bathroom. I look in the bathroom mirror and check to see if anything is out of place on my face. I pull out my shit list to remind myself why I'm here in the first place.

Moments later, I head back toward the garage through the dining room where all the ladies are sitting. My gaze meets Xena's eyes again. As I enter the garage, I hear an eruption of shouts along with giggles from inside.

When I open the door to the garage, I noticed Big Ted is passed out on the couch. Jackson and Mike are nose-to-nose and near blows, Bobby Lee standing in between them as if he is refereeing.

"I didn't take your girl . . . She chose me when your ass expired," says Jackson Reed's punk ass.

Mike throws a punch and misses by a mile. Jackson shoves Mike in the direction of the punch's momentum then stumbles to the ground. Mike can barely stand on his own two feet as he wobbles from side to side.

Mike recovers then picks up one of the empty tequila bottles and throws it in Jackson's direction. He dodges the bottle but ends up falling against the fragile table which collapses under his weight.

"Throw another bottle, and I'll shoot you sum bitches," Bobby Lee says in a stern tone. The ladies enter the garage to help break up the fight.

"What happened?" I ask.

"Same ol' same ol'. They get shit faced . . . Then the shit-talking follows . . . then one of them gets their feelings hurt . . . Then they get into a fight about for the shit they said to each other."

"Mike . . . Let's go home. You had too much to drink," says Leslie.

"You hear that, little bitch," Mike yells. "My wife just saved you from another ass-whooping."

"Come whoop my ass again then, bro," Jackson says, his eyes barely open.

Xena helps Jackson Reed's punk ass to his feet and guides him into the house. As they walk to the backroom, Leslie and Mike exit through the front door. Apple and Big Ted leave right behind them. Bobby Lee and Krystal edge closer to the front door.

"Last chance to come home with us, Buddy Ro." Bobby Lee leans in, "I'd love to see you bang my wife."

"Harass me one more time, and I'll MeToo the shit out you Monday morning."

"It was nice seeing you, man," Bobby Lee says with a chuckle.

Krystal leans in for a hug, and one of her hands slides down toward my groin. I stick my butt back and gave her a church hug.

Xena walks out from the back.

"Everyone left?"

I nod my head yes.

"Are you leaving?"

"Yeah . . . Got to get up early . . . Linking up with Sade tomorrow afternoon."

"Oh Sade!" Xena's eyes jolt when she hears Sade's name. "Hope you guys have fun," she says with a crack in her voice.

The sexual tension between us could be sliced with a plastic knife as we stare into each other's eyes.

"I'll walk you out," Xena says.

Xena walks with me all the way into my parents' yard.

"Your car is cute."

"Thank you. It's a rental. Wanna take a spin?"

"I'd like that," Xena says as she hops in the backseat.

I drive the car down a few blocks and find a perfect place to park. By the time I come to a complete stop, Xena has taken off her clothes. The moonlight glistens off her smooth, beautiful, brown naked body. I jump in the backseat to join her. We start kissing, slow yet sensual. She unbuckles my belt, pulls my pants down, then slides her face into my crotch.

Moments later, she comes up for air and says, "I wanna feel it."

"Turn around," I say as she maneuvers around in the small economy car.

Xena's face is stuffed into the backseat, and her bottom is up. A few strokes, moans, and groans later, I finish then pull my pants up.

Xena ask, "Did you?"

"I did."

"I didn't," Xena said, her ass still sits in the air.

"You might not have come, but you gotta go."

I return to the driver's seat and notice Xena scowling in the rearview mirror. The look on her face is priceless. My petty ass has been waiting for this moment for several years, and it could not have been more perfect.

Several awkward moments later, I pull in front of my parents' house. Xena hops out of the car, runs across the lawn, then enters her house. I pull out the shit-list and scratch Xena and Jackson Reed's names off.

CHAPTER 22

As I try and tiptoe through the house, Haley pops out of nowhere and sprints toward me.

"No! Stop! Heal!" I shout. None of the commands work, and the bitch nips me on the arm.

Mom rushes out from her bedroom with a rolled-up newspaper and smacks the dog on the head.

"Go outside, Haley!" Mom herds Haley outside. From the back yard, Haley scratches at the door and whines. "Oh, shut up, Haley!"

"What's the expiration date for that dog?"

"Boy, hush . . . Coming in my house all late."

"Technically, I came in early."

"Where have you been?" She asks.

"Church."

Mom heaves the rolled-up newspaper at my head. "Don't put them lies on the house of the Lord . . . Smelling like sex and alcohol . . . Just like your damn daddy . . . When are you leaving?"

"I'm packing up and heading to Memphis in a little . . . I need to do some writing before I leave."

"You better not leave before saying bye."

"Come on, Ma. Who do you think raised me?" I walk off and enter the bedroom. I take a seat at the desk, open my laptop, and begin typing . . .

*****

SUCKER FOR LOVE

Basic training would be a piece of cake and life afterward would be a breeze is what my recruiter told me along with a bevy of other lies. I joined the United States Air Force after high school because I wanted to be part of something bigger than myself. It gave me a chance to get away from Blytheville, Armani, and punk-ass Jackson Reed. A year after joining the military, the United States, United Kingdom, Australia, and Poland decided to invade Iraq, kicking off Operation Iraqi Freedom.

A few months later, I was on a nine-month deployment in Iraq. I try not to think much about my military occurrences and delete those memories out of my head as much as I can. Other than the daily mortar attacks, the only significant thing I remembered from that time was the death of Former U.S. President Ronald Wilson Reagan. He had died from complications stemming from Alzheimer's disease. Some of the higher-ranking Sergeants of color threw a barbeque to celebrate his demise. They hadn't forgotten how Reaganomics affected their friends and families within African American communities during the crack epidemic. A couple of tours of Iraq later, I decided to get out.

After separating from the military, Kwesi talked me into moving to Memphis to work with him at his trucking company. There were a few deciding factors in the move, but Kwesi was one of them. He had quit the factory life and gone into business for himself. I wanted to give Kwesi a chance to redeem himself as a father. I wanted us to establish a stronger father and son bond. The bonding didn't go as I had imagined. We worked opposite shifts. In my first year of living in Memphis, we hung out only a handful of times that equated up to about 15 minutes. Our conversations consisted mainly of trucking, ducking, and fucking. We talked trucking because that was our line of work, and we talked about him ducking angry husbands who found out he was fucking their wives. Instead of trying to build a bond with me, Kwesi used my presence as an excuse to be out in the streets. Kwesi told his wife that he was out with me, but it was a cover up for his philandering and debauchery.

I wanted my father's love. But love from Kwesi came with conditions. The times I spent with Kwesi had a transactional nature to them. I would mostly see him when he needed to use me as a scapegoat or to borrow money. One-time Kwesi called and asked, "Hey, Son . . . Let me borrow $160. I'll pay you back once the checks clear." I gave him the money, but he never paid it back. I didn't care much because I just wanted to spend time with my father. I forgot about the cash he had borrowed because I valued the relationship more than the money.

A few months later, Mom needed $500 to cover the mortgage payment and other household expenses. I did not blink because it was my mother. There were plenty of times she went without to provide for me. It was not good timing for me because my rent was due later that week, but I would be fine. Mom had written me a post-dated check for the following week for the amount she had borrowed. I was getting paid $1000 every Thursday. I figured since I worked for Kwesi, he would lend it to me. He knew my pay schedule because I was on his payroll.

I remember calling him and asking, "Hey, Pop. Can I borrow $150? I'm short this week on the rent."

"Let me call you back, Son," Kwesi said as he got off the phone abruptly. A couple of moments passed . . . Then a couple of minutes. A couple of hours turned into a couple of days.

I finally received a call back from Kwesi. I remember answering, "What's up, Pop?"

"I talked with your stepmom," Kwesi said. "We decided that if you can ball out and live downtown in Memphis, you should be able to pay your bills."

Appalled, I stared at the phone for a few seconds before placing it back to my ear, "What about the $160 you owe me from that date you went on a couple of months ago?"

Kwesi started to chuckle and said with a whisper, "I thought I was getting a loan from my homeboy."

"So, when you borrow money from me, you're borrowing from your homeboy. But if I need to borrow money from you, I have to borrow it from you and your wife?" I ended the call in the middle of his response, and I cut him off. It was the first time as an adult that I cut Kwesi off, and it damn sure wouldn't be the last time. Time heals all wounds, and eventually, he would slither back into my verve.

I was ecstatic about living in Memphis. My apartment was in a great spot downtown. It overlooked the AutoZone Park, home of the Memphis Redbirds, a minor league baseball team. The Redbirds are Triple-A affiliate of the St. Louis Cardinals. The town is known as the home of the blues with its iconic Beale Street and Elvis Presley's home Graceland. Growing up, traveling to the ratchet Southland Mall in South Memphis was a vacation. Now I was living in the heart of the city.

One of the benefits of working for Kwesi's trucking company was tripling my income. In three months of driving trucks, I had made more money than I made in an entire year as a staff sergeant. I was on the road a lot, but I was able to support an appealing lifestyle. I envisioned myself having more fun than I did. I had my share of debauchery in Memphis. I was sleeping with random, low-hanging fruit women. Everyone around me tried to hook me up with their single friends, but it never balanced out. It was a reoccurring seesaw: either she liked me more than I liked her, or I liked her more than she had liked me. Grandma even put her two-cents in.

One day on a phone call, I remembered Grandma saying, "You know Sade goes to school out there in Memphis?"

Grandma didn't know that Sade and I had met a few months earlier. I reached out to her when I first moved to Memphis. Reconnecting with Sade was the other deciding factor in moving to Memphis after my military service. Sade had a full ride at the University of Memphis. I didn't have her phone number at the time, so I hit her up on Myspace. From her profile and the pictures she posted, I gathered she was in her final year of college. She led the U of M basketball women's team to three consecutive Sweet Sixteen appearances and a trip to the Final Four. I also noticed her relationship status was single. I looked through all her pictures but didn't see she was in a relationship, thus leaving it to me to fill that void. I didn't know what to expect, but I thought it would be interesting to reconnect with an old friend. Sade and I began to chat via text, and I set up a date for us to meet.

We met on a rainy day at Charlie Vergos' Rendezvous in Downtown Memphis. I could smell the smoky aroma of grilled meats and barbecue up Union Street. The restaurant was relatively large and had several places to eat. Sade and I ate in the downstairs area. We shared an order of nachos and the meatless red beans and rice as an appetizer. Sade ordered the pork ribs and brisket combo, and I chose the chopped chicken breast.

We sat there staring into each other's eyes a few moments. It felt like deja vu. Was this our moment?

A few moments glided by as we stared into each other's eyes. Though Rendezvous was crowded, Sade's pretty face was the only thing my eyes could focus on. Here was my chance.

"Sade, there's something I want to tell you."

Suddenly a short, stocky, muscular guy wearing a University of Memphis lettermen jacket approached us. He leaned in and kissed Sade on the lips.

"Hey, babe," Sade said. "Tre, this is my boyfriend Dray." Her boyfriend, Dray Hopkins, was the star running back on the football team.

"Nice to meet you," Dray said, extending a fist bump.

"Same to you," I bumped him back in greeting.

What the hell just happened? Here I am about to confess my love to Sade, and then I find out she has a boyfriend. It might sound crazy, but I wanted to go outside in the rain and cry.

"Wanna split dinner?" Sade asked.

"No, I got it," I said.

"Are you sure? I can pay half?"

"Sade . . . For real . . . I got it." I said as I placed a $50 bill on the table.

"Was there something you wanted to tell me?" Sade asked.

"Oh . . . I forgot already. I'll remember it next time I see you," I said, hiding my defeat with a big, fake smile. That was the last time I saw Sade in person. As the weeks passed, she posted more photos of her and Dray. I unfriended her from social media because I didn't want to see her happy with another guy. Sade went on to graduate Summa Cum Laude and was drafted seventh overall by the Washington Mystics in the WNBA Draft.

During the same phone call with Grandma, she asked, "Why don't you go to the House of the Lord and find you a good, clean, Christian gal?"

"Good, clean, Christian gal? What does one of those look like, Grandma?"

"I don't know. A pretty girl with all of her teeth. Someone that worships the Lord and a has job."

"You think I can only find a pretty woman with all her teeth in church, Grandma?" I asked.

"Sure, you can! Give it a shot."

For the first time in my life, I took Grandma's advice. I cleaned up, put on a white Easter suit, and headed out. I figured if I was going to church, I wanted to give myself the best chance of meeting a pretty girl with all her teeth.

I found a church with the best reviews and put the address in my GPS. I was on my way. Three Six Mafia blasted through the stereo system as I cruised up Popular Boulevard heading to church. I took my sweet ass time getting to the morning service because I wanted to arrive after the collection plate had been passed around. As I approached an intersection, a car smacked right into the rear of my car.

I punched the steering wheel then jumped out of my car war ready.

The driver who bumped into me was driving a 7-Series BMW. The door popped open, and the person that stepped out of the car was the most beautiful woman I had ever seen in my life. Her aesthetics were impeccable. She had a lovely, round, brown frame with naturally curly hair.

My next thought was, "Nut up! Tell her who you are and get her insurance information." But the only thing that came out of my mouth was, "You OK, sweetheart?"

"Yes . . . I'm so sorry. I'm late again for church service, and my father is speaking to the congregation."

"Is your father a preacher?"

"No, but he's good friends with the pastor."

"What church were you heading too?"

"St. Paul Missionary Baptist Church," the picturesque, olive-skinned lady said.

"Me too!" I said, casually lying. I'd never heard of the place. Hell, I barely knew the name of the church I was heading to. She was so gorgeous I would have told her I was an atheist if that meant getting to know her. I extend my hand. "I'm Tre," I said.

"Maxine!" she said with a smile as her handed greeted mine. When she broke into a smile, I saw her shiny, halo-white teeth. And Grandma would have been happy to know Maxine had all her teeth.

"Let's exchange info, and we'll let the insurance people take care of the rest." I whipped out my phone and we exchanged numbers.

At the time, Maxine had a Myspace page, and I would sneak on to see the pictures that she had posted. She was so gorgeous. I didn't know I could attract a woman like this. My first thought was she was only acting nice because she was at fault for the fender bender. But it turned out she was very receptive to me. It was the first time I found someone that liked me as much as I liked them. Maxine and I talked on the phone for several hours. Our flirty, sexual innuendo-laced conversations flowed as we got to know each other better.

After the insurance companies took care of our damaged cars, we set a date to meet up. We decided to meet at the Mesquite Chop House in downtown Memphis the following weekend. I was a little nervous. I couldn't keep my composure, so I decided to have a few shots at the bar before she arrived.

I drowned my anxiety in liquid courage. When Maxine finally arrived, I remembered awkwardly sticking my hand out to greet her, but she leaned in for a hug. Throughout the dinner, we maintained intense eye contact. I knew if the opportunity presented itself, I would pounce on her like a lion would do to a gazelle. I couldn't wait to kiss her cherry, sweet lips, but I couldn't think about that in the moment. I had to focus on not saying anything stupid that would ruin the mood. So, I shut up and let her lead the conversation until those magic words were annunciated.

"Let's finish this conversation at my place," Maxine said

Maxine lived in a penthouse suite that overlooked the Mississippi River. We headed back to her place to talk. Talking led to kissing, and kissing led to climaxing.

In dealing with me, she had run into a lumberjack, and I laid wood across her back. In the bedroom, I was relentless. I would not stop until she climaxed. I wanted to rock her mind and her body until she fell in love with me. But all that work I put in only made me fall deeper in love with her. I was head over heels. In hindsight, we both fell hard. This was the first time I'd fallen in love with someone who had fallen in love with me. The rest of the world didn't matter when we fell in love. We were suckers for love.

*****

My phone vibrates. I notice I have a few missed calls and a text message from Eva that it reads, *"Please call me if it's not too early."*

CHAPTER 23

Holding the phone to my ear feels like a prison sentence. Eva has been crying the whole time since the call started. I hate hearing her sob like this. I wish I could tell her I slept with another woman so she could go back to calling me bitch and motherfucker in Spanish. I feel like a complete asshole. I've caused more harm to her than she has to me. Eva didn't approach me in the beginning. I was the one that courted her and took her away from her boyfriend. I was the one that encouraged her to move in when she was hesitant at first. I got her pregnant and ran away from my responsibility. This sounds all too familiar.

"This is not how it's supposed to be, Tre," says Eva. "We're supposed to be a family."

If only I had the bravado to tell her I am damaged goods, and she deserves better, but I had to keep the ball in my court.

"If only we hadn't moved so fast," I say. I am quite sure that wasn't the right thing to say, but Eva stops crying after I say it.

"Through it all, I'm still here, Papi. We miss you!"

"I miss you, too. I'll be back in town tomorrow, but I need to get some rest before my travels."

"OK, Papi . . . I love you."

"Talk with you soon, Eva."

The call ends. A few seconds later, I receive a text from Eva that reads, *"You didn't say it back."*

I text back, *"What didn't I say back?"*

"I said I love you and you didn't say it back." Eva texts.

I text it back, *"Sorry . . . Love you too."* I place the phone on silent and start typing where I left off . . .

*****

NO SUCH THING AS LOVE

The start of our relationship was beautiful. We really enjoyed each other's company as we grew to know each other better. She was my Queen, and I was her King. It was a match made in heaven—until our fathers met each other.

Maxine was a nympho, and fortunately for her, I was Kwesi's child. When she stayed at my place, we got it in at least five times a day. At her place, it was even more. Our sexcapades led to the inevitable.

Maxine called me one day and said, "Trevor, I didn't get my period."

I remained quiet and Maxine began to cry. "If my father finds out that I'm pregnant and we're not married . . . He'll hate you. I don't want that for you."

"All will be fine. You're just a couple of days late. Go to the doctor and see what they say, and then we'll go from there."

Maxine calmed down and said, "You're right . . . I'll make an appointment tomorrow." The next day came, and the doctor confirmed that Maxine was pregnant.

We had dinner together that night, and Maxine broke the news.

"What are we gonna do?" Maxine asked. "I can't have this baby . . . I'm married."

"You're married!" I was in complete shock. "How are you married?"

"It's complicated."

"Make it uncomplicated!"

Maxine gathered her thoughts then explained, "My father comes from a traditional Nigerian culture . . . I was in an arranged marriage with the son of a wealthy family in the oil business in Africa, but I broke it off. Legally we're still married, but we're separated. My father is doing everything in his power to get us back together. But maybe if we convinced him . . . Maybe he'd change his mind."

"What's the plan?" I asked.

Maxine thought for a few moments then schemed up something. "Talk to your parents, and I'll talk to mine. Maybe we can set up a Thanksgiving dinner, then we can slowly break the news to them once our families are integrated," Maxine said.

I figured this would be a perfect time for our families to meet.

"One last thing," said Maxine. "My father is quite argumentative. He's a sucker for a great debate."

This will work out better than expected, I thought. That's right up Kwesi's alley. Kwesi is a sucker for a good debate, so it wasn't ironic that he was all-in for a dinner gathering when I contacted him.

When I presented the idea of us all having dinner together for Thanksgiving to my mother, she was all for it. That was before asking, "Will you be inviting your damn daddy to the dinner?"

"Yes," I said.

"If he's going, then I'll pass."

Maxine had daddy issues, but her daddy issues were a lot different than mine. Her father was very controlling, and because Maxine was a daddy's girl, she always did as she was told. Though I understood her frustration, I admired that she had family values. Maxine grew up with both of her parents and her siblings all under one roof. I respected and appreciated her father, but Doctor Abidgun Attah had reservations about me. He had preconceived notions about African Americans. I understood that a lot of people targeted *their family because they were rich and welcoming to outsiders. I never wanted their money; I only wanted Maxine. My agenda for dinner was to express my true intentions. Thanksgiving dinner would be the perfect opportunity for me to make that clear.*

It was the first time I met Maxine's family and my first time at their home. Their home was in a gated community in the heart of East Memphis. I remembered the times riding on Elvis Presley Boulevard and driving by Graceland on our way to The Southland Mall. It was the only mansion I had seen growing up, and now I was about to have dinner in one. It had seven bedrooms and nine bathrooms; it was a Tuscan-inspired light-filled masterpiece, set on over 16,000 square feet of land on one of the highest lots in the area. The home was a mix of old-world elegance and modern open-concept living. When you entered the house, a grand sculpted staircase entry met the glass-lined areas that flowed between indoors and out.

We all gathered at the table in the decadent dining room and sat at the table. At the dinner table sat my father, my stepmom Glenn, Maxine's mother Louise, and her father, Doctor Attah. Maxine's mother, Miss Louise, a southern belle, had prepared a delicious dinner. There was a big honey baked ham, a roasted turkey, cheese grits, and corn pudding. There were mashed potatoes, turkey gravy, and cornbread dressing with cranberry sauce, as well as cracked pepper dinner rolls just waiting to be devoured. Also on the table was macaroni and cheese, collard greens, candied yams, a sweet potato pie with a chocolate crust, and a delicious red velvet cake made from scratch.

At first glance, you would have thought our fathers had known each other for decades. A bromance formed as they joked, laughed, and talked politics. As the conversations flowed, the dinner went from sugar to shit.

Kwesi kicked things off, "The American flag has caused more social injustice than the Confederate Rebel flag has. And I'm tired of white politicians going to black churches to talk about racism when they should be taking their asses to some of those white churches. Them the ones you need to talk to."

"That's a great point," said Doctor Attah.

"When's the last time someone from Black Lives Matter or a member from the Black Panthers shot up a school, a concert, or a nightclub? And if the

shooter turns out to be Hispanic, they wanna build a wall. If it's an Arab, ban Muslims. They form a group to stop social injustices against black folk but are marked as terrorists. But let that sum bitch be white, the narrative is about how our society is failing these poor, troubled, young men. They wanna blame the movies, video games, and music. They wanna rehabilitate people addicted to opioids but they criminalized black folks that were smoking crack in our communities."

Then things got tense.

"Here's one thing I don't understand about black people in America . . . We don't walk around calling each other names an oppressor once called us. If the word nigger is so offensive, why do you call each other it?" Doctor Attah asked.

"We use it as a term of endearment," Kwesi said. "Those terms are antonyms from the word Negus. The Ethiopian name for a black emperor also means King of Kings."

"But you guys don't call each other Negus," Doctor Attah said. "You call each other nigger. That word refers to a group of ignorant people who are economical, politically, or socially disenfranchised. You are not disenfranchised. You may lack culture, but you're not disenfranchised. You live in America. You have clean water and electricity," Doctor Attah expressed. "That's not disenfranchised. You might be classless and entitled, but you're not disenfranchised, my friend."

Everyone at the table cringed at the backhanded comment.

Kwesi nodded his head. "Wow! That's thought-provoking."

"Another thing I don't understand in America is Thanksgiving," Doctor Attah said. "Why do we celebrate a holiday that was genocide masqueraded as dinner?"

"I don't know why we celebrate it, but it's part of our culture."

"Culture! What culture? You guys lack a cultural identity."

"As an African American, we do have culture . . . It's not the same as yours," Kwesi said as he stuffed more food in his mouth.

"Why do you call yourselves African Americans, yet you're not from Africa? "

"*That was something Jesse Jackson came up with in the 80s,*" *Kwesi said.*

"*You guys have never been to Africa. You're an American,*" *said Doctor Attah.*

Kwesi finished chewing then eloquently expressed, "*Yes we are Americans but technically we're from Africa. I was born in America . . . Never have I ever been to Africa. I live my life in a typically American way. I relate to other Americans because of our cultural upbringing, but my DNA is African. To be honest, the European settlers stole our ancestors from Africa, and your ancestors let it happen. They enslaved our ancestors, stole their resources, and your ancestors didn't do a damn thing about it. Some of you Africans look down on us and don't embrace us because we were born in America. Our ancestors were stripped of their culture, their names, and their spiritual beliefs so that you could thrive in America. Therefore, it's frustrating to hear smug bastards like you chime in on something that you benefit from, just like the white man does. The white man divided, conquered, and colonized most of the continent of Africa. Look at South Africa . . . Is it not one of the richest countries in Africa?*" *Kwesi asked.*

"*Sure,*" *Doctor Attah said, encouraging Kwesi to finish his thought.*

"*A country that has a 90% black population but less than 10% of the population, which is of European descent, controls the wealth,*" *Kwesi said.* "*But you guys judge us through the same lens they judge you with. If the media portrays us as poverty-stricken, uneducated, low-class criminals with our pants hanging off our asses, what do you think they portray you guys as?*" *Kwesi questioned.*

"*How are we portrayed?*" *Doctor Attah asked.*

"*You're shown as disease-infested and famine ridden. There are commercials that have starving children with flies on their faces asking for 50¢ a day of my hard-earned money to feed some child I don't know. I have of my own kids to take care of.*"

I laughed out loud but reeled it back in quick. I didn't laugh out loud in a cynical way. I honestly thought Kwesi was joking around when he said he had kids to take care of. Kwesi didn't think it was funny. He knew precisely why I'd chuckled. It was evident at this moment because everyone at the table got quiet as he stared me down from across the table.

Doctor Attah defended his position. "My belief is that you were born here in America, therefore you are American. My daughter, Maxine, is an African American. Her mother was born here in Memphis, and I was born in Nigeria. Both of your parents were born in America, not Africa . . . So, you're an American."

"America doesn't see it that way. Most of you from Africa didn't have to deal with racism in this country, so it's easier for you to relate to white America. Africans come to America and benefit off the backs of our enslaved ancestors but judge their descendants. But answer me this," Kwesi said as he leaned closer to the table. "Rumor has it that Africans don't like the black people in America . . . Why is that?" Kwesi asked.

"We don't dislike you. We know that we are different. Where I'm from, we call you guys Akátá."

"Akátá?" Kwesi repeated.

"Yes. It refers to a wild cat that does not live at home."

Kwesi nodded his head, "Interesting . . . Where I'm from . . . We call you guys African Booty Scratchers."

I took a sip of water to keep from laughing.

"We understand that you are lost and too lazy to find your way," Doctor Attah said. The table grew quiet. "Such a rich history, but your measuring stick is slavery. You think anything after that is progress," Doctor Attah said bluntly. "You guys don't know who you were before."

Kwesi straightforwardly replied, "Who we are as a group today is because of something your ancestors let happen."

"You guys don't take advantage of the opportunities in front of you," Doctor Attah professed. "You're not that educated, but you walk around like you run the world."

"We may not run the world, but we damn sure influence it. Everyone wants to be like us. Everyone doesn't want our struggle, but the world wants our music . . . Our style . . . Our bravado . . . We dominate most sports."

"All you guys have is professional sports," Doctor Attah sneered. "It's like they made you guys into one-trick ponies! Education is our priority because we understand a career in professional sports isn't guaranteed."

The conversation was headed in the wrong direction, so I chimed in and tried to mediate. "Racial inequality is a problem that all black people face. The media pits us against each other. No other race deals with the same scrutiny. A Chinese person can live anywhere because China is respected. Anglo-Saxons get respect because Europe is respected. Wouldn't it be in our best interest to improve the relationship between Africans and the descendants of the African slaves in America? If we want respect around the world, we need to work together," I expressed.

Doctor Attah darted a glare at me, then crudely said, "Boy, don't interrupt us."

Kwesi darted a glare at Doctor Attah. "Don't talk to my son like that. I haven't disrespected your daughter." They started to go back in forth.

I stood up and shouted, "Yo!" The bickering silenced. I had everyone's attention. "You guys made this whole dinner about your opinions. We wanted to gather together because there was something we needed to tell you guys."

Maxine frantically jumped to her feet and pleaded, "Tre . . . No! Not right now."

"We're pregnant," I blurted out.

"No! Hell No! This will not happen," Doctor Attah bellowed.

There was an explosion of emotional rumbles and grumbles from around the table.

"Why won't this happen?" I asked.

"I don't think you're good enough for my daughter."

Kwesi placed his fork down and turned his attention to Doctor Attah. "And why is that?"

Doctor Attah stared me down as if he wanted to fight. "For starters, he doesn't have a college education, he doesn't have a career, and his income isn't sufficient to take care of my daughter. You think working for some classless trucking company will be enough to take care of a family?"

"I work for the same company. As a matter of fact, I own the damn company, and I take care of a family with that income."

"That may be true, but I know my daughter."

"I don't think she's good enough for my son. Other than being pretty and having access to her daddy's bank account, what does she bring to the table?"

Who is this man, and where the hell is Kwesi? I didn't say anything as they went back and forth. I decided I would shut my mouth and stuff it with food. As I reached for seconds, Doctor Attah shouted, "Portion control, boy! This isn't a buffet. You're not in a zoo."

Kwesi snapped back, "Look here, I don't know what crawled up your ass and set up shop, but if you talk to my son like that again, we will have a problem."

Kwesi and Doctor Attah stared at each other down for a few moments.

Doctor Attah paced from side-to-side. "You two will not tarnish my family legacy. Get an abortion!"

Kwesi chimed in and advised, "I agree with him . . . You don't wanna pay child support for 18 years. Learn from my mistakes and get an abortion, Son."

A cantankerous Doctor Attach said, "You, of all people, would say that."

"And what's that supposed to mean."

"It appears you care more for politicking things you have no control over as opposed to the things you do have control over," Doctor Attah said to Kwesi as they stared each other down.

"Doctor Attah, if you have something to say, say it. Keep it all the way funky," Kwesi requested.

"From what I see, you care more about being right in a debate than you do about being a good parent. You're a stereotype," Doctor Attah said. "You do nothing for society. Maxine told me about you. She mentioned how you were not in any of your children's lives."

All I could hear was forks and spoons clashing against expensive china dishes. Kwesi's once prideful demeanor seeped away, and he mumbled, "I can't believe he told these folks my business." Doctor Attah's statement had struck a nerve with him, and the only way out of his shame was to retreat. *"Look here, you spear-chunking asshole, I don't have to take this."*

"You're right . . . you don't," Doctor Attach confirmed. *"I think you all should leave."*

Kwesi took one more bite of his food then yelled, "Fuck you and your overpriced home. I've been kicked out of better places." He stood to his feet and stormed out of the room. From a distance, Kwesi yelled, "Glenn! Bring your ass."

"It was a pleasure meeting you all." Glenn scurried off after Kwesi.

Maxine burst into tears and excused herself from the table. I followed suit.

Moments later, we found ourselves sitting in Maxine's car. I consoled her as she wept. We sat quietly for a good 45 minutes before either of us uttered a word.

"Why are we doing this to ourselves, Tre?" Maxine asked as she looked to the ground, "How can we be together if our families can't get along?"

"We don't need them. We can run away and get married."

Maxine grew cold, "With what, Tre? I marry you, and my father stops supporting me. I refuse to live broke."

"But, Maxine . . . I love you . . . I want to marry you," I pleaded.

"What's love got to do with anything? Marriage is a business. There's no such thing as love."

"Stop repeating your father. You don't believe that."

"He is right . . . I think we need space."

"Space? What does space consist of?" I asked.

"Not dating anymore."

A few moments passed.

Maxine broke the tense silence and requested, "Let's just be friends."

I thought about it for a second, then asked, "You wanna see other people?"

"Maybe . . . I don't know," Maxine said without conviction.

I took a few more seconds to let it all sink in. "You think I'm gonna sit around in a friendship with you, dancing around emotions and thoughts of what could've been, while you get involved with someone else?"

I opened the car door and stepped out of the vehicle. "We can't be friends." I stormed off, never to hear from Maxine again. Last I heard, she had gotten an abortion and moved back in with her parents. There is no such thing as love. I knew I had to elevate my game and do something outside of the box. Knowing that, I packed all my stuff and headed east to jump-start a new life."

*****

I shut my laptop, stuff it in my backpack. I lie across the bed and fall asleep.

Later that morning, I pack up my things and wheel my suitcase out of the room. Mom, Cliff, and Haley are in the living room watching TV. Mom stares at Cliff while he pets Haley. Cliff stops petting Haley and she starts to whine. Cliff begins to stroke her again and she stops whining. Cliff stops petting her. Haley starts to growl. Cliff gently says, "Stop, Haley." He shouts with a high pitch, "She's a good girl!"

"Damn sucker," Mom says, shaking her head. She turns her focus to me, "You rushing off?"

"I'm an American, I'm not Russian."

Cliff chuckles.

"It doesn't pay to be a smartass!"

"Never heard of anyone hiring dumbasses."

"Get out of my house, boy!"

I walk over and kiss my mother on the cheek. "Love you, Ma."

Cliff walks over and extends his hand.

"I'll catch you guys the next trip."

"Come pet the dog before you leave," Mom says.

"Uh . . . I'll pass."

"Bye, boy! Love ya!"

"Love you too, Ma," I say as I roll my suitcase out of the house and carry on with my life.

CHAPTER 24

I see Jackson Reed's punk ass in my peripheral as I approach the rental car. He is standing in front of his mother's house. I continue as if I do not see him walking towards me. I load my suitcase in the trunk, take a seat in the car, and crank the engine. I receive an incoming call. I screen the call then answer it, "Hey Grandma."

"Hey, Tre . . . Thank you for the flowers. They are so beautiful!"

"You're welcome, Grandma . . . Happy Anniversary!"

"Have a safe flight back home. I love you."

"Love you too, Grandma."

Jackson is standing a couple of feet away from the window. I take it he wants to confront me about sleeping with his thirsty-ass wife. I step out of the car and meet him halfway. We stare at each a few moments without saying a word.

"My apologies for last night," Jackson said. "I drank too much . . . I hope the banter didn't offend."

A smile grows across my face knowing that Jackson Reed's punk ass doesn't know any of the intricate things I did to his wife last night while he was a drunken mess. What tickles my fancy is by the time he finds out that Xena and I slept together, I will be long gone. Leaving their marriage in shambles like they did my confidence in high school. I place a hand on Jackson Reed's punk-ass shoulder and sincerely say, "It's water under the bridge, my man."

"Catch you at the next class reunion?" Jackson asks as he leans in for a hug.

I juke the hug and extend my fist out for a pound. "Probably not."

"Next time you come into town, make sure you get a bigger, manlier rental car," Jackson says with a cackle.

"You'd be surprised what you can do in a car like that. Not only are they good on gas, but the backseats are amazing. You should get your wife one," I say smugly. That might be the most satisfying advice I have ever given.

CHAPTER 25

I start to cross the M-shaped through arch Hernando De Soto Bridge or the New Bridge, as Memphians like to call it. I stare at the Pyramid and shake my head. Out of all the things the Memphis Pyramid could have been, it is now a Bass Pro Shop. Sure, it has shopping, a hotel, restaurants, a bowling alley, an archery range, and an outdoor observation deck adjacent to its apex, but I just kind of expect more from such a symbolic structure.

There is one more stop that I need to make before meeting with Sade. Before I stick my neck out and reach out to my siblings, I want to make sure Kwesi is 100% committed to setting up this family reunion. As I pull the rental car into the driveway of his southern-style colonial home, Glenn begins to back her vehicle out of the driveway. I maneuver the car out the way so she can exit without me blocking her way out. Glenn reverses her car past then steps out of the vehicle. I step out of the rental car to greet her.

"Hey, Tre. Your father is in the backyard."

"Oh . . . OK . . . You're heading off?"

"Yeah . . . I have to go to the office and run a few errands," Glenn says. "Make yourself at home. I'll be back soon."

"I won't be here long . . . By the time you get back, I'd be gone already."

"Oh . . . Well, I guess I'll see you over the Thanksgiving weekend."

"That is the plan," I say with a grin.

Glenn stares at me for a few awkward moments, then a grin flashes across her face.

"You look just like your father."

"So, I've heard," I say with a wave. Glenn walks back to her vehicle then backs out of the driveway.

I wave at Glenn until she drives away then I maneuver to the trunk of the vehicle. I open my suitcase and pull out a lavender Polo Ralph Lauren slim-fit button-down shirt that accentuates my build. I put the shirt on and button it to my sternum, then I enter the house.

Kwesi puffs on a joint as he sits comfortably in his chair on the patio. He looks up and notices me entering his space.

"Hey, Son! I haven't seen you in a long time. I guess you don't fuck with your daddy anymore."

"Pop, I was here a couple of days ago."

A perplexed Kwesi thinks on it a second, "Oh, yeah . . . That's right. Well, thanks for coming to see me again, Son."

Kwesi offers me a hit from his joint, and this time I take him up on the offer. I take a few drags from it then pass it back to Kwesi.

"Want something to drink?" Kwesi asks.

I take a seat, "Nah . . . I'm good, Pop. Thanks."

"Don't thank me. You were gonna go get it if you were thirsty."

"No Southern hospitality, huh."

"Southern hospitality my ass . . . This is your home too, Son."

I am sure he meant well by saying that but I'm not sure how to process it. Never have I ever felt at home in any of Kwesi's homes. A couple of beats of silence slither past.

Kwesi stares off into space and rocks back in forth in his rocking chair. He takes a significant drag from the joint. "You see your granddaddy while you were in town?" he asks.

"Sure did."

Kwesi face contorts in a way that looks as if he might be a little jealous.

"It's like I'm in some weird love triangle. Mom gets jealous when I see you, and you get jealous when I see Papa."

We grow quiet as we try to drum up something to talk about. At the same time, we both utter, "So . . ."

I insist, "Go ahead, Pop."

"No, Son. Ladies first."

"I can't stay long. Wanted to stop and confirm with you that we are on for Thanksgiving?"

"Yes, Son. I want to spend a holiday with my children like a normal family."

"I'll set up the trip to the mountains and see you guys in the fall."

Kwesi nods his head, "Sure, Son. Do me a favor and don't beg nobody to come if they don't wanna."

"I gotcha Pop. Well, I stopped by to freshen up before I leave."

Kwesi looks me up and down, "You look fine to me. Why are you freshening up before a plane ride?"

"Well, I'm meeting up with someone before the flight."

"So, you only came by here to get ready for a date?"

"I could have stopped at a gas station if that were the case. But I told you I would stop by before I left."

Kwesi grows curious, "Who is she?"

"Sade."

Kwesi's eyes light up, "Oh! What's up with you two?"

"Just a simple case of none of your business."

Kwesi chuckles. "Asshole . . . You got it, honest. It makes sense why you got your cleavage out," Kwesi says as he takes a drag from the joint.

"I gotta get out of here, Pop."

Kwesi stands to his feet and leans in for a hug. "Safe travels."

As we hug, Kwesi grips me tighter than he has before. It feels as if he is happy to see me and doesn't want to see me leave.

"Don't hesitate to call me, Pop."

Kwesi takes another drag from the joint, "I'll walk you out." Kwesi puts the joint out and leads us inside the home, through the dining room, and out of the garage. He waves goodbye then shuts the garage door.

I enter the rental car and pull out my phone. I send a message to Sade, "*On my way . . . Be yo ass ready!*"

Seconds later, Sade responds, "*I'm pretty sure that's not correct English, Mr. Writer.*"

I reply, "*Whatever . . . See you in about 15 minutes.*"

Sade's message back reads, "*OK . . . Wait for me in the lobby.*"

"*Cool!*"

Before getting on my way, I draft a text message that reads, "*What's up, fam? Listen, I know that we are living our own lives. I hate that we're disconnected. We missed out on having our father in our lives growing up. Whether we want to admit it or not, we've acted as if it didn't affect us or if we didn't care. I know deep down, we all do. I want to invite you all out to Colorado for a trip with our father up in the mountains for Thanksgiving. Let go of the expectations you hold him to. We must be better than his mistakes and turn that negativity into a positive. For our children, our nieces, and our nephews. We didn't ask to come into this world, and we had no control over our mothers' decision to get with Kwesi, but we only have one father. Let's make this happen before it's too late. Love you all.*"

I send a mass text to seven of my siblings. Immediately, I receive a message. In all caps, my baby brother Angelo writes, "*FUCK KWESI!*" It is like a match falling into a tub of gasoline as the group chat floods with messages.

Brice the second youngest responds with the acronym "*LMMFAO*" in all caps, which stands for "LAUGHING MY MOTHERFUCKING

ASS OFF." Jeremy and Armani laugh at Brice's response, and my other brother, Eric, emphasizes Angelo's initial message.

My brother Rod doesn't respond to the group chat but sends a direct message to me outside of the conversation. It reads, *"Baby bro! What's good? Probably won't be able to get the time off . . . It would have been cool to catch up with you but tell your dad I don't have time. Love ya, lil bro!"*

I receive an incoming call from our only sister, Keisha. "Hey, sis!" I answer.

"Hey, bro . . . What's this all about?"

"I'm trying to get the siblings together. Pop is in bad shape, and I wanted to put together a family trip."

"The kids and I are in! It'll be fun to reminisce and catch up with you guys," says Keisha. "It's been 10 years since we first met."

"Has it been 10 years?"

"Yes . . . When you moved to Atlanta, and I was stationed at Fort Benning in Columbus. I found you on Facebook posting those half-naked pictures of yourself. I'm glad you stopped that. I almost unfriended you."

"I'm glad you didn't unfriend me," I say with a chuckle. "I'm gonna go ahead and book the cabin."

"Cool . . . Need me to split the cost?" Keisha asks.

"No . . . I got it. Just show up."

"OK . . . Keep me posted."

"I sure will. Let me get off this horn . . . I got a date!"

"Oh, lord . . . OK . . . But really quick before you go . . . You know we have another sibling nobody knows of," Keisha says.

"Do you have a name?"

"Yeah. Some call him Junior or JR, but have you ever tried to type in the name Junior or JR in a search engine?"

"I'm sure a trillion people popped up."

"Exactly!" Keisha says. "I'll try and make contact with him and invite him out."

"Sounds like a plan, sis. Please do that."

"OK, little bro. Have fun. I love you. See you soon."

"Love you too, sis."

Moments later, I take a right onto Riverside Drive, then turn left onto Union Avenue where I finally reach the historic Peabody Hotel, cushioned in the heart of downtown Memphis, where Sade is waiting for me.

CHAPTER 26

I enter the charming yet elegant lobby of the Peabody Hotel and find an empty chair to sit in. The Peabody Ducks that live on the rooftop of the hotel make their daily trek through the foyer. I feel my phone vibrating in my pocket, and I pull it out.

"Hey, Tre Tre Bear!" Sade says as she approaches me. "Sorry for the delay."

I stand to my feet, and we hug each other. "Stop calling me that."

"I think it's a cute nickname."

"Cute in an emasculating way."

"When did we get so sensitive?" Sade asks with a chuckle. "I like this color on you."

"Thank you," I say, staring into her eyes. The well-put-together Sade is wearing a sexy blue, high-waisted jumpsuit that looks like it was painted on her toned body. Her make-up is light yet also accentuates her natural beauty.

"Wanna grab a drink before dinner?"

"Dinner?" I question. "Who said anything about dinner?"

"You have your whole chest out, and you don't expect to take me to dinner?"

"Stop it."

"I can see your nipples. If you were a woman, you'd be arrested for indecent exposure."

I start buttoning up my shirt.

Sade giggles. "I'm joking. You look good."

"You look good too . . . In a sports broadcaster kind of way."

"In a sports broadcaster kind of way? Cute . . . Let's head to the rooftop bar," Sade says with a smirk as she leads us to the hotel elevator.

We make it to the top floor of the hotel. On the roof, where there are great sky-high views of the city overlooking the Mississippi River, a live band performs The Flamingos' "I Only Have Eyes for You." We find a couple of empty bar stools and park at the bar. A butch female bartender approaches us. "What can I start for you this evening?"

"I'll have an old fashioned," Sade says.

"For you?" the bartender asks.

I scan the drink menu, "Let me get the . . . um . . . I'll take the Citrus Cucumber Cooler. But if that comes in a girlie glass, are you able to put it in a man mug for me?"

The bartender is offended, "I don't like those words," she says.

"What words?"

"Girlie glass and man mug."

"If the drinks I ordered comes in a martini glass . . . I'd prefer to opt-out of using it. Please and thank you," I say, flashing a fake smile that washes away as soon as the bartender walks off.

"What has Mr. Country-boy-turned-city-slicker been up too?"

"Well . . . I'm not married."

"Ok . . . But you're living with someone."

"We're not married, though."

"Why?"

"Marriage is a sucker bet."

"I agree," says Sade. "I don't wanna be tied together by a piece of paper. If I'm gonna be with you . . . I am gonna be with you. I don't want to be with you because some paper says I have to."

"Agreed," I say, staring into Sade's green eyes. I must tread with caution because this could be dangerous for me. The last time we were in Memphis together having dinner, I found out she had a boyfriend. I scan the room to break the tension.

"How does a guy get this far, and no one scooped you up yet? I can't believe you don't have kids," Sade says.

"My pull-out game is lit," I say smugly.

"Whatever," a smirking Sade says, shaking her head. "How's life after Memphis?"

"It's been great. I reinvented myself. I used the GI Bill, graduated from Howard, then moved to Atlanta. Worked for *The Atlanta Journal-Constitution* until my book took off, and the rest is history. I dabbled a little in sports broadcasting, but it wasn't for me. You better be glad I retired though. I'd have come on your show and whooped that ass."

"I don't remember you ever beating me in anything," Sade says smugly.

I neither confirm nor deny.

"That's what I thought," says Sade.

We both share a laugh. A few moments slide past as we stare into each other's eyes.

"Do you know what you want?" Sade asks.

I grab a menu and give a quick look at the list of options. "Not sure yet."

"I'm not talking about the menu, silly," affirms Sade.

"Oh . . . Of course, I do," I say finally catching on to what she's implying.

"OK . . . What type of women do you fancy?"

I ponder for a few minutes. "I've always wanted to be with a woman that's educated and makes me wonder what will happen if she hears the words . . . 'Cash Money Taking Over for the 99 and the 2000.'"

Sade bites her bottom lip to keep from grinning.

"I can't believe you don't remember our pact."

"What was the pact?"

"We were working at Burger King one night, and I told you if we're not married to someone by our 20th high school reunion, we should have a kid together."

"That might have been one of the other guys you were acting fast around at Burger King."

"Oh, shut up . . . I was not fast," Sade says. We both grow quiet as we reminisce on old times.

"Remember that one time in the cooler?" I ask.

"Oh, my God . . . How could I forget?" She thinks on it a second. "That was luck."

"It was luck?"

"Yes . . . Luck," Sade says. "I can't believe we lost our virginity together in a cooler at a Burger King."

"I never told a soul."

"I thought that was the reason why you and Royal got into that fight after graduation."

"He didn't have a clue," I said. "We got into a fight because I called his other girlfriend, Xena, a bitch. But I wish he were still here so I could punch his ass right in the face."

Sade shakes her head, "Petty, petty, petty. Let's not speak bad on the departed."

"I'm just being facetious."

Sade giggles. "I know."

"But on the cool, you have my word, I will not publish anything about our past in my new book. The book is strictly focused on growing up without our fathers and with no proper leadership. How it affected us. I'm using Kwesi as a paintbrush to tell the story."

"He's not gonna like that at all."

"I don't give a damn. Kwesi could've been there to change the narrative. But we're spending Thanksgiving together. What plans do you have for the holiday?

"I'll be in Texas covering the sorry-ass Dallas Cowboys."

"You're gonna get off my Cowboys," I said with a chuckle.

A few moments pass as Sade and I stare into each other's eyes. It ultimately turns into a staring match. Several moments later, I am the first to blink.

"Why do men run away from strong, confident, and beautiful women?"

"Maybe because you stare men down then ask questions like that." I shrug my shoulders. "I don't know . . . Just a thought."

Sade shakes her head in disgust.

"If a man stares at a woman like that, he's a creep; but when a woman does it, she's confident."

"You can't help but being a smartass, can you?"

"I get a kick out of it."

"I read your novel. *The South Hates Me*. It was cool," Sade says.

This info throws me off, and my ego takes a nudge. "It was cool?" I ask.

"Yep!" Sade confirms. "I mean, it was good, but I expected more from you."

"It was a New York Times Best Seller . . . Stop hating."

"So, the south hates you because some chick you were in love with didn't love you . . . Cry me a river."

"It was a fictional story!"

"It was an insanely long cat and mouse game . . . It didn't move me."

"It didn't move you because you're too busy hating from outside the club because you can't even get in."

"Don't be salty. You did the work and people loved what they read. I thought it was a good start, but there's room to grow. You wanna impress me . . . Write a better one."

"Excuse the hell out of me."

"I want you to reach your full potential . . . Steel sharpens steel."

I nod my head, approving her constructive criticism.

"How's Armani?" Sade asks.

"Armani . . . Well, Armani is still Armani."

"Remember when Armani got into a fight with that pregnant girl?" I jokingly ask.

"How could I forget? This fool took his damn shoes off to kick the girl in the head. Armani fought with everyone," Sade says.

"I love my brother from the bottom of my heart, but we fought so much growing up, I didn't wanna fight with anyone else."

"Back in those days, life was simple."

"Remember growing up before smartphones made humans dumb?" I ask.

"Yeah . . . I remember if you wanted to rent the newest blockbuster movie, you had to get to the Blockbuster store early or they'd run out of copies . . . Or if you watched a bootleg movie, it most likely was something someone recorded at a movie theater with a handheld camcorder."

I add, "Or if you were going somewhere and wanted to take pictures, you had to bring a camera with you . . . Got-damn polaroid cameras."

"Remember, if you wanted someone to call you back and they weren't home, you had to leave a message on the answering machine," Sade says.

"You had to memorize everyone's phone number that you called regularly, and if you paged someone, you'd have to wait around the phone for them to call you back. There was no caller ID, so you couldn't screen the call."

"Yeah, I'm kinda glad smartphones were invented," Sade says with a chuckle.

The bartender sets our drinks down. We grab our drinks, clink glasses, and both say, "Cheers." We take a sip and place the glasses on the bar top.

I bounce the conversation back to Sade, "How did you end up in broadcasting?"

"It was my college major, and I knew that once I was done playing ball, I'd go back to it. Hell, it honestly pays more."

"Is that so?"

"Yes!" Sade says emphatically. "I won a championship in the WNBA but made less than a postman. There weren't any million-dollar contracts like the NBA players get."

"I mean . . . Let's be honest. People don't watch the WNBA like the NBA, though."

"Not yet!"

"Who wants to watch layups and bank shots?"

"Were you born a hater, or did that just occur over the years?" Sade asks.

"Why can't men and women accept that we're different?" I ask.

"Because we're not different?"

"Biologically, we're not the same. Men have a dick that women tend to blame for their shortcomings."

"Wow . . . That's not misogynistic at all," Sade says with a hint of sarcasm.

"I'm not misogynistic. You all need to understand that there are things we men can do women can't, and vice versa."

Sade chimes in, "But the things we can do similarly, woman do better."

My eyes roll to the back of my head, "Do you wanna see a UFC fighter like Jon "Bones" Jones fight Holly Holms in a cage match?"

"No! He would destroy her. That is extreme, Tre!"

"Exactly! I understand equal rights for everyone. I'm for women getting paid the same in corporate, entertainment, and professional sports positions. My stance stems from the dating game. Why don't those same rules apply to women and men when it comes to dating?"

"If a woman sleeps with a lot of men, she's a whore. If a man does the same, he's a player."

"If a man sleeps with a lot of men, he's considered gay."

Sade giggles, "You know what I meant. Smartass."

"Most of the pressure is on the man. He has to initiate contact with the female, and then come the demands."

"What demands?" Sade said.

"Some women want to be the boss and be taken care of at the same time. I went on a date with this lady once, and she said going out with her was an investment. Then she followed up saying she didn't like to have sex. How's that an investment? She wanted me to pay for all our dates and not have sex with me? That's not an investment she's proposing. That's blue balls."

"Most of the men I have run into are liars. They lie about their wives and children."

"The great Chris Rock once said . . . Men tell the most lies, but women tell the biggest lies."

"How so?"

"Women lie daily. Some use a ton of makeup, fake nails, fake hair, ass implants, lip fillers, breast implants, push up bras, Spanx, and those deceiving leggings."

"I guess it's hard being a woman with all the social pressures of beauty. I don't need a man to buy me anything. My daughter, her father Dray, and I live comfortably well."

There is the bomb shell. She lives with the father of her child. "You and your daughter's father live together?"

"Yes," Sade said.

"That's so weird!"

"I don't think so," Sade asserted. "Black fathers are depicted as being absent, and I didn't want that for my child. So, her father lives with me on the other side of the house."

My eyes blink as I take a sip of my drink. "The other side of the house?" I ask.

"Yep. I own a 33,000 square foot estate," Sade affirmed. "Because the WNBA wasn't paying well, I started making money outside of the league."

"Doing what? Selling drugs?" I blurt out, momentarily forgetting that her father Rack Daddy was once a drug lord.

"Not funny."

"Sorry," I say.

Sade vents, "My father helped me build a business portfolio. I started investing the money I made from playing basketball, endorsement deals, and the trust fund my father created for me. I work on TV as a hobby."

"Wow! That's impressive."

"The house is big enough. I don't have to see my daughter's father every day, but he can see her every day."

"That's quite the arrangement," I admit. "Are you guys still?"

"Oh no! Hell no! He's banging a different chick every week. We're strictly platonic. Nothing more, nothing less. He lives with me for our daughter's sake. I don't want any child of mine to grow up without both parents in their life. But she turned 13, and when she graduates from high school in a few years, I'm kicking Dray's ass out, and that punk knows it's coming," Sade says.

Sade deliberates as we both sit in silence as the band plays in the background. "Did you sleep with Xena?" Sade asks.

The question comes way out of leftfield. Why would Sade want to know that? I swerve the question and ask, "How's Rack Daddy these days?"

"Please stop calling him that. He hates being called that."

"My bad. What should I call the artist formerly known as Rack Daddy? What about Mr. Cole? How is that?"

"My father is well! Got parole not too long ago," Sade says. "Can you believe he did over 20 years, and it didn't break him?"

"I'm surprised he was able to get out of prison for killing an undercover cop."

"He's changed for the better."

"He would have gotten life in prison had it not been a *black* undercover cop."

"Shut up! We spend a lot of time together these days. I fly him out to D.C. now and again to spend time with us. It's cool reconnecting with him."

"That's good that you get to spend time with your father."

"How's your old man?" Sade asks.

"He's changed," I said. "He has Alzheimer's."

"Alzheimer's?" a puzzled Sade asks. "The only thing Kwesi's forgetting is that he didn't do for his kids. I'm aware that the universe and karma conspire to make things happen, but I'm questioning that one. I feel he's getting off way to easy. Then again, he might forget to go to the bathroom and piss on himself in public . . . That's the only way I'll accept it."

"You have no chill."

"I don't like how he did my Aunt Brandy. But, back to my other question, did you sleep with Xena?"

What is her problem, asking a question like that? I deflect, "Why weren't we a thing in school?"

"Don't answer a question with a question . . . Did you sleep with Xena?" Sade asks again.

"Did I sleep with Xena? What kind of question is that?"

"A question you kind of gave me the answer to."

"What do you wanna hear, Sade? Do you wanna hear that I smashed her in the backseat of a small rental car while her drunk, punk-ass, drunk-ass husband slept."

"Is that the truth?" Sade asks.

I take a few moments before answering, "Let's just say I got mine before she got hers."

A glaring Sade shakes her at me with disgust. "I can't stand you."

"You wanted to hear the truth."

We both stare each other down for a few moments. It ultimately turns into yet another staring match. Several moments later, Sade is the first to blink.

"I don't want you to miss your flight . . . Walk me to my room?"

"Sure," I say.

Several moments later, Sade and I are lying naked face-up, cuddling on a king-sized bed of twisted, drenched sheets.

"Better than the first time?" I ask.

"Yes . . . Considering our first time ended quick."

"Whatever."

Sade rolls over on her side and faces me. I could stare into Sade's beautiful green eyes for the rest of our lives. I'm infatuated with the sweaty, curly hair that's all over her head and with her smooth golden-brown skin. "Heads up, Mister My-Pullout-Game-Is-Lit . . . I'm not on birth control."

I check my phone to see what time it is and notice that I have received several missed calls from Kwesi. He calls back again, this time I answer. "What up, Pop . . . Give me a second."

"Don't put me on hold!" Kwesi shouts. "Glenn . . . She's gone! Oh, my God . . . Glenn's gone, Son!" Kwesi began to sob.

Maybe he's going through a mental lapse, I think. "Yes, Pop . . . Calm down. Glenn ran some errands. She said she will be back in a little."

"No, Son . . . I got a call from the Emergency Room."

"Oh, my God! OK . . . I'll be there in a minute, Pop." I put my clothes on. "I'm so sorry, Sade . . . I have to go."

"What happened?" Sade asks.

"Something happened to my stepmother. I have to go." I walk over to kiss Sade then rush out of the hotel room.

CHAPTER 27

All the way until the funeral, Kwesi has refused to believe Glenn has passed on. "If she had retired from being a lawyer, she would still be here!" An angered Kwesi repeated throughout the week. It hits Kwesi like a ton of bricks once he accepts that Glenn is gone. He reflects on his life, "If I had been a better husband and a better father, this wouldn't have happened to her," I hear him say that day of the funeral.

It is hard watching a man that barely laughed cry. I stand several feet away to give Pop some space as I observe an emotional and devastated Kwesi from a distance.

"That should have been me," Kwesi mumbles to himself. "She should still be here." Kwesi sits alone by the lake in the backyard. Kwesi wears the same tuxedo he was wearing in the wedding photo he is holding. Kwesi grabs the urn and walks closer to the bank of the lake. He dumps Glenn's ashes into the lake.

After the funeral, Kwesi grows reclusive and falls into a deep depression. Lack of nutrition, not getting proper sleep, and drinking runs its course on Kwesi. He stops taking his medication and gives up on life. Kwesi grows bitter and pushes everyone away.

CHAPTER 28

7 MONTHS LATER

The Moose Ridge Cabin sits on a hill in the middle of a glade of pines. The cabin is a short drive from downtown Breckenridge, a Colorado town at the base of the Rocky Mountains' Tenmile Range. The Victorian core of this former mining town is known for its ski resort, year-round alpine activities, and Gold Rush history. The four-bedroom, multi-level cabin with outdoor decks and a traditional interior design accentuates life in the beautiful snowy mountain town. The main living area encompasses the dining room, where a wooden harvest table seats up to eight guests. Next to the table, a breakfast bar seats an additional four guests and separates the dining room from the gourmet kitchen. Chiseled granite countertops provide plenty of space to prepare this years' Thanksgiving meal for the Blacks.

Several months have passed since the death of Kwesi's wife, Glenn. Keisha played an essential part in helping Kwesi lift himself up from his lowest point. Keisha and her children flew into Memphis a couple of weekends a month to keep him company. I popped in a few times over the last few months to check on him and smoke some green out in the backyard. Kwesi accepted his situation and has started coming back to himself.

Smiling from ear to ear, Kwesi sits at the grand piano in the corner with three of his grandchildren: Dustin, Kellen, and Keisha Junior.

"Papa . . . Your shirt is on backwards," Keisha Junior says.

Kwesi looks down and notices that, in fact, his shirt is on backwards. "Well . . . I'll be damned," says Kwesi. "That sum bitch is backwards."

The kids are tickled by their grandfather's comment.

"You guys wanna help ol' Papa light a fire in the fire pit?"

"Yeah!" The kids yell in unison.

"Well, grab your coats, and let's roll." Kwesi and the grandkids put on their jackets then head out into the frigid cold.

Keisha and her wife Michelle Lane brought their kids up to spend the holidays together with Eva and me. Eva and I have worked things out after I accepted my responsibility as a future parent. Not only did I finish the book I was writing, but my literary agent was able to auction it off and garner a huge advance for a memoir.

In the den on the lower level, Keisha and Michelle, my eight-month pregnant Eva and I sit. The den has couches, chairs, and high bar tables for cozy nights with the whole family.

"I think now is a good time to talk about who's gonna take care of daddy when his condition worsens," Keisha says.

"It has to be a child that he has done right by," I interject.

The room grows silent.

"Does Glenn have children?" Keisha asks.

"No . . . Glenn couldn't have kids. Probably why Kwesi stayed with her as long as he did."

"You and daddy seem to be in a better place. How did he feel about what you wrote in your book?" Keisha asks.

"First of all, he doesn't know, secondly, he doesn't read, and lastly, if he finds out, I'm banking on him forgetting."

Keisha probes, "Did he get mad?"

Eva and Keisha both shake their heads.

"When he finds out you wrote a book about him— "

"I'm banking on him forgetting," I say, cutting Keisha off from finishing her statement.

"If daddy finds out you wrote a book about him, he may never talk to you again," Keisha says.

"It wouldn't be the first time."

"At some point, you're gonna have to let that go, big bro."

"I did, and I have . . . That's why I wrote the book. It was therapeutic . . . I feel much better now."

"Well, you need to tell him."

"Why?"

"How can you act as though everything is cool but trash him in a book?"

"I didn't trash him, Keisha. What I wrote was actual facts."

"That's beside the point, Tre."

My eyes roll to the back of my head. "Ok . . . So . . . What? You want me to go tell him right now, Keisha?"

All four of us glance outside and see a happy Kwesi in the middle of a snowball fight with his grandchildren.

"OK . . . Maybe not at this moment, but sometime when you guys are alone."

"You want me to tell him during this trip?" I question. "I think we should let sleeping dogs lie."

"The sooner, the better. Wouldn't you wanna talk to daddy now while we're here having a good time as opposed to when times are not so bright?" Keisha suggests.

"No! I think it'll ruin the whole trip."

"I don't think so," Michelle interjects. "Your father appears to have thick skin."

I signal for Keisha to lean closer to me. "Who was talking to Michelle?" I whisper dryly.

Eva swallows her laughter and pats me on the leg to calm me down. "Papi, don't be an asshole," Eva says. "Just talk to your father about the things you wrote. I'm sure he'll understand why it was written if you explain it to him."

I can see they make a solid point, and it makes no sense to argue with three women, so I segue, "Have you tried to reach out to any of the other kids?"

"Not since the initial text you sent to everyone."

"I saw Angelo and Brice's mother, Brandy, at the funeral . . . She only showed up to make sure Glenn was dead."

Keisha chuckles then blurts, "Don't say that . . . How do you know?"

"Because she walked right up to us at the funeral and said, 'I only showed up to make sure that bitch was dead.'"

The room grows quiet.

"I invited JR and his family up. They should get here sometime tomorrow."

"OK, cool . . . Is he Kwesi Junior?"

"I think so . . . Guess that's why people call him JR."

"I wonder if he's like your daddy."

A burst of energy rushes in as all three of the animated kids enter the den.

Eva rises to her feet. "I'm going to bed. See you guys mañana," she says. "Mi Hijo, Cállate! Come with mamá now!" Eva gives me a kiss then wobbles off.

Keisha spots Kwesi entering the den. "Uh, kids, it's time to go to bed. Hug your Papa and tell him goodnight."

"Can we stay up for another hour?" Kellen pleads, "Please, mama."

"Yeah . . . Let the kids stay up," I chime in to avoid alone time with Kwesi.

Kwesi shakes his head no. Michelle asserts, "You guys will have a few more days to play with your Papa. Let's call it a night."

"Papa will take you guys to Peak 8 tomorrow."

"What's peak 8, Papa?" Keisha Junior asks.

"There are rollercoasters, a super slide, minigolf, a maze, rock climbing, trampolines, zip lines, a bounce house, and Gondolas," says Kwesi.

"What's a gondola?" Kellen asks.

As Kwesi is talking, I try to sneak out of the room, but Michelle blocks the path for me to escape.

"You'll find out tomorrow," Keisha says. "Let's go upstairs. Make sure you brush your teeth before getting in bed."

Keisha, Michelle, and the kids exit the den leaving me and Kwesi alone.

CHAPTER 29

It is a nostalgic moment for Kwesi and me as we sit in silence by the lit fire. This was the longest time we have spent around each other. I dreamed of moments like this as a child. *Better late than never*, I think as I try to stay in the moment.

Kwesi takes the last sip of his drink and asks, "Wanna another one?"

"Sure," I say.

Kwesi pours two glasses of Johnnie Walker Blue Label King George scotch. He hands me the drink and we clink glasses and say, "Cheers." We take a sip together. "That's some good-ass scotch, right there, Buddy Roe," says Kwesi.

I nod my head. I take another sip, this time bigger than the last, and let the scotch sit on my tongue.

"I understand why your sister loves women," Kwesi reflects. "Pussy tastes better than chicken."

I choke on my scotch.

"Talk to any of the other kids?" Kwesi asks.

"Yep."

"Are they coming out?"

"Keisha said JR is coming up tomorrow."

"I don't know if I ever met him. I thought he was named after me, but his mama named him after the guy she was married too."

"So, he's not Kwesi Junior?"

"Nope. His mother calls him Junior, though. What about the rest of the kids?" Kwesi asks.

I shake my head no.

Kwesi's eyes grow tight, and he lowers his head. "Fuck em . . . I fuck with those that fuck with me on the level that they fuck with me on," Kwesi segues. "I heard you wrote another book."

"Yep . . . Just thoughts on a piece of paper."

"I don't know how you do it." Kwesi admits. "Staring at a computer for endless hours . . . Painting your thoughts on a blank sheet of paper. I'd lose my mind . . . I'd rather be fucking."

I deflect, "How are you?"

"I'm good. Taking it day by day. It's the life we live, you know. We're all passing through. Father Time is the enemy none of us can beat. Flesh dies, but energy never dies," Kwesi says solemnly. We sit on the couch quietly as Kwesi words drift through the room.

"How are you and your girl?" Kwesi asks.

"Life's good . . . We are better. Eva's good to me, and I question if I'm good for her."

"Eva seems like a good woman, but you have to ask yourself: if she died today, how would you feel?"

I cogitate a few beats. "I would fly to D.C. and propose to Sade. I feel Sade and I have always had a strong bond."

"Have you let her know that?"

"No."

"You have to let Eva know how you feel. But don't be Tre when you do it. Be someone else. Be anyone else other than Trevor. That motherfucker is an asshole."

We both chuckle at Kwesi's statement.

"I love Eva, and I may be in love with someone else," I say. "But, honestly, I don't wanna be like you. I have to be with Eva because we're having a child together. Sometimes I reminisce what would've been if my parents had stayed together. I see families from white communities or even families from other countries . . . I wonder what if I had that same family structure growing up? Where would I be in life? They had a head start because of the family values instilled in them. We are disenfranchised, and that lack of knowledge was passed down from generation to generation. For that reason alone, I will never leave any of my children behind."

Kwesi takes a long sip of his drink. "Losing yourself in the process isn't fun either. I busted up with your mama because I didn't like her."

I dart a glare at Kwesi. Did this fool just say that to me?

"I'm bullshitting," says Kwesi. "Your mother was cool. She left me. And she was well within reason to. Your mother and I would've worked well together. It was all about me. I wasn't loyal to her but don't tell her I said that. I know I wasn't shit, Son. I was arrogant. I had no business having kids that young. My folks didn't show me how to be a parent, and it has affected all my children. I needed to find me to be better for you guys, but I failed miserably. I wanna make it better."

I say nothing as I take another sip of scotch.

Kwesi sits back and reflects, "As a child, I got everything I wanted . . . My folks bought me everything I wanted, but they didn't teach me how to raise a family."

"As a child, we didn't get everything we wanted, but Papa and Mom made sure we got everything we needed."

Kwesi meditates a few moments then responds, "Son . . . I helped some too."

"In what fashion?"

"Child support checks."

"That was only $81 a week for two children, Pop."

"That adds up."

"It adds up to a little over four grand a year for two children."

"I did the best I could . . . I was the best father I could be, Son."

"No . . . You weren't . . . And you're a damn fool if you believe that."

Kwesi grows defensive, "Don't you know I was paying $400 a week to Brice and Angelo's mother?"

"Sounds like their mother had a great lawyer."

"I could barely maintain my lifestyle," Kwesi says defensively.

"So, I'm supposed to feel sorry for you? We didn't ask to be here."

We grow quiet; the tension in the room could be cut with a dull pencil.

"I don't wanna talk about that stuff. Can we just enjoy each other's company?" Kwesi said.

We raise our drinks and clink glasses.

"The doctor recommended some brain exercises to strengthen my short-term memory. One of them is reading."

I take a big gulp of scotch.

"Your last novel was the very first book I read. I just want to say that the south doesn't hate you, Son. We love you."

"Yeah . . . It was a fictional story, Pop."

"What's the next book about?" Kwesi asks.

The question catches me off guard. "Huh?" I utter.

"Your book," Kwesi reiterates. "What's it about?"

"My next book . . . It's about the lack of leadership in our communities."

Kwesi takes a second to process the subject in his mind. "You got a point there, Son!" he utters without knowing the true subject of the manuscript. "Millennials complain about politicians, but don't vote. They'll protest their asses off when things doesn't go their way, but they won't vote."

"True . . . You also have people that'll vote their asses off but don't take care of their kids." I add. We both grow quiet as we stare each other down.

The tension creeps back into the room as we stare at each other. Kwesi nods his head as a smug grin grows across his face. "You're trying to bait me into an argument."

"No, Pop. It's accountability. You didn't instill confidence in me as a child, and that is what our community lacked. Our community is fractured and riddled with a lack of leadership. So . . . I wrote a book highlighting elements of my upbringing so that someone can learn from our mistakes."

"Our mistakes?" Kwesi sets his drink on the table and processes my statement. "You wrote a book about our mistakes? What were our mistakes?"

"You know how many times I heard mom say. . . You look like your daddy. I wish your damn daddy were in your life. Your daddy ain't do this . . . Your damn daddy ain't do that... Your daddy should spend more time with you . . . Ask your daddy this . . . Ask your daddy that . . . But you were nowhere for me to ask."

Kwesi takes a moment to collect his thought. "What's the title of the book?"

"Daddy Issues," I say.

"Daddy Issues?" an offended Kwesi asks. "What will you be disclosing?"

I take a few seconds to gather my thoughts, "Most of my peers and all of my siblings grew up without their father, and they're trying to be the best parents they can be."

"And what does that have to do with me in this damn book, Son?"

"I wrote the book to express that a righteous father protects his children with his time and his presence. If you had been a better father to your children, they would've all been here with you. I didn't want kids because I thought I would disappoint them like my father did his children. But when I have children, I want them to know their daddy is there. I'm gonna tell them every single day they can do anything if they put their mind to it."

Kwesi's temper flares as he takes a second to dissect the thoughts running through his brain. "How dare you write a book about my life?"

"First of all, it's not just about your life . . . It's about other lives you affected. And why do you care? You're gonna forget about all of this in a year or so."

"Is your Papa in the book?"

"Well . . . Yeah . . . He raised me, Pop!"

Nope!" Kwesi roars, "Are you using my real name?"

"There are other people in the world named Kwesi."

"How many of them are named Kwesi that are from Blytheville, Son?"

He has a point, but that is another problem he will forget.

"You can't release that book," Kwesi utters. "You're gonna tarnish my legacy."

"What legacy, Pop? You've done nothing for society but increase the population of children with daddy issues, and you're worried about a legacy."

Kwesi rises to his feet, "You will not publish that damn book!!"

I stand to my feet, "What is it to you if it's already published?"

"I'll just have to whoop that ass if I find any of my business in it," Kwesi says meekly as he sizes me up.

I get right in Kwesi's face. "I guess you're gonna have to whoop my ass then, Pop."

We both stare each other down for a few moments. Kwesi rubs his jaw then rubs his chin. He takes a deep breath and takes a step back then catches me with a sucker punch to the eye. The blow is hard enough to knock me to the ground.

Like a mouse running away from a cat, Kwesi circles around the furniture using it as a barricade between us.

Kwesi manages to get the bathroom and lock the door. "Exodus 20:12 says, "'Honor thy father,'" Kwesi shouts. "I'm still your father, asshole!"

"How about John 17:1?"

"What does that say?" Kwesi asks from the other side of the bathroom door.

"'Glorify thy Son that the Son may glorify you.'" I throw back at him then bang on the door.

"Well . . . Austin 3:16 says I just whooped your ass," says Kwesi.

I punch the door.

"Calm down, Son."

"Open the door, Pop!"

"Don't publish that book, Son!"

I calm myself down and gather my composure. "It's too late, Pop." I walk over to my backpack and pull out a paperback copy of the book. I place it on the coffee table and then walk off.

"There's a copy of the book for you on the table. I'm going to bed."

Several moments later, Kwesi peeks his head out of the door to see if the coast is clear. He struts out of the bathroom and walks over to the table where I placed the novel. Kwesi picks it up, not knowing it is a booby-trap for me to catch him outside of the bathroom. I stampede toward Kwesi like a bull in a pit. Barely escaping, Kwesi manages to get inside of the bathroom yet again and lock the door.

"Punk ass!" I shout.

"Goodnight, Son!" Kwesi yells from the other side of the door.

I take a sit on the couch then shout, "We can do this all night, Pop!" I get comfortable and patiently wait for Kwesi to step out of the bathroom.

CHAPTER 30

Several hours have passed. I awake from falling asleep on the couch in the den. Dustin, Kellen, and Keisha Junior are all standing around staring at me.

"You got knocked the fuck out!" Kellen says boldly.

"Boy, watch your mouth!" I say in a stern tone. "Where did you hear that from?"

"We watched that movie 'Friday' with Papa this morning," Kellen says. "Then he gave me $20 to say it.

I gaze at the bathroom, and notice Kwesi had snuck away while I was asleep.

"What happened to your eye, Uncle Tre?" Keisha Junior asks.

"My eye?"

I rush to the bathroom and see my left eye is swollen and has a dark ring around it. Kwesi maimed me pretty bad. "Oh . . . OK!" I shout as I rush out of the bathroom and upstairs.

Kwesi, Keisha, and Michelle are all upstairs in the main living area watching ESPN. "Daddy says you know this woman on TV," Keisha says. Sade is on the screen speaking, but the TV is muted.

"We watch her show all the time," Michelle says. "She's stunning."

"She looks like she's pregnant."

I grow uneasy, "Why do you say that?"

"Look at her . . . She looks like she put on some weight these last couple of months," Keisha says.

I look over at Eva, who is seated at the breakfast bar eating. A buffet-style breakfast has been prepared in the gourmet kitchen. On the buffet tariff are French toast, oatmeal, scrambled eggs, bacon, turkey bacon, apple sage chicken sausages, pancakes, waffles, sliced strawberries, and orange juice. Eva takes a big bite of her turkey bacon. "Sorry, Papi, but I couldn't wait for you," Eva says. "What happened to your eye?"

"Oh, damn! I just noticed that," Michelle says. "Your shit is jacked all the way up, homie."

I direct my rage toward Kwesi. All I see is red as I stalk Kwesi down like a cheetah preying on an antelope. Kwesi circles around the furniture to avoid getting mauled.

"Keisha! You better get him before I fuck him up again." Kwesi says.

"Calm down, guys," Michelle says. "Let's be civil about this."

"When I get my lick back, we can be civil," I say.

"That's what you get for telling all my got-damn business." Kwesi holds the balled up copy of my novel in his hand. "I read what you wrote. Talking about how you was better off growing up without me . . . Fuck you!"

"Fuck you back. Let's take a walk through the pines and see who comes back, Pop?"

A frightened Kwesi answers, "Nope."

"Chicken shit!" I say, trying to bait him.

"Ask your left eye who's chicken shit!"

I circle the furniture, attempting to get one solid swing on Kwesi.

"You think you can write a book about me?" Kwesi roars. "You try to ruin my life . . . I'm gonna ruin yours, you gotdamn stereotype."

"It's your fault I'm a stereotype. You stereotype creating motherfucker!"

"So," Kwesi says with a nonchalant shrug.

"Children, stop," Keisha says.

"He started it," Kwesi and I say in unison.

"Guys . . . Please!" Michelle pleads. "The kids are watching." They are staring at Kwesi and me like we are an iPad.

"It's my fault. I should have never encouraged Tre to talk to you about the book."

"It's not your fault, baby-girl," Kwesi says. "He shouldn't have ever written the damn book about me in the first place."

"No . . . You should've been a better father. Then I would not have had nothing to write about."

"From what I read, I did you a favor. Your book ain't nothing without me."

"Daddy, take the kids to Peak 8 like you promised," Keisha says. Kwesi scurries over to the front door where his jacket and boots are. I jump at him as if I am about to chase after him.

A frightened Kwesi rushes out of the door and shouts, "Keep it up and get fucked up again, Son!"

"Tre! Let the kids go with their Papa," Eva says.

"Papa, my ass," I scoff. "All those years of crying because your punk ass wasn't there . . . When I should've been praising the real Papa for doing your damn job."

Kwesi flips me the bird.

"Daddy, please!" Keisha yells.

Kwesi and the kids stroll off.

"You see now why I didn't wanna tell Pop about the damn book? I told you we should let sleeping dogs lie," I say as I storm off to my room.

CHAPTER 31

I pace back and forth in the master bedroom suite like a deranged, caged wildcat. Though I must admit that the suite is very nice. It has a king size bed, private access to a large outdoor balcony, and its own sitting area with leather chairs and a 70-inch TV. I take a seat on one of the leather chairs and pull out my phone. To my surprise, I have a miss call from Papa.

I send a text to Sade, *"Hey . . . Everything cool?"*

Sade replies, *"Remember when I told you I wasn't on birth control . . . Well... I'm pregnant."*

I text back, *"Are you serious?"*

Sade replies, *"Yes."*

My hand starts to tremble. I don't know if I'm nervous because the child could be mine or if I'm afraid the unborn child is somebody else's. Can I handle her being pregnant by another man? If Sade's pregnant by another man, there will never be an opportunity for us to get together. Either way, I type back, *"Is it mine?"*

Sade sends a text back, *"What do you think?"*

I type, *"We're having a baby together?"*

Sade sends back, *"Yes. "*

I'm not sure how this is supposed to feel. I am excited, sad, and mad all at the same time. Excited because it feels right to be connected with Sade this way. She was always my first choice. This situation is sad because I have two different women pregnant at the same time. I can't even fathom where to start with Eva. What will I tell her? How will she react? Will she be mad at me? I'm angry at myself. How the hell did I carelessly get two women pregnant at the same time? My mind fills with a thousand thoughts. I type, *"What do you wanna do about it?"*

Some moments later, Sade replies, *"I don't believe in abortions . . . so God-willing, I'm having this baby, whether you are in or not. Let's talk later . . . I have to get back on set."*

I walk into the elegant bathroom with polished granite countertops, a double vanity, and a contemporary walk-in shower. I turn the water on for the shower then walk over to the mirror and examines my swollen eye. Kwesi stuck me pretty good.

"I'm getting my lick," I say to my pathetic reflection in the mirror. "Carelessness got you here."

My pocket starts to vibrate. I pull out my phone; it's an incoming call from Papa again.

"Hey, Papa! Happy Thanksgiving!"

"Hey . . . Happy Thanksgiving! What's going on there?"

"Nothing much . . . Up in the mountains with my family."

In the background, I hear Grandma fussing and cussing, then suddenly she picks up the other phone, "Robbie got all that junk outside," Grandma says through the receiver.

"What about all the junk you got inside the house, woman?"

"I just wanna run away."

"You don't have to run away . . . You don't even have to walk. They got companies that'll pick yo crazy ass up from the house."

"You hear how he talks to me, Tre?"

"Gotdamn it! Where's my saw? I'm gonna saw yo head if you don't get off the phone."

"How's everything back home?" I say with a chuckle.

"I want a divoce," Papa mumbles.

"I'm sure there are situations that are worse than Grandma's fussing and cussing." Compared to my current situation, I'd take Grandma's fussing and cussing any day.

"Getting a tetanus shot sounds better than hearing that hag yap."

"You guys are silly, Papa."

"The IRS contacted me about some money I supposedly owe. They said it's back taxes from the money I made selling candy."

"They might have found out through me."

"Yeah, that's what the folks at the courthouse said."

"I wrote a book about my childhood and mentioned you in the book."

"You sapsucka. Why you putting my business out in these streets?"

"I'm sorry, Papa . . . I'll take care of it."

"You better. Call me when it's done," Papa ends the call.

I undress and walk my defeated ass into the shower. Maybe I can scrub some of this misery off. Things can't get any worse than this.

CHAPTER 32

Michelle, Keisha, and Eva are in the kitchen preparing Thanksgiving dinner. The doorbell rings.

"I'll get that."

An overzealous Michelle runs to the sink and washes her hands. She dashes past me as I enter the living room.

Eva hands me the remote then takes a seat at the dining table next to me. "Football should be on, Papi." I flip to the game and see that Sade is broadcasting live from Dallas, Texas.

"That's kind of cool you know her," Eva says studying the TV. "Did you see her at the class reunion?"

"Yes . . . I mean . . . No! I saw her but, we didn't speak."

"Tre! Keisha! Someone's here to meet you!" Michelle yells.

"That might be Junior." Keisha walks to the sink and washes her hands. She dries them off and leaves the kitchen.

As we approach the front, I notice a familiar face I wasn't expecting. My face turns into a scowl.

"Jackson Reed? What the hell are you doing here?"

"My sister Keisha invited me. What are you doing here?" Confusion strikes the room.

"Keisha is my sister."

"Yes . . . Well, I guess I'm both of your guys' sister," Keisha clarifies.

"Wait . . . You're Junior?" I ask.

"Yep. I'm Jackson Reed Junior. My mother named me after my stepfather, but she calls me Junior."

Kwesi and the kids have returned from Peak 8 and are headed toward the door.

"Kids, come say hi to your Uncle JR." Michelle says. They wave.

"Nice to meet you all," Jackson Reed's punk ass says to my family.

"How was it?" Keisha asks.

"It was so much fun, Mama!" Keisha Junior says. "We played while Papa read Uncle Tre's book."

"You wrote another book? Congrats, bro!" an applauding Jackson says.

"Thanks!" I say, rubbing my head.

"Papa got us lost coming back." Dustin blurts out.

"No, I didn't get lost, stoolpigeon," says Kwesi.

Kwesi extends his greeting, "Kwesi Black . . . Sorry, we're doing this so late in life, but nice to see you if I haven't already!"

An enthusiastic Jackson expresses, "I'm excited to know that you were always my real father. If it weren't for the ancestry test, I never would've known."

"So, do you go by Junior?"

"Junior or Jackson . . . Whatever you want to call me, Dad."

"So, what's your full name again?"

"It's Jackson Reed Junior."

"Jackson Reed," Kwesi repeats as he scratches his beard and cogitates on the name.

Jackson places his arm around my shoulders. "I've always had suspicions you were my little brother . . . That's kinda why I picked on you growing up."

"Cool," I say with the biggest, fakest smile my cheeks can handle.

"Jackson Reed, huh? My mind is off these days," Kwesi interjects. "But that name rings a bell. Anyway, I'm gonna freshen up and finish reading Tre's book. You should get him a copy, other son," Kwesi says as he tries to walk around me. I jump at Kwesi, and he flinches and then breaks into a light jog.

"Alright . . . Get your ass whooped again, Son!"

"What's that all about?" Jackson asks.

"Don't mind them. Just family drama." Keisha says. "Make yourself at home. Your bedroom is on the lower level."

"My wife Xena is bringing in the luggage."

"Why is your wife bringing in the luggage? You brought her here?"

"Uh . . . Yeah," Jackson says with a little chuckle. "She's my wife. Why wouldn't I bring her with me to spend time with my family?"

"Of course, he's bringing his wife, Tre."

"I'm Eva . . . Trevor's fiancé!" She extends her hand in greeting, but Jackson Reed's punk ass pulls Eva in for a hug.

"I'm a hugger, love. You are so beautiful." Jackson says. "Is that my future niece or nephew in the oven?"

"It's your future niece," Eva says proudly.

"How did a jackass like Trevor get a woman like you pregnant? What are the secrets, bro?" Jackson says as he places his hand on my shoulder. I remove it.

"Eva . . . Stay away from him. I'm gonna help with the luggage."

"I'll help you."

"Don't worry about it . . . Make yourself at home."

I rush off. "Xena!" I angrily whisper.

Xena is in the back of the car digging through one of her suitcases.

"Tre! What are you doing here?" A now seven-month pregnant Xena asks.

"This is a family trip with my father."

"Oh my god? I did it again . . . Are you and Jackson related?"

"Apparently so . . . We have the same deadbeat father."

"Why didn't anyone tell me?" she says frantically.

"I just found out. Just be cool . . . Don't act weird."

Xena scurries off as I grab their suitcases and roll them up to the front door of the cabin.

"I'm sure you guys want to freshen up . . . Kellen!" Keisha shouts! "Show your Uncle Junior and Auntie Xena to their room. Dinner will be ready in a few."

Jackson and Xena grab their luggage while Kellen guides them downstairs to their room. Everyone ventures off too his or her perspective corners to prepare for dinner. Keisha Junior is the only one left behind. I nod Keisha Junior over and whisper, "I'll pay you $20 if you find Papa's book and bring it to me." Keisha Junior shakes her head then runs off.

I sneak off to the fire pit and dial up a number.

"Armani . . . Did you know Jackson Reed was our brother?"

"Yeah . . . I knew a long time ago but uh . . . I heard what you wrote about me in your little book," Armani said.

"You don't even read, bro."

"Kris does . . . And she told me everything you said about me. Talked about me like a dog."

"I only wrote facts, little bro."

"To think . . . I'm the one that helped your little career."

"What are you talking about?" I ask.

"I'm the one that talked to Kris. She was way done with you. But I talked her out of it. I told her not to punish you because of my actions. So, whatever your animosity with me, I want no part of."

"I have no issues, and I'm not trying to argue with you today. I don't have time for this."

Armani chuckles, "You're the one mad . . . Telling everyone but me. But you don't have time for it? You had time when you were writing about me. People ask me why you don't like me, and I tell them I don't know."

"They know why I don't like you, but they're not telling you the truth. But you don't wanna hear the truth."

"Nah . . . I wanna hear the truth."

"Every time you get in trouble, you bring everyone with you. You never handle your business like a responsible adult. Everyone has their own problems to deal with, Armani."

"Is that why you're mad? Live your life, Tre! Stop worrying about what I got going on, and we'll be good."

"Nobody wins if the family feuds." Armani begins to laugh as if I said something funny. He only makes me feel as if I said something dumb to anger me. But I'm not going down that rabbit hole today.

"Go argue with somebody else. I only called to ask you about Jackson. I have too much going on. Happy Thanksgiving!" The call ends abruptly. I leave the fire pit and head back into the cabin to join the rest of the family.

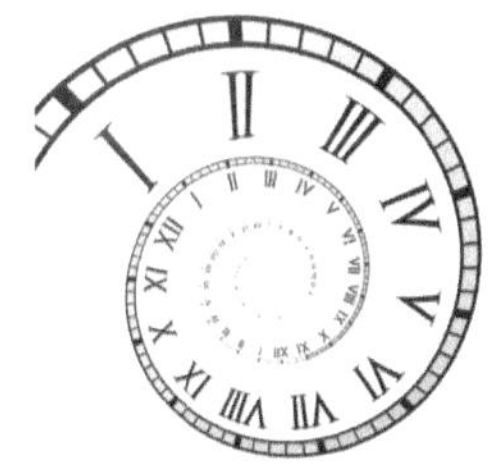

CHAPTER 33

The family gathers around the dining table. Kwesi sits at the head, and I sit on the opposite end. As soon as we take our seats, our gaze meets. Though no words are spoken, we are communicating. My body language reads *I'm whooping that ass when I get a chance.* But something is different about this stare down. Kwesi's fire is back. That little vulnerability I once saw in my father's eyes has vanished. He has grown a dangerous, smug smile, and Kwesi's body language reads, *You better whoop it good because I'm earning this ass whooping today.*

As I start to make a plate, Kwesi stands to his feet and begins to speak, "Let's say grace before we eat. Jackson, why don't you lead us in prayer since you're my eldest and my favorite son?"

"Let us bow our heads," Jackson says. Everyone bows their heads except for the three nosey children, Kwesi, and me.

Jackson begins the prayer, "OK . . . uh . . . Lord . . . Thank you for blessing this family. Thank you for gathering us all here."

At this juncture in the prayer, the stare down between Kwesi and me is as intense as it has ever been.

"Bless our children that are in our wives' wombs and let this delicious food nourish our bodies . . . In your name, we pray. Amen."

Everybody repeats "Amen."

Everyone takes their seat, all except for Kwesi and me. Kwesi gestures for me to take a seat first. I decline and gesture for Kwesi to take a seat before me. Kwesi declines and throws it right back at me.

"Please, guys . . . It's Thanksgiving." Keisha says. Kwesi and I simultaneously take our seats.

Lots of delicious food awaits us on the table. There is a big, honey-roasted turkey, mashed sweet potatoes, turkey gravy, and cornbread dressing with cranberry sauce. There is a dish of creamy macaroni and cheese, a kale dish, a peanut butter sweet potato pie with chocolate crust, and a delicious homemade red velvet cake. Everyone prepares their plates—all except for Kwesi, who has not stopped staring at me since we got to the table.

"I see someone has an eye problem."

"Oh, it damn sure looks like an eye problem," Kwesi adds.

"I didn't want to say anything . . . But, what happened to your eye, bro?" Jackson asks.

All eyes are on me. "I walked into a lucky demented punk ass tree branch when I wasn't expecting it," I say, the whole time staring Kwesi down.

"Maybe you had it coming from that lucky demented punk ass tree branch," Kwesi interjects.

"Next time I see that slow, demented punk-ass branch coming my way, I'll duck and fuck that twig up."

"Please! Kids at the table." Michelle utters.

"I'm sorry, kids, but your Uncle Tre is a piece of shit."

"Says the sorry ass deadbeat father that didn't raise any of his children."

The kids snicker at the exchange.

"Children cover your ears," Keisha demands.

"Tre, chill! You shouldn't talk to our father like that," Jackson says, trying to mediate the situation.

"That's right with your mark ass!" Kwesi says.

"Daddy! Grow up. That's your son," Keisha wails.

"That ain't my son. He doesn't have my last name. He changed that it to his granddaddy's name," Kwesi mocks.

"That's life! That's the man that raised me! If you have a problem with it . . . You should've done something about it years ago."

"Oh . . . I'm inclined to think I've already done something about it, Left Eye."

"Please, Pop! Let's take a long brisk walk through the pines."

Kwesi turns his attention to Jackson, "How's my new favorite son?"

"He doesn't have your last name, though," I say, mocking Kwesi.

Kwesi pats his pockets then scans around the room for the book.

"Where did I put it?"

Keisha Junior holds up the book as if she's holding baby Simba. I dig in my pocket and flash her a $20 bill.

"I'll double it," Kwesi says.

Keisha Junior and the other kids stare at me to see if I up my offer .

"OK . . . I'll triple it." I pull out a wad of cash.

"Papa will take you guys out to eat and I'll let you curse in public."

Keisha Junior hands Kwesi the mangled-up book.

"Stool-pigeon," I mumble under my breath.

Keisha Junior shrugs. Kwesi slams the book on the table. I grow a little uncomfortable.

"Speaking of names," Kwesi said. "Jackson Reed, isn't it?" Kwesi thumbs through the pages. "Have you read Tre's book yet?"

"No, not yet, but I can't wait to read it."

A sinister smile grows across Kwesi face as he finds the page, "Let's see . . . You once robbed his precious Papa's candy store."

"I made it into your book. Wow. I can't believe you wrote about that," Jackson says with a chuckle. "Not my proudest moment . . . We were young and Armani talked me into doing it." Jackson confesses.

"Oh, I'm fully aware," Kwesi asserts. "It's all in the book, Son."

"What else does he say about me?" a curious Jackson asks.

"Oh, you wanna know, Son?" Kwesi teases.

"Pop . . . You don't have to do this right now," I plead.

"Throughout the book, you are referred to as 'Jackson Reed's punk ass.'"

Jackson's smile vanishes.

"I must confess," Kwesi searches for the right words, "Yes, there are things in my past that aren't great. I was married to Trevor's mother and was cheating on her with Keisha's mother. Keisha . . . You were conceived in the backseat of my old 1987 Cutlass Supreme."

"What's conceived mean?" Kellen asks with his hands covering his ears.

"Keep your ears closed, boy," Keisha shouts.

"Jackson, your mother and I were just fucking," Kwesi says.

"OK . . . Kids . . . " Michelle interjects. "Grab your plates, and let's go downstairs to the den," Michelle and the kids scurry off.

"We had an affair while she was married to the guy you were named after. But that's not in the book," Kwesi says. "What's in the book?" He turns toward the end of the book and finds the right page. "What's your name, sweetheart?"

Jackson gets uncomfortable and states, "Xena!"

"Xena! Like the Warrior Princess. Beautiful name by the way," Kwesi confirms as he studies a page then flips to another. "While I look for the page . . ." Kwesi looks up at Eva then says, "You know Tre slept with Sade."

"I never told you I slept with Sade, nor is that in the book," I say defensively.

"But you did say you were in love with Sade. You met up with her when you came home . . . You and your lady were beefing about some personal trainer she slept with back in the day. You used that as an excuse to get away, and you told me you were meeting up with Sade," Kwesi says bluntly.

"What?" I blurt out as I attempt to act as if I don't know what the hell he is talking about.

"You don't remember?" Kwesi asks. "Ain't I supposed to be the one with the bad memory disease?" The room is eerily quiet. "You said it last night before I readjusted your vision. You may or may not have slept with Sade, but uh . . . As for Xena, you definitely hit that" Kwesi lifts the bald-up manuscript to the air. "The proof is in the pudding . . . Sorry, daughter-in-law." Keisha stands up from the table, grabs her plate, and heads downstairs to den with the others. The room is uncomfortably quiet.

Jackson is in a state of delusion. "No . . . No, that's fiction. Trevor writes fiction. That's the only reason he would write something like that," Jackson says.

"If it's fiction, why is it so precise?" Kwesi emphasizes.

The table grows quieter. All I can hear are forks and spoons clashing against the dishes. It feels like déjà vu from the last Thanksgiving Kwesi and I spent together years ago. This time I am the villain.

"Is it?" Eva asks. "Is this fiction?"

There is nothing that I can say to defend myself. Even if I wanted to lie, my mind cannot process any thought for my mouth to enunciate.

"You thought you would never see your brother Jackson again, and yet here we all are," Kwesi says. "You tried to expose me . . . Writing a book about my whereabouts or lack thereof. But you exposed yourself."

Jackson is still in denial. "I know they may have had a thing in high school, but that's the past. Whatever she did before me is none of my business. I love the lady I'm with today."

Kwesi pulls out the book and searches for the page. "They never slept with each other in high school," Kwesi says. "Not until the class reunion."

Kwesi flips through a few more pages and unearths what he's been looking for, "Found it! It reads, 'While Jackson Reed's punk ass was passed out from drinking too much, I had his wife Xena bent over in the backseat of a little rental car he had made fun of. There was nothing spectacular about it. I only did that so that I could kill two birds with one stone on my shit list. Revenge is a dish that is best served cold, and I just served one of the coldest dishes of my life.'" Kwesi moves the book away from his face and smiles at me. And with that verbal blow, Kwesi wins the joust. He doesn't stop there, though.

"He spoke highly of all your other classmates that showed up," Kwesi expresses. "Tre also said . . ." He brings the book back up to his face.

"'Most of the popular kids from high school ended up working at dead-end jobs and married women who were washed up and shaped like elbows.' Little snide of you, Tre."

Kwesi throws the book on the ground and expresses, "Now let's feast. I'm starving." The vengeful Kwesi starts preparing his dinner plate. Jackson Reed stares at Xena while an angry Eva stares at me.

"Papi . . . Did you sleep with her?"

I shake my head no. Xena makes eye contact with me. I shake my head no to subtly signal her to stay silent. But I can tell the pressure is too much for Xena.

"I'm so sorry. We were drunk during the class reunion and . . . Oh, my God . . . I didn't know you guys were brothers."

"Find another way home," Jackson says as he storms out of the cabin.

Xena says nothing. She notices Eva holding a steak knife, observes Eva's livid energy, and darts off. Eva wobbles after Xena, who rounds the corner and manages to escape into the bathroom where she locks the door.

"Fuck you, Tre!" Eva shouts. "We are done." Eva starts to sob as she walks toward the master bedroom. The door slams shut.

The only people left at the table are me and Kwesi.

"Just the two of us . . . Building shit castles in the sky," Kwesi sings. "Guess the apple doesn't fall too far from the tree . . . Huh, Son?"

"I'm nothing like you."

"Son, we're the same."

"We're not the same, Pop. We might be the same, but we are not the same."

"Son, hate it or love it, we're the same. You might have your grandfather's last name, and he might've raised ya, but my blood still runs through your veins." Kwesi takes a bite from his plate, "That's pretty damn good."

I sit tranquilized from the Thanksgiving dinner thrashing. Kwesi takes several more bites from his dinner. "Yummy! This food is so delicious . . . You can whoop my ass now."

I rise to my feet, "Fuck you, Pop!"

"That's no way to speak to your father," Kwesi says with sarcasm.

"You can have this moment," I say. "You're gonna die alone anyway."

Kwesi takes a few seconds to digest what I said. He takes a bite from his plate and chews it up, then he swallows. "It is what it is, Son. I came into this world alone."

I storm off and exit the cabin, leaving Kwesi by his lonesome to finish eating a cold yet delicious Thanksgiving meal.

CHAPTER 34

As I open the door to the master suite, I find a teary-eyed Eva pacing the room. She wobbles back and forth, screaming and cursing in Spanish. She spots me peeking my head in and storms toward me, "Some high school crush?" Eva shouts. "Hijo de puta! Did you sleep with her?"

"Calm down . . . It's not what you think," I say.

"Then what is it, Papi?" Eva says as she moves close enough to hit me. I can see her beautiful brown eyes start to well up as she stares deep into my eyes.

"I . . . I . . ." I stutter. "I wrote some things . . . That may or may not be true."

"Did you sleep with that woman before or after us?"

I don't answer. My silence is a dead giveaway.

"I may have withheld information about my past, but I never cheated on you," Eva admits.

"Withholding information is the same as cheating," I say, defending what little ground I have left to stand on.

"I never slept anybody else while we were together. You told me all those stories you wrote happened before our time together. So, is that why you left me when I told you I was pregnant? I had panic attacks thinking I destroyed our relationship while you were sleeping some high school crush."

"No . . . I told you. I was under a lot of stress, and I needed some space."

"You needed space so you could sleep with that."

"No," I say as I rub the sweat that has formed on my forehead. "This might sound stupid, and it may not be what you want to hear, but I only did that for revenge. There are no feelings there. No attachment. I've been over that."

"What about Sade? Is what Kwesi said at the dinner table true?"

If at first, you don't succeed, play dumb. "What did Kwesi say?" I ask.

"Pendejo! Don't play me."

I lower my head, breaking eye contact with Eva. A few moments of the most uncomfortable silence I have ever experience slither by. At this point, there really is nothing to say.

"I'm so sorry, Eva."

"You slept with her too?"

My silence answers her question yet again.

"What do you want, Tre? Do you want her? Or do you want me?"

"I don't want Xena. That was nothing," I say to deflect from Sade.

"I'm not talking about her. I'm talking about the other bitch."

"Why would you call her a bitch when you never met her?"

"Why are you defending her?" Eva asks.

"I'm not defending her . . . I was just saying—"

"What are you saying, Papi?"

"I may or may not have gotten Sade pregnant."

Suddenly, Eva grows still. She doesn't mumble even a single word. It is hard to assess her state of mind because a grin flashes across her face. She walks over and hugs me. I can taste her salty tears on my lips as I press my face against her cheek. Like the eye of a hurricane, Eva is calm, unlike the raging bull she was before I entered the room. The aura is perfectly peaceful. We hold each other as if everything is OK. *Maybe this could work*, I think, but just like a hurricane, outside the eye, everything is hell on wheels.

"Hijo de puta!" Eva violently screams as she pushes me off her and smacks me across my face. She starts heaving any and everything at me that is not attached to the ground. Eva grabs a lamp and flings it at me, but I manage to dodge it and escape out of the room. I guess I will be sleeping on the couch again.

CHAPTER 35

Keisha and I sit by the fire pit in the frigid cold. Keisha sips hot green tea as I chuck logs onto the open flame. The morning after the Thanksgiving dinner debacle has us all in our feelings. The smell of burning lumber on a cold, snowy day makes up for all those mosquitos-biting, hot summer days in Arkansas. I find tranquility in throwing pieces of wood into the fire. It feels as though I'm tossing every problem I have into the pit. With each chunk, a tribulation swelters in the blaze. But I can only wish that was actually the case.

"I didn't envision yesterday happening the way it did . . . I feel like it's my fault it all happened," Keisha confesses.

"I'm not gonna disagree with you," I say. "But I wish I could've been more honest. I can't believe I got two women pregnant at the same time."

"You got two different women pregnant at the same time. Do you not believe in condoms, Kwesi Junior?"

"Do not put me in the same box as your daddy, OK! I'm reversing that curse. I'll be there for my children."

"I'm teasing, bro!" Keisha says. "I heard Eva last night.

"Nah . . . Not really. After she trashed the room, she packed up and left with Dustin."

A few beats slide by as we stare into the fire. A flurry of snowflakes starts to fall.

"I was never their first choice," I profess.

"What are you talking about?"

"Xena . . . Eva . . . Sade . . . or Kwesi . . . I was never their first choice. I only slept with Xena to get back at her for playing me in school. If I had known Jackson was my brother, I would not have targeted him or his wife. When I first tried to get with Eva, she wasn't feeling me. I chased after her until I got her attention. Once I got her, I didn't know how to treat her. I wasn't even my mother's first choice. She worked more than she should have because Kwesi wasn't around. Pop not being around caused all this dysfunction. He's the reason why I'm out here making dumb ass decisions."

Keisha takes a few moments to process what I said. "I get that, and I understand, bro," Keisha says. "But at some point, you're gonna have to stop blaming daddy for your dumb-ass decisions. Especially if you know, they're dumb-ass decisions you made as a grown man. You have to take responsibility for your actions."

"You're right, sis."

"Don't beat yourself down because you made mistakes. That's life."

We stare into the blaze for a few moments.

"What am I gonna do, Keisha? If I chose to be with Eva, I'll miss the opportunity to be with Sade. If I choose to be with Sade, you can bet your bottom dollar Eva will have me in child support court. I don't wanna do that to my children. I'm damned if I do, damned if I don't."

"Just be honest."

"But who should I be honest with?" I ask.

"Everyone . . . But most important, be honest with yourself. Do you know what you want, Tre?"

I've never considered that. On the surface, I have wanted many things. I wanted a beautiful girlfriend. Then I wanted to be single. I tried to sleep with all the women that ever told me no. I wanted to be successful. I wanted a condo in the city. I tried not to become my father, but that's not trending well at the moment. I got revenge, and it blew up in my face like a grenade. I wanted kids . . . Now that I'm about to have them, I don't know if I even want them. "I don't know what I want, sis."

"That's OK . . . You're a smart man. You'll find what you want or what you want will find you. Just try to be the father you wish you had growing up. Don't blame your life problems on a lack of leadership . . . Fix the problem by becoming the leader you needed."

"Thanks for the chat, sis." We hug each other. "Let's head back in," I advise as the arctic winds begin to pierce my cold-weather gear.

As we enter the cabin, a distraught Xena is sitting in the same seat she sat in the night before. She has her suitcase packed along with Jackson's bag. Michelle sits at the barstool, reading the crumbled copy of the manuscript I gave Kwesi. Kwesi rushes in fully dressed, wheeling his packed suitcase.

"Pop, you don't have to leave. I don't think you're in good condition to leave."

"You ain't the boss of me. What makes you think I'm not in good condition?"

"Your shoes are on the wrong feet."

Kwesi, along with everyone in the room, stares at his feet and sees that his left shoe is on his right foot and his right shoe is on his left foot.

"Well, I'll be," a stunned Kwesi says. "That sum bitch is right." Kwesi kicks his shoes off then struggles to get each shoe back on its proper foot. I pick one of his shoes up off the floor. Kwesi smacks the shoe out of my hand. "I don't need your gotdamn pity. All you're gonna do is write a book about it."

"The place is booked a few more days. I'm driving to the airport tonight so you guys can have the place for yourself."

"I'm good. You paid for this place with the blood money you made from that damn book." Kwesi then yells, "Glenn! Let's go!"

"Pop."

"Glenn!" Kwesi shouts as he searches around for her.

"Pop."

"Don't Pop me," Kwesi shouts, "Glenn! Bring your ass!"

"Daddy!"

"Glenn! Let's go . . . I ain't got all day!"

"Daddy!" Keisha says stern. "Glenn . . . She's gone."

"Gone?" a perplexed Kwesi asks. "When will she be back?"

"Glenn died several months ago."

Kwesi tries to conceal his dismay and confusion.

"Oh . . . Yeah . . . I remember."

He turns his attention to Xena. "Ready to ride out, baby-girl?"

Xena nods her head, stands up, and the two of them stroll out of the cabin together.

"If my calculations serve me right, Kwesi could potentially sleep with Xena on the way to the airport," Michelle announces as she turns to the next page of my manuscript. I shake my head and walk out of the room

CHAPTER 36

Luckily for me and my deposit, the master bedroom suite was not declared a state of emergency. After the departure of the category five hurricane named Eva, I was expecting to walk into a site of devastation. A couple of lamps were broken, and the chairs were knocked over but there was no other real damage. Honestly, I would not have blamed her if she trashed the place. If the shoe was on the other foot, I would have burnt this bitch down to the ground. It was my fault that I brought her here. I flip one of the wooden chairs then take a seat. I grab my phone and FaceTime Sade.

"Hey," Sade says as she brushes through her long curls. Her face is free of make-up, and her skin is clear. She is naturally prettier without make-up. "How was your Thanksgiving?"

"Uh . . . Ladies first." I deflect.

"It was good," Sade says. "The Cowboys lost . . . That made my day. How was yours?"

"Were you ever gonna tell me that you were pregnant?"

"I was getting to it . . . Yes. Never thought I'd have children by different men. I needed time to accept that I was pregnant. And I needed to accept the fact that you may or may not be there."

"What are you talking about, Sade? I'd die before that happened."

"How do I know that? I mean . . . Kwesi is your daddy," she says with a giggle.

"Yes. We're the same, but we are different . . . That's why we are the same . . . because we're different."

"What's that mean, Tre?"

"I don't know . . . I heard Kat Williams say it one time . . . Thought the timing was appropriate. Just understand I would not ever leave you hanging."

"I know you wouldn't. But honestly, I don't wanna be in some love triangle. You live with someone."

My face contorts, "But you're living with your ex."

"Yes, but we're not romantically attached," Sade assures. "We have an arrangement, but that's only for our daughter."

"How will that change now that I am in the picture?"

"I don't know . . . Maybe you can live with me."

That would not be weird to live under one roof with the love of my life and the father of her first child . . . Not. "There is no chance in hell I'll be in the same house with a man that has seen my lady naked. So, I don't know if that's gonna work. But . . . There is something I need to tell you."

"What's that?"

I take a few seconds to get my thoughts together. "The lady I live with . . . Eva . . . She's pregnant as well."

"What kind of soap opera shit did you get me involved with, Trevor Russell?" Sade shouts. I wouldn't say I like like the nickname Tre Tre Bear, but even that sounds better than how she says my government name.

"I'm sorry I brought you into my mess. I'll make it work . . . I promise. I love you."

"What?"

"I said, I love you."

"Tre . . . You may be caught up in the moment—"

"I've always had a love for you." I say, cutting her off. "Always have, always will."

"How would I know that . . . You ghosted me . . . remember?"

"Yes but . . . No . . . I didn't ghost you. I had the deadline for my book, my father's drama, along with my stepmother's passing. Eva and I were going through our thing. But even before when you and I met at Rendezvous . . . I knew then that I only had eyes for you. But I have this other woman in my life that I have love for, and now she's pregnant."

A few moments float in between our dialogue.

"Do you know what you want, Tre?" Sade asks.

"I want you."

"How do you know that?"

"I know."

"Tre . . . I love you. Take care of what you need to with your lady . . . We'll work this out somehow. Goodnight, Tre. Have a safe flight back to the A."

I blow her a kiss. Sade blows one back then waves goodbye, and the phone call ends.

CHAPTER 37

couple of months later, Eva gives birth to my first child, a beautiful baby girl. A month later, Sade delivered a beautiful baby boy. I try to make things work with Eva. It is difficult for her to get over the fact that I had gotten another woman pregnant while we were together. I travel from D.C. to ATL every other week for a few months to spend time with my children. All is well until I arrive back at the condo one day, and Eva's things are gone. On my desk is a note that reads, *"Sorry, Papi. I can't live like this."* At first, I think she is just mad. Eva will get over it and come back home the next day. The next day comes, and she doesn't return. Several days pass, which becomes several weeks. The several weeks turn into a month. I realize she is gone forever this time.

I act as if I didn't miss her. I am happy she has left. Then I get mad. *To hell with her,* I think. I'll attract her replacement. Eva will regret leaving. As I cogitate a bit more, I reflect on if I had respected her a little more, spent a little more time with her, maybe she would have stayed. Had I been more honest with what I wanted; I wouldn't have pushed Eva away. As much as I had wanted to show strength, I was afraid. I questioned if

I was fit to be a child's father. A dark cloud covers me as I doubt my life. Sure, I am single and can commit to Sade, but am I even worthy of love? I have thoughts of suicide, but then it hits me: Eva leaving might be a healthy choice, and this life is not about me anymore. From the moment I saw my children's little faces, I knew I would do whatever it takes to protect and nurture them. I would die for them.

A year after our little girl is born, things heat up. Eva takes our affairs to the family court system. Her lawyer fights for alimony because we are common-law married. They use my father's infidelities as well as my own to sketch some parallel conclusion that I will abandon my child based on trends within the African American community. *When they go low, we go high* doesn't apply to us. My lawyer digs up old text messages of her threatening to take my little girl away from me if we don't work things out. I submit racy photos she had posted online, and my lawyer alludes to suspicions of prostitution based on her profile on Instagram. Eva knows I am nothing like Kwesi, and I know she wasn't a whore, but that's how the cookie crumbles in the family law system sometimes. Child support is for children, not failed relationships.

CHAPTER 38

7 YEARS LATER

I imagined myself to be one of those cool fathers. You know, the type of dad you see wearing trendy clothes. The kind of dad that drives a sports car and wears a three-piece Tom Ford suit to business meetings. I thought I would be the type of dad that listened to all the fresh music the young folks were jamming to, or even the dad that knew all the new dance moves. But all of the stuff these young kids do now hurt my whole body.

Not only do sports cars sit too low, but they also hurt getting in and out of, and they attract the wrong kind of women. They don't make three-piece suits that are four-way stretch, quick-drying, and wrinkle-resistant with excellent shape retention. I can't relate to what some of these kids are rapping about in their music. I retired from dancing a few years ago because I tried to do that Flossin' dance and damn near dislocated my hip, my knee, and my shoulder. I have a new appreciation for the Electric Slide. I hung up the young man's boots. I have reached a different stage in my life, and that is fatherhood.

I'm standing here in the mirror plucking gray hairs out of my beard in my Polo Ralph Lauren pajamas and the SpongeBob SquarePants house slippers my daughter got me for my birthday.

My fractured love affairs never recovered from the infamous Thanksgiving dinner that exposed my philandering ways. Things didn't work out well with Eva. We tried to make it work, but she couldn't get past my horrendous acts and the embarrassment I caused her. We remain friends for the sake of our daughter. We share custody of our daughter, Little Kwesi Russell, who is seven years old. Eva keeps her during the school year. I get her every other weekend and during the summer.

I sold the condo in Atlanta and moved closer to Sade and my seven-year-old son Trevor Russell Junior, also known as TJ. Sade and I have an on-and-off kind of relationship. I couldn't handle being under the same roof as Sade's firstborn's father, Dray. I moved back down south to restart my life as a single father. I went back to sports journalism and cover the Miami Dolphins in South Florida. I bought a cozy three-bedroom condo in Miami Beach that overlooks the Atlantic Ocean. The condo is more of a vacation spot because of the amount of time I spend traveling for work. Marble flooring is laid throughout the condo, which has an open kitchen with stainless steel appliances, granite countertops and European-style cabinets. The balcony has spectacular views of the water and the city. There is something more intricate that is in the condo. It's not the chestnut-colored Arch Nomad leather corner sectional with chaise centered perfectly in the living room. It is more what is sitting on the beautiful couch. A cute little lady named Kwesi, and her brother Trevor Junior are enjoying a relaxing morning on the couch in their pajamas watching old Looney Tunes clips.

It is summer break for the kids and off-season for football. We've spent a lot of quality time together over the past several weeks. We have had quite a busy summer so far with a Disney cruise to the Bahamas. Not to mention the countless visits to the Magic Kingdom, Universal Resort, SeaWorld, Busch Gardens, and LEGOLAND. We have gone to a few Miami Marlins games, played some competitive minigolf, and had countless bowling games. We are taking a small break from all the travels of the previous weekends.

I enter the living room dressed in a Polo T-Shirt and cargo shorts. "Happy Father's Day, Daddy!" The kids shout in unison.

"Thanks, kids."

"We got you some something." Little Kwesi hands me a neatly-wrapped gift. "Open it, Daddy."

I rip open the first gift, and it's a coffee mug with a picture of us from our Disney Cruise plastered on one side. "*Best Dad In The Whole World*" is printed on the other side of the mug, and it's signed by both of the kids.

"Nice! Thank you, guys."

TJ hands over a half-assed, newspaper-wrapped gift. "TJ wrapped that one up," Little Kwesi says.

I chuckle as I open up the second gift. It's six popsicle sticks attached to one another. The first one is inscribed with crayon that reads: "*5 Things We Love About Daddy*." The five sticks read: "*You play with us,*" "*You spend time with us,*" "*You are funny,*" "*You are strong,*" and "*You are the loudest parent at our games.*"

"Thank you, guys. Bring it in." I open my arms, and they fall right into my big bear hug. I squeeze them tight and lift them off their feet.

"You guys want breakfast?"

Little Kwesi and Trevor Junior simultaneously say, "Yes!"

I walk over to the kitchen, "What do you want? Eggs, pancakes, oatmeal, or cereal?"

"Daddy, can you fix me a bowl of cereal?" Little Kwesi asks.

"Yeah . . . Me too, daddy." TJ repeats.

"My kind of party . . . Cereal it is!" I confirm.

"Daddy!" TJ yells. "Are aliens real?"

I take a few seconds to collect my thoughts. "Earth is in space. We float around a star called the sun. At night when you look to the sky, other stars are sprinkled in the sky. To some other being out in the universe, those stars are equivalent to our sun. Does that make sense, son?"

TJ nods his head.

My pocket vibrates. I pull out my phone and receive a text message from Keisha. The message reads, *"Have you talked to daddy lately?"* I ignore the message and place the phone back in my pocket.

I grab the box of Cinnamon Toast Crunch and pour two bowls for the kids, then place the bowls on the table. "OK . . . Come and get it."

"Thank you, Daddy." Little Kwesi says.

They migrate to the kitchen table.

I dig my hand in the box, grab a handful of cereal, and stuff it in my mouth. Little Kwesi pulls out her phone and places it on the table. The two kids' eyes are glued to their phones. The video puts the kids in a hypnotic state.

I hear the crinkle of a package and a soft lulled narrator's voice giving a play by play of something.

"Pete and repeat . . . What the hell are you guys watching?" I grab the phone and notice perfectly-manicured hands unboxing a brightly colored unopened toy box on the screen. I study the video for a few moments.

"What's so fascinating about watching someone you don't know open up the same toys you guys have already? Whatever happened to kids watching TV like I did growing up?" I place the phone back on the table.

"Daddy . . . It's not the 1900s anymore," Little Kwesi says.

A chuckling TJ mimics an old man and shouts, "Get off my lawn." The kids chuckle at his impression of a grumpy old man.

" Ha-ha! Whatever . . . Finish eating so we can go."

The kids don't budge. Their little eyes are glued to the phone.

"If y'all don't finish eating, I'm throwing that damn phone off the balcony!" I say with a stern tone.

"Don't do that, Daddy!"

The kids start devouring their food until it's gone.

"Hurry up and change so we can get to the theater on time. You know I hate missing the previews." The kids rush out of the kitchen and into their rooms to change.

CHAPTER 39

We ride along in my blacked-out Ford F-150 Raptor. As I drive, I glance in the review mirror. Kwesi and Trevor Jr. sit in the back, staring at their phones.

"You kids have it easy," I say, "When I was growing up, we had to do this thing called going outside and using our imagination. We didn't stare at a phone all day."

"Get off my yard!" Little Kwesi says as she does her rendition of a grumpy old man.

TJ takes off his headphones and joins his sister in teasing their father. "Yeah . . . Get off my yard!"

"Stop it . . . I don't sound like that."

"Yes, you do, Daddy." Little Kwesi says.

"Fine... Enjoy your stupid little devices. I don't wanna talk to you guys anyway."

They say nothing, as their little eyes remain glued to the phone screen.

"Daddy!" TJ says.

"Stop touching me," TJ yells with a whine.

"I'm not touching you . . . You're touching me." Little Kwesi howls.

"No, I'm not!"

"Yes . . . You are."

"Both of you stop—or else," I threaten.

"He started it," Little Kwesi says.

"No, I didn't . . . You started it." TJ defends.

"I don't care who started it . . . I'm gonna come back there and finish it with a crowbar upside your heads."

"Daddy . . . What's a crowbar?" Little Kwesi asks.

"You wanna find out, little lady?" I say deadpan.

Little Kwesi shakes her head no.

"Daddy, I have a question," TJ says.

"I might have an answer . . . What's up, Son?"

"Are you and mommy ever gonna get married?" I grow quiet.

Why is this seven-year-old thinking about this right now? I think. What the hell made him ask me that?

"I don't know. I've asked your mom Sade to marry me several times . . . But, sometimes things don't work out, and you have to make the best of it . . . We're happier this way."

"What about my mommy, Daddy?" Little Kwesi asks curiously.

"Eva and I don't think marriage was written in the stars for us. That and she can't stand to be in a room with me longer than she has to. We're raising you guys our way instead of the traditional way . . . You got me?" They both nod their heads yes. A few moments later, I find a parking spot.

Little Kwesi makes an observation, "Daddy, why are you sweating?"

"Uh . . . I'm sweating because I'm ready to see this movie." I segue. "Who's with me?"

"We are!" The kids roar with excitement.

"Then, let's roll." We hop out of the truck and walk towards the entrance to the movie theater.

"Alright, let's huddle," I say right before we enter the theater. The three of us form a circle as if we're drawing up a football play. I whisper, "I'm gonna teach you guys a valuable lesson about candy and movies . . . OK?"

The kids nod their heads in compliance.

"We don't buy candy at the theater." I declare. "We buy it beforehand."

"Is it like stealing?" Little Kwesi asks.

"Nope . . . It's the opposite, baby girl."

TJ raises his hand, "Is this like smuggling?"

"Correct, Son. Give your brother a high five!"

Little Kwesi sticks her hand up and gives TJ a high five.

Little Kwesi raises her hand then asks, "Isn't that being cheap, Daddy?"

I nod my head yes! "You wanna be rich, right?"

The kids nod their heads yes.

"Rich people stay rich by acting like they're broke while broke people stay broke by living like they're rich. You don't pay full price for anything . . . You try to get a deal every which way possible."

I dig in my pocket and pull out a few bags of M&M's and Sour Patch Kids then hand them over to the kids.

"Hide these in your pockets." They stuff the candy into their pocket, but Little Kwesi has trouble concealing the candy in her pants.

"TJ . . . Pull your sister's shirt down so we don't get caught."

TJ pulls his sister's shirt down to hide the contraband candy. "Alright, let's head in." I utter as I lead the way into the theater.

"Be cool. Don't walk like you stole something . . . Walk like your daddy." I strut in fresh, or at least I think I do. I get a glimpse from the reflection of the entrance of these fools imitating how I walk. We all look guilty as hell as they try to mimic my strut into the Silverspot Cinema.

Right before we approach the ticket counter, I lean closer to them and whisper, "I'll do all the talking."

They nod their heads in compliance.

I approach the ticket counter. "Two kids and one adult . . . A veteran adult if you have any discounts."

"Sorry, we don't have a veteran's discount, and they can't bring candy into the theater," the ticket seller says.

I look down and notice the kids are eating the candy out of their pockets. I shake my head and chuckle, "Damn stool pigeons! Y'all better eat every bit of it . . . And I mean it, too." I hand the cashier my credit card, and she slides back three movie tickets. My pocket vibrates. I pull out my phone and receive another text message from Keisha. The message reads, "*Call me ASAP*."

"Give me a second, kids." I dial up Keisha.

"Hey, what's up, sis?"

"Happy Father's Day."

"Thank you, sis."

"Daddy's not doing too well," Keisha says. "He checked himself into a retirement home a few years ago, and he's not taking his medicine."

"Good for him. That's not my problem, Keisha."

"They say he's in pretty bad shape."

"Ok. so . . . What am I supposed to do? I live in Miami now."

"He's in Pompano Beach, Florida."

"That's like 40-something minutes away from me. But I'm with the kids, and right now is daddy-time . . . Right, guys?"

"Yeah!" The kids roar.

"Gotta go, sis . . . Love you," I say as I end the call. "Let's get some popcorn . . . I can't believe you guys ate all my damn candy." We walk toward the ticket taker then enter the theater.

CHAPTER 40

A couple of days later, the kids and I load up in the truck to make a small road trip up north. The journey is a bit different from all the others we have taken. We are heading to Pompano Beach, Florida. What is fascinating about this drive is that the kids are not glued to their phones. I glance at the rearview mirror, and I can see curious Little Kwesi and TJ both staring at their quiet yet pouty father. The kids are staring at me as if they were staring at their phones. "Take a picture . . . It'll last longer." I say deadpan.

"Daddy," Little Kwesi utters. "Why do you have a poop face?"

TJ snickers and teases, "Daddy has a poop face . . . Daddy has a poop face . . . Daddy has a poop face." The kids start giggling together.

"Ha . . . Ha . . . Hell!" I say disdainfully. "I don't have a poop face."

As we ride along in the truck, Little Kwesi says, "Mommy says that me and Grandpa have the same name."

"Yep, baby girl . . . Your name means Sunday born like your Grandpa."

"Grandpa was also born on a Sunday?" Little Kwesi asks.

"Yep, but please curb your enthusiasm. Your grandfather is not your regular walk in the park."

"Mommy said that she named me after Grandpa to piss you off," Little Kwesi confesses.

"That she did, baby-girl," I say with a frown. "That she did."

"Daddy, why do you hate your daddy?" TJ asks.

"I don't hate him."

"You shouldn't be like that with your daddy . . . Daddy," Little Kwesi says.

"It's hard for you guys to understand. My father and I didn't have the type of relationship that I have with you guys. I didn't see my father much growing up."

"Was he in jail like Mommy's daddy?" An inquisitive TJ asks.

"No, Son . . . It wasn't jail."

Moments later, I pull the truck into the parking lot of the Rehabilitation & Nursing Center. I shut off the engine. My hands start to tremble, and my heart starts pounding in my chest. I think I may be nervous.

Several moments later, I re-ignite the engine and begin to back out of the parking spot. A car pulls in and blocks me from leaving. I kick the gearshift into the parking position and turn my attention to the children, "We don't have to go in kids."

"We wanna meet Grandpa," an enthusiastic TJ says.

"Fine . . . Come on . . . Let's go," I say with no enthusiasm. We all hop out of the truck.

"When we get in there, sit down. When I say, it's time to go, it's time to go. Don't touch anything . . . Don't break anything . . . If you break anything, I'm breaking you . . . Got me?"

"Yes, Daddy," they both say with shit-eating grins on their faces.

I lead the way into the nursing facility.

"Wait here, kids." I say to the kids as I walk up to the receptionist's desk and approach one of the nurses' aides.

"Hello . . . I'm looking for a Kwesi . . . Kwesi Black."

The nurse's aide asks, "OK . . . And you are?"

"I'm one of his children, Trevor . . . Trevor Russell."

The nurse types his name into the system. "I'm sorry . . . I don't see that you're on his visitation list. I don't know if I can allow you to see him." The nurse's aide declares. "He cannot distinguish faces except for his closest friends and relatives, and no-one has visited Mr. Black in several years."

"Can I see my father? I brought my children up to see their Grandpa. They never met him."

The empathetic nurse's aide studies the children and me, "I'll allow it. They're so cute, and you look a lot like how your father did when he first checked himself in."

My curiosity is spiked by the past tense the nurse's aide used. "How long has he been here?"

"About six years now," she said. "Follow me."

The nurse's aide leads us down the hallway of the nursing home. We walk several feet from the receptionist's desk and reach Kwesi's room.

The nurse's aide knocks on the door, "Mister Black . . . You have visitors." The children and I enter the room. Kwesi and I make eye contact, but no words are exchanged.

"I'll leave you all alone," the nurse's aide says as she exits the room.

A furred white beard covers Kwesi's frail face. He looks to be undernourished, but still has a strong, military bearing. Kwesi and I don't greet each other . . . Nor do we hug . . . or even shake hands. Not one word is mumbled between the two of us as we stare each other down. With confusion and distress, Kwesi poses the question, "Who the fuck are you?"

"Pop . . . It's me . . . Trevor!"

A puzzled Kwesi can't register the name. "Trevor?"

"Yes . . . Trevor. I brought your grandchildren to see you."

Kwesi starts to chuckle, "I have grandchildren?"

I awkwardly start to chuckle with him. "Yeah, Pop. I have children now."

"But this can't be . . . I never had children."

A cloud of confusion covers my face. "Pop . . . Stop messing around."

Kwesi ignores me as he stares out the window.

My eyes well up and a tear rolls down my cheek. I take a few steps closer to my father and walk into an invisible cloud of funk. I notice that Kwesi's clothes are soiled and haven't been changed in days. Kwesi's condition is worse than I imagined as I notice bed sores on his body. There appears to be rug burn markings around his wrists. "Kids . . . Let's go." We storm out of the room.

Moments later, we all rush to the receptionist's desk. "Kids . . . Give me a moment with the nurse's aide."

Little Kwesi and TJ walk over to a bench, pull out their phone, and start staring at it.

"My father smells like piss and ass," I sternly verbalize to the nurse's aide. "Why is he in this condition?"

"Mr. Black . . . Your father . . . is in severe decline. He refuses to take his medication, which is only accelerating that decline. Mr. Black needs constant supervision and requires professional care. He wanders around at night . . . At times, we have to strap him down. He is sometimes unable to control his bladder and bowels," the nurse states.

"Is there something I can do to help him?" I ask.

"Unfortunately, no." the nurse confirms. "People in this stage are approaching the end. In the final stages of Alzheimer's, he may lose his ability to swallow. He'll lose the ability to communicate. Though he may still be able to utter phrases, they will give no insight into his condition."

"Thank you, Ma'am," I say, deflated by the news. I walk down the hall to take one more look at the snoozing and decrepit Kwesi.

"I wish we had spent more time together." I walk up and put my hand on top of my sleeping father's head. "I forgive you, Pop." The tears fall from my face like an April shower. "I forgive you . . . I hope you found it in your heart to forgive me."

CHAPTER 41

Some weeks later, a composed Keisha and I sit quietly in a lawyer's office at Atlantic Tower in downtown Pompano Beach, Florida. The Atlantic Tower is the tallest office building in the downtown area. My palms are clammy, and my leg shakes a million times a minute. I have a special kind of loathing for places like these. The last time I was in a lawyer's office, was when I was in court with Eva.

"I have a special kind of loathing for places like this," I say reminiscing. "Reeks of bullshit, scams, and lies."

Keisha chuckles, "Relax, Bro." We grow silent for a few moments.

"Keisha . . . I'm so sorry. He wanted me to do it . . . He said if I ever found him somewhere in a hospital room unable able to talk." A tear rolls down my face. "He wouldn't wanna live . . . Not like that . . ."

Keisha puts her arm around me. "Daddy was in bad shape. He would've appreciated you doing it." We grow silent for a few moments.

"Where the hell is this guy?" an impatient Keisha asks.

Kwesi's quirky estate attorney enters the office, "Sorry about the wait," he says as he extends his hand.

We shake. "Trevor Russell."

"William Garts."

"Keisha Black . . . Nice to meet you."

"The pleasure is all mine. Sorry for the delay. I am handling your father's estate. I want to extend my condolences to you and the family on your loss. Your father was . . . He was quite charismatic."

We all share a laugh.

"He left a video," says the attorney. "After the video is played, I'll need a couple of signatures, and then you guys can be on your way." Garts grabs the remote, presses play then hands the remote over to Keisha. He exits the room to give us privacy.

We see a healthier, cleaner-cut visual of Kwesi wearing a pair of glasses and holding a sheet of paper. He stares into the camera. "If you're watching, one of three things has happened. Either I can't talk anymore and done shitted and can't wipe myself , or Tre pulled the plug on his ol' man." I lower my head in guilt.

"I'm fucking with ya, Son."

I shake my head with relief.

Kwesi takes a deep breath then continues, "My apologies for the way I acted at our family dinner. That should have been one of the most special moments of our lives, and I let my ol' ego get in the way. I wish we all could've gotten a better understanding of one another."

"Keisha . . . You've made your daddy so proud. Retiring from the Marines and raising my two beautiful grandchildren. And you married well with Michelle. Hell, I wish I was the one that told you to stay away from little boys, but it looks like you got it right," Kwesi said.

Keisha chuckles.

"Unlike your brothers, thank you for loving me unconditionally."

"Keisha and Tre , you guys wanted me in your life . . . You looked past the mistakes I made and accepted me as is . . . Well, Keisha more so than you, Tre . . . I ain't mad at ya, Son. You did what you felt was the right thing to do when you wrote that stuff about me. I learned a lot from it, and hopefully, the message in it changes the course of our family dynamics. The leadership programs you set up back home was pretty cool . . . Donating the money you made from writing that book about me was honorable . . . I wouldn't have done it, but that's what makes you and me different. Your Papa, Grandma, and Mama did a great job raising you."

Kwesi tears up and walks away from the camera. Several moments pass before Kwesi reappears in the frame.

"With that said, I feel it's only right to not leave your ass with anything. Keisha will be my executor, but I will make it better for any child you have. Genesis 17:6 says, 'I will make you very fruitful; I will make nations of you, and kings will come from you.' I want my legacy to be helping set my grandchildren up for success. That is why I will leave my assets to all my grandchildren in the event of my passing." Kwesi pulls the sheet of paper to his face and starts to read:

"I, Abilene Kwesi Black being of full age and sound mind and memory, do make, publish and declare this to be my last will and testament, hereby revoking and annulling any last will and testaments or codicils at any time heretofore made by me. I direct that all my debts, secured and unsecured, be paid as soon as reasonable after my death, provided, however, I direct that my executor may cause any debt to be carried, renewed, and refinanced for its repayment as my executor may deem advisable taking into consideration the best interest of the beneficiaries hereunder. All of the rest and residue of my property, real and personal, of every kind and description and whosesoever situate, which I may own or have the right to dispose of at the time of my death, I give, devise, and bequeath in equal shares to pay the college tuition for the children of my children. The grandchildren's inheritance will be contingent upon making regular visits to the lake house. They will have to sign a registration book to prove they have shown up. Donate any funds that are leftover to a nonprofit charity the executor creates. I see things differently, and I want to make the world better."

"I leave my home to Keisha. Use the ol' lake house for family gatherings. And I leave Tre my old truck. Crank that sum bitch up from me and take it for a spin now and again. And lastly, cremate my body and scatter the ashes over the lake. Don't mourn this spacesuit I was in. Celebrate my life and homecoming. I direct that my executor and beneficiaries abide by any written statement or list by me directing the disposition of tangible personal property not specifically disposed of by this last will and testament. This directive is mandatory to the extent allowed by law," reads Kwesi.

"I hereby name, constitute, and appoint Keisha Black as my executor and direct that my executor shall serve without bond. Should my executor be unable or unwilling to serve or continue to serve, then I guess I hereby name, constitute, and appoint Trevor Russell formerly known as Trevor Black."

The camera flips on its side. And we hear Kwesi say, "Cut this damn thing off . . . Need to roll up some dope."

We both share a chuckle that transmutes into a long, somber silence.

"I'm gonna miss that old man," Keisha says.

I put my arm around my little sister, and she begins to weep.

CHAPTER 42

We are back in a familiar setting: the backyard of Kwesi's old, southern-style, colonial home in a suburb of Memphis, Tennessee. It is chilly and gusty, and autumn leaves fall in flurries each time the wind blows. I rock back and forth in my father's old rocking chair. As I stare off into the lake, I take a big drag from a joint I rolled from Pop's stash.

"Tre," my mother shouts. "You out here smoking that skunk weed?"

I shake my head yes, but say no, choking on the smoke. I put the joint out in the ashtray and conceal the rest under the chair.

"You don't smoke that stuff around the kids, do you?"

"No, Ma. Pop had a stash in one of the rooms. He would come out here, look out into the lake and puff a little bit. I'm showing homage to him, that's all."

"Armani ain't coming. Said he had to work."

"Armani has a job?"

"Yes. Can you believe that?" Ma says with a chuckle.

I chuckle. I never thought there would be a day I would hear Armani working an actual job in a sentence. "I don't blame him for not coming."

TJ runs up to hug his grandma, "Hey, Mimi."

"Hey, boy."

TJ moseys over and sits in my lap.

"Grown people back here talking, little man . . . Whatcha want?"

"Daddy, will we all die?" TJ asks.

My eyes well up, but I hold back the tears. "On Earth . . . Yes. Father Time is undefeated." I point to the sky. "But out there, we never die, Son. Energy never dies. We're just passing through . . . But while you're here, do the best that you can. Do what you can to make this world a better place . . . Leave it better than it was before you got here. If you're not trying to make someone's life better, why are you here? You got me, little man?"

TJ nods his head yes.

"Go find your sister and meet us in the back for the memorial service." I pat TJ on the bottom, and he scurries off.

Mom stares me down for a few awkward moments. I feel like a little boy who's about to get a spanking.

"I didn't do it, Ma."

"Boy, stop," she says with a little snicker. There is a different glow about my mother that I have never seen.

"Raising you guys through the years, I became bitter," Mom says. "I probably took my frustration out on you more than I should've. I know your father, and I weren't in your life as much as we needed to be . . . I want you to know I see you. You're a great father, Son. You've become the father you always wanted in your life. I'm so proud of the man you've become, and so grateful to call you my son."

"Damn it, Ma." I say, choking up.

"Watch your mouth, boy," Mom says with a chuckle. "Come here." She opens her arms and hugs me tight.

I can't hold back the tears and they fall freely from my eyes.

"It's OK . . . I love you, Son." She kisses me on the forehead.

"Love you, Ma. Let's get this thing over with," I say as we walk out of the patio.

Several moments later, a small group of people congregates on the field next to the lake behind Kwesi's house. In attendance are Keisha, her wife Michelle, their teenage children Keisha Junior, and Kellen. Mom takes a seat next to TJ and Sade. Sitting next to Sade is her father, Rack Daddy. Little Kwesi sits with her mother, Eva, and her older son, Dustin, who recently graduated from high school. Eva casts a regretful gaze and rolls her eyes. Coach Rocky Hoffman, Kwesi's ex-coworker, is also in attendance.

The preacher Reverend Percy James stands up in front of the gathering next to Kwesi's urn and a larger portrait of him smiling. The preacher is a round, chubby man wearing what looks to be a 50-button, navy blue Steve Harvey Easter suit.

"We're here today to pay tribute and respect to our brother, Abilene 'Kwesi' Black. We're here today to show our love and support for Brother Kwesi's precious family."

A few more people walk up and join the service. Approaching is Xena and a little boy that looks to be around the same age as TJ and Little Kwesi. Following right behind them is Jackson Reed. We make eye contact, and a few tense moments follow. He takes a seat right next to me then whispers, "Relax chump . . . We did a paternity test, and the kid is mine."

I give them a thumbs up. That is excellent news to hear on a sad day.

"We're here today to seek and to receive comfort. We would be less than honest if we said that our hearts have not ached over this loss. We're not too proud to acknowledge that we have come here today, trusting that God would minister to our hearts, and give us strength as we continue our walk with him," says Reverend James. "And now, Kwesi's son, Trevor, will give us some final words."

What the hell? Speaking is not on the itinerary of things for me to do. Keisha looks over at me. She shrugs her shoulders and mouths the words, "I don't know."

"Let's give Brother Trevor a round of applause."

Everyone starts to clap their hands. I saunter to the front of everyone.

I scratch my head, "Uh . . . I wanna thank everyone for showing up." I say, as my voice cracks. "I didn't prepare a speech or anything like that . . . I wasn't expecting to speak. You would've thought Reverend James had consulted me beforehand, but let's give him a round of applause for putting me on the spot," I dart a glare over at Reverend James, who seems oblivious.

"Pop . . . Kwesi and I were sitting on the porch in the backyard one time . . . We were staring out into the lake, and he said . . . Middle-age is the awkward period when Father Time starts catching up with Mother Nature."

Coach Rocky blurts out, "You gotdamn right, it does."

The people in the attendance erupt in laughter.

"Pop had all the virtues I admire and all the vices I despise. He and I got testy every now again because we shared a love-hate kind of relationship . . . I hated to love him and loved to hate him. For some odd biological reason, we tend to act alike."

Keisha, Sade, my mother, and Eva all chuckle in unison. It is obvious they each individually had to deal with the good, the bad, and the ugly of our shared tendency towards debauchery.

"When Kwesi was here, he was self-centered. That is where he and I bumped heads the most. He was anti-social and anti-family. A lot of which came from his upbringing. Leadership starts with parenthood. Good fathers make better mothers. We need strong fathers back in our communities. Pop wasn't the best father, but he tried to make it right at the end." I lower my head as a tear rolls down my cheek. "For those reasons and in honor of my father, we're turning his home into a nonprofit leadership headquarters that will be named 'The Kwesi Center.' The program will provide funding, mentorship, and strategic planning to help mend broken homes within African American communities. The goal will be to start a society within a society. The center will be used to groom talented, at-risk children and mold future trailblazers. Thank you all for showing up." Everyone applauds as I take my seat.

Reverend James returns to the front of the flock. "Thank you, Brother Russell, for those beautiful words. Please join us for Brother Kwesi Black's final request." Reverend James grabs the urn, and we all walk to the bank of the lake. Reverend James opens the urn, "Ashes to ashes . . . Dust to dust." The preacher dumps Kwesi's ashes into the lake.

CHAPTER 43

Most of the visitors from the memorial service depart after dinner. The remaining guests are inching out one by one except for Reverend James. Keisha thought it would be cute to hire Reverend James because he was a friend to Kwesi at some point in his life. Every other sentence he speaks around me starts with, "I remember your Daddy and I doing this," or "The Bible says that . . ."

The majority of the guests go away because they are simply turned off by Reverend James's presence. Some visitors leave because he reeks of cheap cologne which gives them a headache. Others probably leave because of his loquaciousness. Hell, I almost left the house because he talked so damn much. He is lingering around obnoxiously, interjecting his thoughts and religious beliefs into the small talk.

It takes seven minutes for the preacher to ask a simple question. And if asked a 'yes or no' question, it turns into long-winded, dragged-out answer. Most of his responses lead to him trying to recruit people to his new church. In the middle of dinner prayer, Reverend James mentions how he turned an old grocery store into a house of praise, and how it would be a blessing for us to join his congregation for tomorrow's service.

I never really knew Kwesi had friends, but I imagined them to like the same things that Kwesi liked. Which is why I have kept my eyes on him since the memorial service. This fool is slick flirting with my mother. He sits next to her during dinner, and if he isn't talking ears off, he is in my mother's face. Wherever my mother is, the preacher is following nearby like a homeless, hungry puppy. I know enough is enough when she makes firm eye contact with me. She gives a half-strength smile that reads, *get this fool away from me.*

I maneuver through the kitchen and walk over to the refrigerator where they are standing. Reverend James is in mid-sentence when I approach.

"And the Bible says, 'Ask, and you shall receive' . . . Does anybody hear me?" the preacher shouts.

"Yes!" I say. "We've been hearing you all day."

Mom bites her bottom lip to keep from laughing out loud.

"Can I borrow you a second, Reverend?"

"Sure . . . Give me one second, darling."

I lure the preacher out back to the patio.

"How can I help you, brother?"

"You do know that happily-married woman you're stalking is my mother."

"Stalking? I meant no disrespect," the preacher says with a nervous chuckle.

"None taken."

I fire up a joint and wave it in the air in the hope that the smell of marijuana does what sage does to bad energy. I take a long drag from the joint then exhale, "The strippers should be coming through soon," I say deadpan then pass the joint to Reverend James.

"Strippers?" he says as his face lights up like a Christmas tree.

I nod my head yes.

The preacher's mind says no, but his deflated posture says otherwise. "I remember your Daddy and I use to mess around with them strippers back in the day. Of course, that was before I gave my life to the Lord," the preacher says, placing his hand over his heart. "I will not be partaking in the inhalation of that devil's lettuce," Reverend James says as he scurries off the patio and back into the kitchen where the rest of the folks are hanging out.

"My thoughts and prayers are with you all," he says then makes his exit.

The room grows silent for a few moments. As soon as I enter the kitchen, everyone erupts into clapping and cheering. Not sure if the applause is for the preacher's departure or me coaxing him to leave. Either way, we are all glad the preacher is gone.

Jackson and his family are the next bunch to leave. They edge their way in my direction. *This is about to be uncomfortable,* I think.

"Wait for me in the car," Jackson says to Xena and their son.

Xena does not make eye contact, nor does she speak a word to me. She leans in and sticks her butt out to give me an awkward, one-arm church hug then walks off with my nephew.

Jackson and I stare each other down for a few moments. I'm not sure if he wants to fight or hug me.

I take a step back. "Jackson . . . If I knew you were my brother, it wouldn't have gone down with Xena and the book and—"

"Don't sweat it," Jackson says, interrupting me. "Growing up, I might've done things to you that weren't brotherly. If I had known you were my brother, I would've treated you better than I did. I probably would've helped you in that fight at graduation. Water under the bridge," he says, extending his greeting.

I hesitate a second, then grip his hand.

Jackson pulls me in for a hug. "Love you, little bro."

"Love you too, big bro," I say, still trying to fathom Jackson Reed is my older brother.

"Take care, brother," Jackson says as he exits the house.

Sade, Mom, Keisha, Michelle, Rack Daddy, and TJ are out back on the patio. I take a seat in my father's old chair. We all watch the sun dip behind the trees that surround the lake as the afternoon disappears into evening.

TJ rushes over and starts wrestling with me. I scoop him up, playfully body slam him to the ground and pin him to the floor as if we are in a WWE wrestling match. "One . . . Two . . . Three . . ." I count. "The winner and still the heavyweight champion of the world . . . Your damn daddy!"

"Rematch, Daddy!" TJ says.

"Go wrestle Mimi."

TJ rushes over to his grandma.

"Don't you even think about it, little boy," Mom says to TJ. "Looking like your damn daddy."

Those are words I'm too familiar with, I think with a chuckle. Seconds later, Little Kwesi walks onto the patio and joins the rest of us. "Hey, baby girl . . . Your mama left already?"

Little Kwesi nods her little head, yes.

"Let me get on back to Blytheville. I'm sure my husband misses me," my mother says. "He's probably in the backyard smoking that skunk weed."

"That's a strong possibility," I say, chuckling. "I'll walk you to your car, Ma."

"Nice seeing you again, Miss Renita," Sade says as she stands to give mom a big hug.

"Kids, come hug your grandma and tell her bye," I say.

Little Kwesi and TJ rush over to hug their grandma goodbye.

"I'm getting out of here, too," Rack Daddy says. "Pleasure finally meeting you, Renita. Despite Kwesi's DNA, you raised a fine young man."

"Daddy! Be nice," Sade shouts.

"What? I am being nice," Rack Daddy says. "I came to the damn funeral, didn't I? You know I didn't like Kwesi."

"Drive safe, daddy." The two of them hug.

"Nice seeing you again, Tre," he extends a handshake.

"You too, Mr. Rack Daddy."

Sade gives me a sharp glare. I forgot he doesn't like to be called that anymore.

"I meant Mr. Cole." We shake hands, and Rack Daddy departs.

"Tre, I'm taking a nap," Sade says.

"OK . . . I'm gonna take the kids for a spin around town. See you in a bit." I kiss Sade on the forehead, and she walks off to the bedroom.

Moments later, Mom, the kids, and I make it out to the driveway where she parked. "When are you two getting married?"

My eyes roll to the back of my skull.

"Don't roll your eyes at me, boy. Y'all ain't getting any younger, and you look cute together."

"Hey, kids," I segue, "Give Grandma another big hug before she goes."

Mom starts chuckling as the kids wrap around each of her legs. "OK, boy . . . I see what you're doing," she says.

"Love you, Ma." I lean in for a hug.

"Love you too, boy."

Mom enters her car, cranks the engine, and backs out of the driveway. We wave goodbye as she heads out of the neighborhood.

We stroll over to the side garage that is not attached to the house. I punch in a code and the door opens. There, we discover Kwesi's classic, red 1989 Chevy Silverado. I open the door of the truck then sit inside. I down the sun visor, and a pair of keys falls from it. I grab the keys from the floor, place one in the ignition, and attempt to crank the engine. It doesn't turn over. I notice that there is half a tank of gas in the truck and that the dashboard lights and radio popped on. I take the key out, blow on it, place it back in the ignition then attempt to crack the truck one last time. This time the engine turns over, and the truck rumbles raucously through its Flowmaster exhausts. I pull the truck out of the garage.

"Let's ride, kids," I yell over the thunderous engine.

Little Kwesi and TJ jump in the truck, and we take off.

Little Kwesi and TJ stare at their phone as we ride along in my father's old truck. I speed along, reaching speeds of 100 miles per hour down the highway.

"When I was your age . . . I thought this was the coolest thing ever. Riding along with my father in his loud truck." I notice the words are landing on deaf ears.

"You guys don't even care." The kids say nothing, as their eyes stay glued to the phone. "I guess I'll entertain myself," I say to myself as I fumble around with the old radio, but none of the stations work because the receiver has weak reception. I pull out a dusty cassette tape from the side of the door. I blow off the dust and insert the tape into the cassette player.

A grin creeps across my face as a familiar melody blares through the aftermarket Cerwin Vega stereo system. It's none other than "Reminiscing" by Little River Band.

As the song reaches the chorus, I sing along, "Hurry, don't be late . . . I can hardly wait. I said to myself when we're old. We'll go dancing in the dark, walking through the park. And reminiscing."

Moments into the song, Little Kwesi shouts, "Daddy!"

I turn the volume of the stereo down. "Yes, baby-girl."

"I don't like this song," she says bluntly.

"Which part?"

"The part you sing," Little Kwesi says as TJ snickers.

"Oh . . . Us that so?" I turn the volume up louder. Little Kwesi covers her ears as I sing, "Hurry, don't be late . . . I can hardly wait. I said to myself when we're old. We'll go dancing in the dark, walking through the park. And reminiscing." We were in the wind as we drove off into the sunset.

THE END

ACKNOWLEDGMENTS

At this moment, I would like to celebrate my mother, Janice (Ware) Anderson. I appreciate you for always being my mother and my father at times. Thank you for supporting me without judgment. Like any mother, I am sure there were times you were not happy with some of the decisions I made, but you never tried to play me. I am appreciative of you nurturing and loving me unconditionally. I want to acknowledge all the strong single mothers who have had to raise children because the father chose not to be in the life of his kids. Shoutout to all of the parents raising children because their significant other passed on to the next life. I want to acknowledge all who have had to raise children of incarcerated fathers. I want to send a shoutout to all the good fathers who grew up without their fathers and who are doing the best they can to put their children in a position to win. I honor all fathers that want to be fathers to their children.

I would like to recognize a few great fathers that I have spent significant time with. I'll start with Corey L. Pugh. Thank you for being a great brother-cousin. Growing up, you roughed me up like a brother-cousin should have. It's your fault I am in love with all of this hippity-hoppity music. I will forever enjoy our time together. Your son Corey Jr. has one of the best fathers on the globe. Jamaal Phillips has been my best friend since the first grade. Never have I ever met someone that has been down to the ground like you. Some years have passed since the first grade, but we still cut up like little kids. Thank you for always being there for me. You once told me that I should focus my love on people who show me that same love back. That was the best piece of advice I have ever received, and my life has been significantly better since I have absorbed those words. Lauren and JJ are lucky to have a father like you.

Shantario "Rod" Parks, you have always been a big brother to me. I have known you longer than anybody, and you have always embraced me through the good and the bad. I truly appreciate you for always showing love and supporting me. There is no GirlDad on the planet that is better than my guy Rod. Twinkie, Muffin, Savannah, and Pudding got themselves a real one starting at the daddy position. I want to acknowledge Jason R. Anderson for being one of the sharpest people I have ever been around. If you know Jason as I do, you'll know he is the first person to do everything I didn't know anybody could do. Your determination to get something done is quite impressive yet overwhelming at the same time. To my stepfather Dewayne Anderson. I am grateful for you being there for my mother. Your presence allowed me to venture off into this world and obtain knowledge to put our family in a better position.

I want to send a shoutout to my brother Jamal Robinson. Thank you for the laughs and the memories growing up. I appreciate you for making me a better brother, and I will always be here for you. I want to send a shoutout to my sister Candace Smith. Even though you were in the Navy, you are still my favorite sister in the whole wide world. Raissa and Royston have one of the coolest mothers on the planet. Brandon Robinson, you light up a room, little brother. I appreciate you for always embracing me as your big brother. Don't let anyone steal your joy, and keep smiling. To my baby brother Antjuan Robinson. Continue to be the best father you can be for AJ and Alandis. Do not let anger or disappointment from our upbringing get in the way of the ultimate goal. That goal is to be the father and leader we wish we had growing up. And shoutout to my oldest brother Vonzell Smith. I look forward to meeting Elia and Andreus. I love you all dearly and wish the stars had aligned that we all could have grown up together.

To Timmy White Senior, thank you for embracing me as if I were one of your own. I appreciate you for being a father figure in my life. Thank you for allowing me to live vicariously through your family during my childhood. I also want to acknowledge Thomas Moses, Markus Richardson, Shameek Belsches, Jesse Beal, Leonard "JB" Williams, Randy Henderson, Kelly Cardenas, Alvin Hancock Jr., Elrico Tunstall, Ladarius Parks, Robert Lucas II, Robert "Trey" Lucas III, Garrick Dixon, and Alan White for putting in the work and being great fathers. A special shoutout to Eric Flowers. He is not only a great father, but he is an even better grandfather. Thank you for believing in me a very long time ago when my biological father questioned you about my career choice as a writer.

Shoutout to my military buddies who are great fathers: Malik Shahid, Adam Warren, Joshua Webster, Carey Presha, David Sims, Anthony Nixon, Ronnie "Tank" Woods, and even you, Lance Horan. Thank you all for the laughter during our tumultuous times downrange. I want to acknowledge the editors for this novel: Emily Crawford-Margison, Jemiscoe Chamber-Black, and Jesse Coleman. My profound thanks to you all for the guidance, confidence, and eye for detail needed to complete *Father Time*. If I forgot your name, it was not in vain.

ABOUT THE AUTHOR

TORTHELL ROBINSON was born on the Eaker Air Force Base located in Blytheville, Arkansas. He enlisted into the United States Air Force at age 17 and served as a Security Forces troop United States Air Force. During his military service, Torthell served two deployments to LSA Anaconda in Balad, Iraq (Operation Iraqi Freedom) and deployed to Manos, Kyrgyzstan (Operation Enduring Freedom). After separation from the military and with the help of the GI Bill, Torthell packed up and relocated to Los Angeles. There he advanced his knowledge in film production. Torthell studied at the Los Angeles Film School, the New York Film Academy, and UCB Upright Citizens Brigade, where he crafted his skill as a well-rounded writer.

Instagram: @Torthell

Twitter: @Torthell

Blog & Podcast: SitYourAssDown.co

www.ingramcontent.com/pod-product-compliance
Lightning Source LLC
Chambersburg PA
CBHW061620190726
48288CB00007B/2407